Raves for the Work of Erle Stanley GARDNER!

"The best-selling author of the century...a master storyteller."

—*New York Times*

"Gardner is humorous, astute, curious, inventive—who can top him? No one has yet."

—*Los Angeles Times*

"Erle Stanley Gardner is probably the most widely read of all...authors...His success...undoubtedly lies in the real-life quality of his characters and their problems..."

—*The Atlantic*

"A remarkable discovery...fans will rejoice at another dose of Gardner's unexcelled mastery of pace and an unexpected new taste of his duo's cyanide chemistry."

—*Kirkus Reviews*

"One of the best-selling writers of all time, and certainly one of the best-selling mystery authors ever."

—*Thrilling Detective*

"A treat that no mystery fan will want to miss."

—*Shelf Awareness*

"Zing, zest and zow are the Gardner hallmark. He will keep you reading at a gallop until The End."

—*Dorothy B. Hughes,*
Mystery Writers of America Grandmaster

Evaline Harris was standing in the door, peering down the corridor with sleep-swollen eyes. She didn't look either mousy or virginal. She said, "What do you want?" in a voice that was rough as a rasp.

"I'm an adjuster for the railroad company. I want to make an adjustment on that trunk."

"My God," she said. "It's about time. Why pick this hour of the morning? Don't you know a girl who works nights has to sleep sometime?"

"I'm sorry," I said, and waited to be invited in.

She stood in the doorway. Over her shoulder I caught a glimpse of a folding wall-bed let down, the covers rumpled and the pillowcases wrinkled.

She continued to stand in the doorway, doubt, hostility, and avarice all showing in her manner. "All I want is a check," she said...

SOME OTHER HARD CASE CRIME BOOKS YOU WILL ENJOY:

THE KNIFE SLIPPED *by Erle Stanley Gardner*
JOYLAND *by Stephen King*
THE COCKTAIL WAITRESS *by James M. Cain*
THE TWENTY-YEAR DEATH *by Ariel S. Winter*
THE SECRET LIVES OF MARRIED WOMEN *by Elissa Wald*
ODDS ON *by Michael Crichton writing as John Lange*
BRAINQUAKE *by Samuel Fuller*
EASY DEATH *by Daniel Boyd*
THIEVES FALL OUT *by Gore Vidal*
SO NUDE, SO DEAD *by Ed McBain*
THE GIRL WITH THE DEEP BLUE EYES *by Lawrence Block*
PIMP *by Ken Bruen and Jason Starr*
SOHO SINS *by Richard Vine*
SNATCH *by Gregory Mcdonald*
FOREVER AND A DEATH *by Donald E. Westlake*
QUARRY'S CLIMAX *by Max Allan Collins*

TURN *on* *the* HEAT

by **Erle Stanley Gardner**

WRITING UNDER THE NAME 'A. A. FAIR'

A HARD CASE CRIME NOVEL

A HARD CASE CRIME BOOK
(HCC-131)
First Hard Case Crime edition: November 2017

Published by

Titan Books
A division of Titan Publishing Group Ltd
144 Southwark Street
London SE1 0UP

in collaboration with Winterfall LLC

Print edition ISBN 978-1-78565-617-0
E-book ISBN 978-1-78565-618-7

Design direction by Max Phillips
www.maxphillips.net

Typeset by Swordsmith Productions

Printed in the United States of America

Visit us on the web at www.HardCaseCrime.com

TURN ON THE HEAT

Chapter One

I opened the door marked *Bertha Cool—Confidential Investigations—Entrance.* Elsie Brand looked up from her shorthand notes, and, without missing a beat on the keyboard, said, "Go on in. She's waiting." The staccato rhythm of her typing followed me across the office and through the door marked *Bertha Cool—Private.*

Bertha Cool, profane, massive, belligerent, and bulldog, sat back of her desk, her diamonds flashing in the morning sunlight as she moved her hand over a pile of papers, sorting and rearranging. The thin man in the middle forties seated in the client's chair looked up at me with anxious, apprehensive eyes.

Bertha Cool said, "You were long enough getting here, Donald."

I said nothing to her, but sized up the client, a slender man with grayish hair, a gray, close-clipped mustache, and a mouth which seemed more decisive than the general anxiety of his appearance would indicate. He wore blue glasses so dark that it was impossible to distinguish the color of his eyes.

Bertha Cool said, "Mr. Smith, this is Donald Lam, the man I told you about. Donald, Mr. Smith."

I bowed.

Smith said, in the voice of a man who has disciplined himself to subordinate general impressions to exact accuracy, "Good morning, Mr. Lam." He didn't offer to shake hands. He seemed disappointed.

Bertha Cool said, "Now, don't make any mistakes about Donald. He's a go-getter. God knows he hasn't any brawn, but he has brains. He's a half-pint runt and a good beating raises hell with him, but he knows his way around. Don't mind my cussing, Mr. Smith."

Smith nodded. I thought the nod was somewhat dubious, but I couldn't see his eyes.

Bertha Cool said, "Sit down, Donald."

I sat down in the hard, straight-backed wooden chair.

Bertha Cool said to Smith, "Donald can find her if anyone can. He isn't as young as he looks. He got to be a lawyer, and they kicked him out when he showed a client how to commit a perfectly legal murder. Donald thought he was explaining a technicality in the law, but the Bar Association didn't like it. They said it was unethical. They also said it wouldn't work." Bertha Cool paused long enough to chuckle, then went on: "Donald came to work for me, and the first case he had, damned if he didn't show 'em there was a loophole in the murder law through which a man could drive a horse and buggy. Now they're trying to amend the law. That's Donald for you!"

Bertha Cool beamed at me with a synthetic semblance of affection that didn't mean a thing.

Smith nodded his head.

Bertha Cool said, "In nineteen hundred and eighteen, Donald, a Dr. and Mrs. James C. Lintig lived at 419 Chestnut Street, Oakview. There was a scandal, and Lintig took a powder. We're not concerned with him. Find Mrs. Lintig."

"Is she still around Oakview?" I asked.

"No one knows."

"Any relatives?"

"Apparently not."

"How long had they been married when she disappeared?"

Bertha looked at Smith, and Smith shook his head. Bertha Cool kept looking at him, and he said finally, in that precise, academic manner which seemed characteristic of him, "I don't know."

Bertha Cool said, "Get this, Donald. We don't want anyone

to know about this investigation. Above all, no one is to know who our client is. Take the agency car. Start now. You should get there late tonight."

I looked at Smith and said, "I'll have to make inquiries," and Smith said, "Certainly."

Bertha said, "Pose as a distant relative."

"How old is she?" I asked.

Smith knitted his brows thoughtfully, and said, "I don't know exactly. You can find that out when you get there."

"Any children?"

Smith said, "No."

I looked across at Bertha Cool. She opened a drawer in her desk, took out a key, unlocked a cash box, and handed me fifty dollars. "Keep expenses down, Donald," she said. "It may be a long chase. We'll have to make the money go as far as possible."

Smith put his fingertips together, rested his hands on the front of his gray, double-breasted coat, and said, "Exactly."

"Any leads to work on?" I asked.

"What more do you want?" Bertha asked.

"Anything I can get," I said, my eyes on Smith.

He shook his head.

"Know anything about her, whether she had a commercial education, whether she could do any work, who her friends were, whether she had any money, whether she was fat, thin, tall, short, blonde, or brunette?"

Smith said, "No. I can't help you on any of that."

"What do I do when I locate her?" I asked.

"Notify me," Bertha said.

I pocketed the fifty dollars, scraped back my chair, said, "Pleased to have met you, Mr. Smith," and walked out.

Elsie Brand didn't bother to look up from her typing as I crossed the outer office.

The agency car was an antiquated heap with tires worn down pretty close to the fabric. It had a leaky radiator, front wheels that developed a bad shimmy at anything above fifty, and so many rattles the engine knocks were almost drowned out. It was a hot day, and I had trouble getting over the mountains. It was hotter in the valley, and my eyes began to feel like hard-boiled eggs. The hot glare from the road cooked them right in their sockets. I couldn't get hungry enough to make stopping worthwhile, but grabbed a hamburger along the road, ate with one hand, and drove with the other. I made Oakview at ten-thirty that night.

Oakview was in the foothill country, and it was cooler up there, with moisture in the air, and mosquitoes. A river came brawling out of the mountains to snake smoothly past the foothill country around Oakview, and spread out on the plains below.

Oakview was a county seat which had gone to seed. They rolled up the sidewalks at nine o'clock. The buildings were all old. The shade trees which lined the streets were old. The place hadn't grown fast enough to give the city fathers an excuse to widen the streets and rip out the trees.

The Palace Hotel was open. I got a room and rolled in.

Morning sun streaming through the window wakened me. I shaved, dressed, and got a bird's-eye view of the town from the hotel window. I saw a courthouse of ancient vintage, got a glimpse of the river through the tops of big shade trees, and looked down on an alley full of old packing-cases and garbage cans.

I looked around for a place to eat breakfast, and found a restaurant that looked good on the outside, but smelled of rancid grease on the inside. After breakfast I sat on the steps of the courthouse and waited for nine o'clock.

The county officials came straggling leisurely in. They were mostly old men with placid faces—browsing along the streets, pausing for choice morsels of gossip. They gave me curious stares as they climbed past me up the steps. I was a stranger. They knew it and showed they knew it.

In the county clerk's office an angular woman of uncertain age stared at me with black, lackluster eyes, listened to my request, and gave me the great register of 1918—a paper-backed volume starting to turn yellow. Its fuzzy-faced type indicated a political plum had been handed to a local newspaper.

Under the L's, I found: *Lintig:—James Collitt, Physician, 419 Chestnut Street, age 33*, and *Lintig:—Amelia Rosa, Housewife, 419 Chestnut Street*. Mrs. Lintig hadn't given her age.

I asked for the 1919 register and found neither name. I walked out feeling the deputy's black eyes staring at the back of my neck.

There was one newspaper, the *Blade*. The lettered sign on the window showed it was a weekly. I went in and tapped on the counter.

The noise made by a typewriter came to a stop, and an auburn-haired girl with brown eyes and white teeth came from behind a partition to ask me what I wanted. I said, "Two things. Your files for 1918, and the name of a good place to eat."

"Have you tried the Elite?" she asked.

"I had breakfast there."

She said, "Oh," and then, after a moment, said, "You might try the Grotto, or the Palace Hotel dining room. You want the files for 1918?"

I nodded.

I didn't get any more glimpses of her teeth, just two tightly closed lips and opaque brown eyes. She started to say something, changed her mind, and went into a back room. After a while she came out with a board clip filled with newspapers. "Was there something in particular you wanted?" she asked.

I said, "No," and started in with January 1, 1918. I glanced quickly through a couple of issues, and said, "I thought you were a weekly."

"We are now," she said, "but in 1918 we were a daily."

"Why the change?" I asked.

She said, "It was before my time."

I sat down and started poring through the papers. War news filled the front page, reports on the German drives, the submarine activities. Liberty Loan committees were making drives to reach their quotas. Oakview had gone "over the top." There were mass meetings, patriots making speeches. A returned Canadian veteran, disabled, was making a lecture tour telling the story of the war. Money was being poured into Europe through a one-way funnel.

I hoped what I was looking for would make a big enough splash to hit the front page. I went through 1918 and found nothing.

"Could I," I asked, "keep this temporarily, and see 1919?"

The girl brought me the file without a word. I kept on going through the front pages. The Armistice had been signed. The United States was the savior of the World. American money, American youth, and American ideals had lifted Europe out of the selfishness of petty jealousies. There was to be a great League of Nations which would police the world and safeguard the weak against the strong. The war to end war had been won. The world was safe for Democracy. Other news began to filter into the front pages.

I found what I wanted in a July issue, under the headline: *Oakview Specialist Sues for Divorce—Dr. Lintig Alleges Mental Cruelty.*

The newspaper handled the affair with gloves, mostly confining itself to the allegations of the complaint. Poste & Warfield were attorneys for the plaintiff. I read that Dr. Lintig had an extensive practice in eye, ear, nose, and throat, and that Mrs. Lintig was a leader of the younger social set. Both were exceedingly popular. Neither had any comment to make to a representative of the *Blade*. Dr. Lintig had referred the reporter to his attorneys, and Mrs. Lintig had stated she would present her side of the case in court.

Ten days later, the Lintig case splashed headlines all over the front page: *Mrs. Lintig Names Corespondent—Society Leader Accuses Husband's Nurse.*

I learned from the article that Mrs. Lintig, appearing through Judge J. E. Gillfoil, had filed an answer and cross-complaint. The cross-complaint named Vivian Carter, Dr. Lintig's office nurse, as corespondent.

Dr. Lintig had refused to make any comment. Vivian Carter was absent from the city and could not be located by telephone. There was some history in the article. She had been a nurse in the hospital where Dr. Lintig had interned. Shortly after Dr. Lintig had opened his office in Oakview, he had sent for her to come and be his office nurse. According to the newspaper account, she had made a host of friends, and these friends were rallying to her support, characterizing the charges contained in the cross-complaint as utterly absurd.

The issue of the *Blade* next day showed that Judge Gillfoil had asked for a subpoena to take the depositions of Vivian Carter and Dr. Lintig; that Dr. Lintig had been called out of town on business and could not be reached; that Vivian Carter had not returned.

There were scattered comments after that. Judge Gillfoil charged that Dr. Lintig and Vivian Carter were concealing themselves to avoid service of papers. Poste & Warfield indignantly denied that, and claimed that the accusation was an unfair attempt to influence public opinion. They claimed their client would be available "in the near future."

After that the case drifted to the inside pages. Within a month, deeds were recorded conveying all of Dr. Lintig's property to Mrs. Lintig. She denied that a property settlement had been made. The attorneys also registered denials. A month later, a Dr. Larkspur had purchased from Mrs. Lintig the office and equipment of Dr. Lintig and had opened an office. Poste & Warfield had no comment to make other than that "in due time, Dr. Lintig would return and clear matters up satisfactorily."

I turned through the issues after that, and found nothing. The girl sat on a stool behind the counter watching me turn the pages.

She said, "There won't be any more until the December second issue. You'll find a paragraph in the local gossip column."

I pushed the file of papers to one side and said, "What do I want?"

Her eyes looked me over. "Don't you know?"

"Yes."

She said, "Then just keep right on the blazed trail."

A gruff, masculine voice from behind the partition said, "Marian."

She slid off the stool and walked back of the partition. I heard the rumble of a low-pitched voice, and after a while a word or two from her. I retrieved the file of papers and turned to the December second issue. In the gossip column was a paragraph to the effect that Mrs. James Lintig planned to spend the Christmas holidays with relatives "in the East" and was leaving by train for San Francisco where she would take a boat through the Canal. In answer to queries about the status of the divorce action, she had stated that the matter was entirely in the hands of her lawyers, that she had no information as to the whereabouts of her husband, and branded as "absurd and false" a rumor that she had learned of her husband's whereabouts and was planning to rejoin him.

I waited for the girl to come back out. She didn't show up. I went to a corner drugstore and looked in the telephone directory under *Attorneys*. I found no Gillfoil, no Poste & Warfield, but there was a Frank Warfield having offices in the First National Bank Building.

I walked two blocks down the shady side of a hot street, climbed rickety stairs, walked down a corridor slightly out of plumb, and found Frank Warfield with his feet on a desk littered with law books, smoking a pipe.

I said, "I'm Donald Lam. I want to ask a few questions. Do you remember a case of Lintig versus Lintig which was handled by—"

"Yes," he said.

"Can you," I asked, "tell me anything about the present whereabouts of Mrs. Lintig?"

"No."

I thought back over Bertha Cool's instructions, and decided to take a chance on my own.

"Do you know anything about the whereabouts of Dr. Lintig?"

"No," he said, and then added, after a moment, "He still owes us court costs and retainer fees on that original action."

I said, "Do you know whether he left any other debts?"

"No."

"Have you any idea whether he's alive or dead?"

"No."

"Or about Mrs. Lintig?"

He shook his head.

"Where could I find Judge Gillfoil, who represented her?"

His pale blue eyes made a watery smile, "Up on the hill," he said, pointing in a northwest direction.

"On the hill?"

"Yes, the cemetery. He died in 1930."

I said, "Thank you very much," and went out. He didn't say anything as I pulled the door shut.

I went back to the clerk's office and told the suspicious-eyed woman that I wanted to see the file in the case of Lintig versus Lintig. It didn't take ten seconds to dig it up.

I looked through the papers. There was the complaint, the answer, the cross-complaint, a stipulation giving the plaintiff ten days' additional time within which to answer the cross-complaint, another stipulation giving him twenty days, a third stipulation giving him thirty days, and then a notice of default. Apparently, summons had never been served on Vivian Carter, and for that reason the case had never been brought to trial, nor did it appear that it had ever been formally dismissed.

I walked out feeling the suspicious hostility of her eyes on the back of my neck.

I went back to the hotel, sat in the writing-room and scribbled a note to Bertha Cool on hotel stationery:

B. Check through the passenger lists on ships leaving San Francisco during December 1919 for the East Coast via the Canal. Find the one that carried Mrs. Lintig. Check the names of other passengers, and see if you can locate some fellow-traveler. Mrs. Lintig was full of matrimonial troubles, and may have spilled the beans to some fellow-passenger. It's a long time ago, but the lead may give us pay dirt. The trail looks pretty cold at this end.

I scribbled my initials on the report, put it in a stamped, addressed envelope, and was assured by the clerk it would catch the two-thirty train out.

I tried the Grotto for lunch, and then went back to the *Blade* office. “I want to run an ad,” I said.

The girl with the thoughtful brown eyes stretched a hand across the counter for the ad.

She read it, reread it, checked off the words, then vanished into the back room.

After a while a heavyset man with sagging shoulders, a green eyeshade pulled low on his forehead, and tobacco stain at the corners of his lips came out and said, “Your name Lam?”

“Yes.”

“You wanted to put that ad in the paper?”

“Uh huh. How much is it?”

He said, “There might be a story in you.”

I said, “There might, and then again there might not.”

“A little publicity might help you get what you want.”

“And again it might not.”

He looked at the ad, and said, “According to this, there’s some money coming to Mrs. Lintig.”

“It doesn’t say so,” I said.

“Well, it might just as well say so. You say that a liberal reward will be paid to anyone who can give you information as to the present whereabouts of Mrs. James C. Lintig, who left Oakview in 1919, or, in the event she is dead, as to the names and residences of her legal heirs. That sounds to *me* as though you were one of these heir chasers—and that fits in with some of the other things.”

“What other things?” I asked.

He turned, focused his eyes on the cuspidor, streamed yellow liquid explosively. He said, “I asked you first.”

"The initial question," I said, "of which you seem to have lost sight, was the cost of the ad."

"Five bucks for three insertions."

I gave him five dollars of Bertha Cool's money, and asked for a receipt. He said, "Wait a minute," and went back behind the partition. A minute later the brown-eyed girl came out, and said, "You wanted a receipt, Mr. Lam?"

"I did, and I do."

She hesitated over the receipt, holding her pen over the date line, then looked up at me. "How was the Grotto?"

"Rotten," I said. "Where's the best place for dinner?"

"The hotel dining room if you know what to order."

"How do you know what to order?"

"You have to be a detective," she said.

I let that pass, and after she saw that it had passed, she said, "You go in for a little deduction, and reason by elimination. In other words, you need a licensed guide."

"Do you," I asked, "have a license?"

She glanced over her shoulder toward the partition. "It isn't quite as bad as that."

"Aren't you a member of the Chamber of Commerce?"

"I'm not. The paper is."

I said, "I'm a stranger in town. You can't tell. I might be looking for a good manufacturing site. It would be a shame for me to get a false impression of the city."

Behind the partition the man coughed.

"What do the local people do for good cooking?"

"That's easy. They get married."

"And live happily ever afterward?"

"Yes."

"Are you," I asked, "married?"

"No. I eat at the hotel dining room."

"And know what to order?"

"Yes."

"How about eating with a perfect stranger," I asked, "and showing him the ropes?"

She laughed nervously. "You aren't exactly a stranger."

"And I'm not exactly perfect. We could eat and talk."

"What would we talk about?"

"About how a girl, working in a country newspaper office, might make a little extra money."

"How much extra?" she asked.

"I don't know," I said. "I'd have to find out."

She said, "So would I."

"How about the dinner?" I asked.

She glanced swiftly over her shoulder toward the partition, and then said, "It's a date."

I waited while her pen fairly flew over the receipt blank. "It'll start day after tomorrow. We're a weekly now," she said.

"I know," I told her. "Shall I call for you here?"

"No, no. I'll be in the hotel lobby about six o'clock. Do you know anyone in town?"

"No."

She seemed rather relieved by that.

"Any other newspaper in town?" I asked.

"No, not now. There was one back in 1918, but it folded in '23."

"What about the blazed trail?" I asked.

"You're on it," she said, smiling.

Back of the partition, the man coughed again, this time, I thought, warningly.

I said, "I'd like to get the file for '17, '18, and '19."

She brought them out, and I spent most of the afternoon checking the society columns, getting the names of the persons who had attended social gatherings at which Dr. and Mrs. Lintig had been present. I arranged the names in columns and checked those which were repeated frequently enough to give me an idea of the social circle in which the Lintigs had moved.

The girl back of the counter spent part of the time on the stool, watching me; part of the time behind the partition, clacking away on the typewriter. I didn't hear the masculine voice again, but I remembered that warning cough and didn't try to talk with her. The name on the receipt she had given me was Marian Dunton.

Around five o'clock I went back to the hotel and freshened up. Then I went down to the lobby and waited for her. She came in about six.

"How's the cocktail bar?" I asked.

"Pretty good."

"Would cocktails make our dinner taste better?"

"I think they would."

We had a dry Martini apiece, and I suggested another one. "Are you," she inquired, "trying to get me tight?"

"On *two* cocktails?" I asked.

"Experience has taught me that two make a swell beginning."

"Why should I want to get you tight?"

"I wouldn't know," she said with a laugh. "How could a girl working in a newspaper office in Oakview make some extra money?"

"I'm not certain yet," I said. "It depends on the blazed trail."

"What about it?"

"How far it's been blazed, and who blazed it."

"Oh," she said.

I caught the bartender's eye and indicated the two empty glasses. While he was fixing the second cocktail, I said, "I'm listening."

"It's an excellent habit," she told me. "I try to cultivate it."

"Ever make any money at it?" I asked.

"No," she said, and then, after a moment: "Have you?"

"A little."

"Do you think *I* could?"

"No. I think you could make more money by talking. How does it happen you're the only pretty girl in town?"

"Thank you. Have you taken a census?"

"I have eyes, you know."

She said, "Yes, I'd noticed that."

The bartender filled the glasses. She said, "The cashier at the picture show says the traveling salesmen all ask her why she's the only pretty girl in town. Perhaps that's just the urban approach."

"I don't think much of it," I said. "It doesn't seem to get one anywhere."

"Why don't you try another one?"

"I will," I said. "In 1919 this town supported an eye, ear, nose, and throat specialist. It doesn't look as though it would support one now."

"It wouldn't."

"What happened?"

She said, "Lots of things. We never list them all at once. It sounds too depressing to strangers."

"You might give me the first installment."

She said, "Well, the railroad had shops here. It changed the division point and moved the shops, and there was a depression in '21, you know."

"Was there?" I asked.

"So they tell me. Business fumbled the ball, but recovered it before the politicians grabbed it."

"What," I asked, "are the *Blade*'s political affiliations?"

"Local," she said, "and in favor of the incumbents. There's quite a bit of county printing, you know. We'd better finish the cocktails and get to the dining room before the local talent higrades the best of the food."

We finished the cocktails, and I escorted her into the dining room. After we were seated, I toyed with the menu and asked, "What do we eat?"

"Well," she said, "you don't want corned beef hash. I wouldn't take the chicken croquettes because they had the chicken Wednesday. If there's veal potpie, it was left over from Thursday. You're pretty safe on roast beef, and they do have good baked potatoes."

"A baked potato," I said, "with lots of butter would make up for a lot of other things. How did you happen to go to dinner with me?"

Her eyes grew large and round. "Why, you asked me."

"How did I happen to ask you?"

She said, "Well, I like that!"

I said, "I happened to ask you because you brought the subject up."

"I did?"

"Indirectly, and you brought it up because the man who tried to pump me, and couldn't, went back of the partition and suggested to you that it might be a good idea."

She let her eyes grow very large and said, "Oooh, Grandma, what big ears you have!"

"And he made that suggestion because he wanted some information, and he intimated that he had some information that he might give me in exchange for information I could give him."

"Did he really?"

"You know he did."

"I'm sorry," she said, "but I'm not a mind reader."

A waitress came and took our orders. I noticed her looking around the dining room. "Worried?" I asked.

"About what?"

"Whether Charlie will see you dining with me before you have a chance to tell him that it was a business assignment the boss gave you."

"Who's Charlie?"

"The boyfriend."

"Whose?"

"Yours."

"I don't know any Charlie."

"I know, but I didn't think you'd tell me about him so we might as well call him Charlie. It'll save time and simplify matters."

She said, "I see. No. I'm not worried about Charlie. He's really quite broad-minded and tolerant."

"No firearms?" I asked.

"No. It's been almost six months since he shot anyone, and even then it was only a shoulder shot. The man wasn't in the hospital over six weeks."

"Admirable self-restraint," I said. "I was afraid Charlie might have a temper."

"Oh, no. He's very patient—and kind to animals."

"What does he do?" I asked. "I mean for a living."

"Oh, he works here."

"Not the hotel?" I asked.

"No, no. Here in town."

"Does he like it here?"

The bantering look left her eyes. She jabbed her fork into her roast beef, and said, "Yes."

I said, "That's nice," and she didn't say anything for a minute or two.

The dining room was fairly well filled. I didn't figure the hotel rooms furnished the patronage. Apparently, a good deal of it was steady trade. Several of the diners showed an interest in Marian Dunton and her escort. I figured the girl was pretty well known to the local trade. I asked her a few more questions about the town and got short, informative answers. She wasn't trying to kid me anymore. Something had put a damper on her spirits. I tried to figure whether it was someone who had come into the dining room about the time the light went out of her eyes. If that was the case, I could divide responsibility between two middle-aged men who seemed utterly engrossed in the food and their own conversation, and the family party who looked like automobile tourists, a middle-aged man with a bald head and faded gray eyes, a chunky woman, a girl about nine, and a boy about seven.

After we'd had dessert, I offered her one of my cigarettes. She accepted. We lit up, and I took out the list of names I'd made and handed it to her. "How many of these people are still in town?" I asked.

She studied the list for a few minutes, and then said grudgingly, "You *are* smart. I mean you *really* are."

I waited for her to answer my question. After a while she said, "You have fifteen names here. Not over four or five of them are still in town."

"What happened to them?"

"Oh, they went the way of the railroad shops. Those people made up the younger set when Dr. Lintig lived here. I've known some of them. Quite a few left when business started to get bad. We had another setback in 1929. A canning factory that was here folded up."

"How about those who're left? Do you know them?"

"Yes."

"Where could I reach them?"

"You could find the names in the telephone book."

"Couldn't you tell me?"

"Yes, but I'd prefer you got the information from the telephone book."

"I see," I said. I folded the list and put it back into my pocket. There was a movie with a second-run picture that I'd seen. I suggested we go, and she accepted. From the way she acted, I was pretty certain she'd already seen the movie. Afterward, we had ice cream, and over the ice cream I took out my list again.

"Suppose you check the persons who are still here," I said. "It would save wear and tear on the telephone directory."

She thought that over for a while, then took the list and checked four names. She said, "That's an intelligent way of going about it, but I don't think it'll get you any place. I don't think anyone in town knows where she is."

"Why do you seem so positive?"

"It attracted a lot of attention, you know."

"That was back before the depression," I said. "A lot of things have attracted attention since then."

She acted as though she wanted to tell me something, but felt that she shouldn't. I said, "Go ahead. Give me a break."

She said, "*You* don't give *me* any."

I said, "If I could find Mrs. Lintig, it might be very much to her advantage. She might fall heir to a large estate."

Marian Dunton laughed, and said, "And then again, she might win a sweepstakes."

I grinned.

"Won't you tell me why all this activity about Mrs. Lintig?"

I kept the interest out of my eyes. "I don't know," I said.

"Are you working for someone, or are you on your own?"

I said, "Well, if I could find her, there might be something in it for me."

"How about me," she asked, "if I found her?"

"If you know where she is, and would jar loose with a little information, there might be something in it for you."

"How much?"

"I wouldn't know until I asked some questions. Do you know where she is?"

"No. I wish I did. There'd be a story in it. I gather news for the *Blade*, you know."

"And you'd get your wages raised?" I asked.

She said, "No."

I said, "I might be able to put you in touch with someone who would pay for the information—more than the *Blade* would."

"The *Blade* would pay nothing."

I said, "Then I'm *sure* we'd make the highest bid."

"How much?"

"I don't know. I'd have to find out. How about the others?"

"What others?"

I seemed surprised. "Why," I said, "the others who were looking for her."

She said thoughtfully, "I guess I shouldn't have made that crack about the blazed trail."

I said, "No. The man who's running the paper didn't like that crack."

She focused her eyes on a big glass mug that had evidently been a beer glass at some time in the history of the place. Turning the glass stem slowly in her fingers, she asked, "How long have you lived in the big city?"

"All my life," I said.

"Like it?" she asked.

"Not particularly."

"I should think you'd be thrilled to death."

"Why?"

"Being out in the thick of things," she said, "instead of a little backwater hick town where you know everyone and everyone knows you. You can really live your life in a city. There are thousands and thousands of people, unlimited opportunities for contacts and friendships, shows to see, department store windows, decent beauty shops—and restaurants."

I said, "There is also chiseling, traffic signals, parking limits, one-way streets, grind and noise and confusion, and as for friendships—well, if you want to be really lonely, try a big city. Everyone's a stranger, and if you don't have just the right kind of contacts, they remain strangers."

She said, "It would be better that way than to see the same old faces day after day, to be living in a place that's eaten up with dry rot, where people know more about your business than you do."

"Do people," I asked, "know more about *your* business than you do?"

"They think they do," she said.

"Cheer up," I told her. "You have Charlie."

"Charlie?" she asked. "Oh, yes, I get you now."

"If you went to a big city," I said, "you'd have to leave Charlie behind. Remember, he likes it here."

"Are you kidding me," she asked, "or just showing me a good time?"

"Just asking questions. How about getting me some information I could use?"

She chopped at a little dab of ice cream with the edge of her spoon, cutting it into little particles, and then tapping those little particles until there was nothing but a liquid in the bottom of the glass dish. She said, "Let's see if I get you right, Donald. You're working for someone. You're trying to get information. If I gave you any information that was worthwhile, you couldn't pay for it—not until you talked with someone."

"That's right," I said.

"Then why should I tell you anything?"

"Just being friendly and cooperative," I said.

"Listen. I don't want money. That is, I don't know anything that's worth money, but I might be able to help. If I did, would you help me get a job in the city?"

"Frankly, I don't know of any jobs. I *might* be able to introduce you to someone who would know of some."

"If I helped you and then came to the city, would you—well, sort of show me the ropes?"

"If I could, yes."

She stirred her spoon around in little circles. She said, "You're playing a game with me. It's your job. You're here to find out something. If you think I have any information, you'll try to get that information without telling me why you want it. Is that right?"

I said, "That's right."

She said, "All right. I'll play the same kind of a game. If I can get anything out of you, I'm going to use it."

"Fair enough."

"Don't say I didn't warn you."

"I won't. You're warning me now."

"What do you want to know?" she asked.

"Do you know where Mrs. Lintig is?"

"No."

"Are there photographs of her in your newspaper morgue?"

"No."

"Have you ever looked?"

She nodded slowly, her manner preoccupied, her eyes focused on her ice-cream spoon.

"When?"

"About two months ago."

"Who," I asked, "was looking for her then?"

"A man by the name of Cross."

"You don't remember his initials, do you?"

"He was registered here in the hotel. You could look it up."

"What did he want?"

"The same thing you did."

"What did he look like?"

"In the forties, chunky, mostly bald, and a continuous cigar smoker. He kept the office stunk up all the time he was reading."

"Who was next?"

"A young woman."

"A *young* woman?"

She nodded.

"Who?"

"Her name was Evaline Dell. Does that sound phony to you?"

"Lots of names sound phony."

"Well, that sounded particularly phony."

"That must have been because she looked phony then," I said.

She thought that over and said, "Perhaps you're right. There was something about her that didn't just—I don't know, just didn't click."

"What did she look like?"

"I think you've put your finger on it. She looked phony. She looked as though she should be loud and—well, a little brazen. She wasn't. She was quiet and very mousy, as though she were walking on tiptoe all the time. She had a swell figure, and her clothes were up to the minute, and, believe me, they were clothes that showed off the figure. But she was just a little too nice, too mealy-mouthed, too virginal."

"And she didn't give the impression of being virginal?"

"No. You'd better look up Evaline Dell. I think she's related."

"Did she say so?"

"I gathered the impression she was a daughter by a former marriage."

"How old would that make Mrs. Lintig?"

"Not very old, around fifty. I believe Evaline Dell was just a child when her mother married Dr. Lintig—a secret child."

"That would make her around twenty-eight or something like that now."

"About that. No one here knew Mrs. Lintig had a daughter."

"Did she stay here at the hotel?"

"Yes."

"How long was she here?"

"A week."

"What did she do during that time?"

"She was trying to find a good picture of Mrs. Lintig. She bought up four that I know of, old shots from family albums. She was sending them away somewhere. They told me here at the hotel she'd posted several photographs and was very particular to get corrugated cardboard for the packing."

"Did the hotel give you the addresses?"

"No. She mailed them from the post office, but she got the materials for packing them here. The hotel people knew they were photographs."

"Anything else?" I asked.

"That's all."

I said, "Thanks, Marian. I don't know how much this will help. I hope it will help some. If it does, I might be able to get a little piece of money for you, not much, but some. The people I'm working for aren't very generous."

"Never mind. I'd rather play it the other way."

"What other way?"

"You find out what you can from me, and I'll find out what I can from you. Up to a certain point, I'll help you. If I should come to the city and look for a job, you do anything you can for me."

"I can't do very much."

"I understand. You do what you can. Will you?"

"Yes."

"Are you going to be here long?"

"I don't know. It depends."

"Perhaps something might turn up. In case it should, where could I reach you?"

I took a card that had only my name on it, and wrote the name of the building and the number of the room in which Bertha Cool had her office. I said, "A letter sent to me there will be delivered."

She studied the card for a minute, tucked it in her purse, and smiled at me. I helped her on with her coat and took her home in the agency car. She lived in a two-story frame building that needed paint. There was no sign in front intimating that it was a rooming house, so I figured she was living with a private family. I didn't bother too much about it because I knew I could find out all about her any time I wanted to. As she herself had said, the people in that town knew more about her business than she did.

I could tell from the way she acted she hoped I wasn't going to try to kiss her good night, and I didn't.

I got back to the hotel a little before midnight. A cigar made the night clerk communicative. After a while I checked through the register and found the signatures of Miller Cross and Evaline Dell. I figured the addresses were phony, but made a surreptitious note of them just on general principles while the clerk was busy at the switchboard.

When he came back to the desk, we chatted for a while, and he mentioned that Miss Dell had arrived by train, that her trunk had been damaged, and she'd secured affidavits from the hotel porter and the transfer man. He hadn't heard whether the claim had ever been settled.

I found I could send a wire from the telephone booth, and sent one to Bertha Cool:

Making slow progress. Get complete information on claim against Southern Pacific Railroad Company for damaged trunk shipped to Oakview about three weeks ago. Claim may have been made under name of Evaline Dell. Can I pay twenty-five bucks to party giving helpful information?

I hung up the telephone and went up to my room. I tried my key, and it didn't work. While I was trying to figure that out, the door was jerked open from the inside, and a big man, whose figure loomed against the light seeping in from the window, said, "Come on in, Lam."

He switched on the lights as I stood there on the threshold, looking up at him.

He was around six feet and weighed over two hundred. He wasn't thin, and he wasn't fat. He was broad across the shoulders, and the hand which shot out and grabbed my necktie was a big, battered paw. "I said, 'Come on in,' " he observed and jerked.

I shot on into the room. He gave a swing with his shoulders, and I went spinning across the carpet to crash down on the bed. He kicked the door shut, and said, "That's better."

He was between me and the door—between me and the telephone. From what I'd seen of the service the night clerk gave at the hotel switchboard, I figured it would take at least thirty seconds to get any action on the telephone. Nor could I picture this guy standing idly by while I tried to telephone the police.

I straightened my necktie, pulled down the edges of my collar, and said, "What do *you* want?"

"That's better," he said, drawing up a chair and sitting down, keeping between me and the door.

He grinned, and I didn't like his grin. I didn't like anything about him. He was beefy and assured and acted as though he owned the town and the hotel.

"What," I asked, "do you want?"

"I want you to get the hell out of here."

"Why?"

"The climate," he said. "It's bad for little pipsqueaks like you."

"It hasn't disagreed with me so far," I said.

"No, but it will. It's the malaria, you know. Mosquitoes buzz around at night. They bite you, and the first thing you know you feel sick."

"Where should I go," I asked, "to avoid the *insects*?"

His face darkened. He said, "No more of that, pint size."

I fished a cigarette out of my pocket, and lit it. He watched me put the match up to the cigarette and laughed when he saw that my hand was shaking.

I shook the match out, inhaled a lungful of smoke, and said, "Go ahead. It's your party."

He said, "I've said it. There's your bag. Pack it. I'm here to escort you down to your car."

"Suppose I don't want to be escorted?"

He said amiably, but significantly, "If you left now, you could leave under your own power."

"And if I waited?"

"You might have an accident."

"I don't have accidents. My friends know that."

"You might walk in your sleep and fall out of the window.

Your friends could back track on that and never get any place."

"I could start yelling," I said. "Someone would hear me."

"Sure, they would."

"And notify the police."

"That's right."

"Then what would happen?"

"I wouldn't be here, and you wouldn't, either."

"Well," I said, "I'll try it," and let out a yell: "Help! Pol—"

He came out of the chair like a cat. I saw him looming over me, and put everything I had in a right to his stomach.

It never connected.

Something hit the side of my head, seemed to pull my neck loose, and the lights went out. When I came to, I was in the agency heap rolling along pavement. My head hurt, and my jaw was so sore I could hardly move it. The big man was sitting at the wheel, and when I moved, he looked over at me, and said, "Jesus, what a heap! Why doesn't your damned agency give you decent transportation?"

I put my head out of the window so the cool night air would help clear my head. The big man kept a heavy foot on the throttle, and Bertha Cool's car, rattling its protest, swayed from side to side along the road.

It was a mountain road, winding and twisting up a canyon. After a while it came out on a level place with pine trees standing in dark silhouettes against the starlit sky. The big man slowed down the car, apparently looking for a side road.

I watched my chance and lurched across the seat. I grabbed the steering wheel with both hands and jerked. I couldn't turn the wheel, although the car swerved to one side of the road and then back to the other as he exerted pressure to counteract mine. He snapped up his elbow without taking his hand off the wheel, and it caught me on the point of my sore jaw, making me loosen my grip. Something like a pile driver caught me on the back of the neck, and the next I remembered I was lying flat on my back in the dark trying to figure where I was.

I put events into some sort of hazy sequence after a while, and groped in my pocket for matches. I found one and lit it. I was inside a log cabin, lying flat on dry pine needles. I sat up on the bunk, which was covered with old, dried pine boughs, and struck another match. I found a candle and lit it, then looked at my watch. It was quarter past three.

The cabin evidently hadn't been used for a while. It was dirty and smelled musty. The windows were boarded up. Rats had been rummaging around the place, dragging stale bread crusts out of a cupboard. A spider, hanging in a big cobweb, seemed to be staring ominously at me. Dried pine needles from the branches on my bunk had got in my hair and, as I stood up, worked down my neck.

I felt as though I'd been run over by a steam roller.

I was all alone in the cabin. I looked at the boarded windows and tried the door, expecting to find it locked. It wasn't. Cool mountain air, filled with the tang of pine, struck my nostrils. Something black was out in front of the door. I brought out the candle and saw it was the agency car.

A mountain stream was making noises, apparently close to the cabin. I did a little exploring with the candle, and found a trail which led to the water. I wet my handkerchief in the ice-cold water and put it on my forehead, on my eyes, and then on the back of my neck. A gust of wind blew the candle out. I sat there in the dark letting the cold water do its stuff.

After a while I groped with cold, wet fingers for my matches, and lit the candle at the second try. I went back to the cabin. I didn't have the faintest idea where I was.

I blew out the candle, closed the cabin door, and got in the agency car. The keys were in the ignition. I switched on the motor. The tank was half full of gas. The headlights showed a rugged mountain road leading from the cabin. I put the car into gear and found a paved highway within a quarter of a mile. I didn't know directions, but I turned the car on the down grade, figuring I wanted to get toward the valley.

Chapter Two

Bertha Cool pushed aside the Monday-morning accumulation of mail, lit a cigarette, looked across the desk at me, and said, "For God's sake, Donald! You've been fighting again!"

I sat down in the chair across from the desk. "It wasn't a fight."

"What was it?"

"I was escorted out of town."

"Who did the escorting?"

"From the way he acted, I would say he was a member of the local constabulary, but his tactics were a little too sophisticated for Oakview. I don't think he was local. He must have had a friend who followed along behind in another car, or else he had one staked out for a getaway car. He left me the agency heap. He even bought gas for it."

"What makes you think he was a cop?"

"He looked like it, he talked like it, and he acted like it."

She beamed at me, and said, "Donald, you *do* have the damndest times."

"Don't I," I said.

"Did you go back?"

"No. I didn't go back."

Her eyes hardened. "Why not?"

"The climate," I said, "isn't so hot. They have malaria. There are mosquitoes."

She said, "Nuts."

"And," I said, "I think we can do more at this end than we can at that."

"How so?"

"Two people have been there ahead of me. They wanted the same thing I did. I figured they took away more than they left."

"Then why did they want you out of town?"

I said, "I'll bite."

Bertha Cool studied me through a blue haze of cigarette smoke. She said, "That's funny as hell, Donald."

"I'm glad you think so."

"Now, don't get sore, lover. You know it's all in a day's work. It's what you get for being a little runt. People figure it's easy to push you around. Who was this guy?"

"I don't know. He was sitting in the hotel room when I came up, right after I'd sent you that wire. I started to go back to Oakview, and then figured I had a lead I could follow to better advantage at this end."

She said, "Tell me about the lead."

I took out my notebook and gave her a summary of the information.

Bertha Cool said, "It's a bum steer on Mrs. Lintig. She never did sail through the Canal—not in 1919, nor the early part of 1920—not under her own name anyway, and if she used an assumed name, we're licked. It's too far back to trace anyone by a description, and we can't pay twenty-five bucks for information. They pay *us* for getting that, and we keep the dough for salaries, office expense, and profit. Don't ever waste words in a wire asking a question like that again."

"It was a night letter," I said. "I had fifty words coming. It didn't cost you anything extra."

She said, "I know. I counted the words to make sure—but don't do it again. Who gave you the information?"

"A girl. I don't feel so generous toward her now. The guy who ran me out of town might have been Charlie."

"Who's Charlie?"

"I don't know. It's a nickname. What did you find out about the trunk?"

"An Evaline D. Harris made a claim for seventy-five dollars' damage to a trunk and wearing apparel."

"What happened to the claim?"

"Still in process of adjustment. The railroad company caved in one end of the trunk. They claim the trunk was old and defective. They say the claim for damages is exorbitant."

"Get Evaline Dell's address?" I asked.

"Evaline Harris," she said.

"They're the same. She was there for about a week."

"Yes, I have it. Let's see. Where is it? Hell's fire, I can't *ever* find anything!" She picked up the telephone, and said to Elsie Brand, "Find the address of Evaline Harris. I gave it to you.... Yes, I did....Oh....In my right-hand desk drawer, eh? Thanks."

Bertha Cool opened her right-hand desk drawer, rummaged around among some papers, and brought out a slip of paper. I copied the address into my notebook.

"Going to see her?" she asked.

I said, "Yes. Here's another hunch. The state medical board may have been asked to transfer a license from Dr. James C. Lintig to some other name."

"What makes you think so?"

"Lintig was an eye, ear, nose, and throat specialist. He skipped out. His office nurse went with him. Figure it out. A man doesn't throw away his right to practice his profession."

"What makes you think he'd be practicing in this state?"

"Because he couldn't go to any other state without accounting for the time he'd spent in this state. That would make for inquiries. He probably got a court order changing his name, sent a certified copy to the state medical board, and had his license issued in a new name as a matter of routine. That would be dead simple."

Bertha Cool looked at me, her frosty gray eyes twinkling approvingly. "Donald," she said, "you're a brainy little runt. It's a good hunch." After a minute, she went on: "Of course, our instructions were to concentrate on Mrs. Lintig."

I said, "After we find Mrs. Lintig, no one will ever know how we found her. I need fifty bucks for expenses."

She said, "You sure do go through money. Here. Try to make this last. You think he knows where she is?"

"Dr. Lintig," I said, "gave her everything. He probably gave her a secret property settlement." I counted the money and pocketed it.

"Well, what if he did?"

"If he was going to give her everything, he could have stayed right on in Oakview where he had a practice built up. A court couldn't have stripped him any cleaner than he stripped himself. He *wanted* to go away. If there was a secret property settlement, he probably knows where she is now."

Bertha Cool narrowed her eyes. "There's something to that," she admitted.

"Do you have Smith's telephone number?"

"Yes."

"Well, give him a ring and—" I broke off, and Bertha Cool said, "What is it, Donald?"

"Let's not let Smith know just what we're doing right now. We'll find Mrs. Lintig in our own way. I can get in touch with Evaline Harris as a claim adjuster, for the railroad company. I'll pay her seventy-five dollars for damage to her trunk and take a receipt. Later on, I can come back and crab that I made the adjustment under false representations. It'll give me an angle of approach."

Bertha Cool's eyes popped wide open. "My God, Donald,"

she said. "Do you think this agency is made of money? *We* should go around adjusting the claims of the railroad company!"

I said, "You can charge it as a necessary expense."

She said. "Be your age, Donald. There'll be other expenses. The more we pay to other people, the less we have for Bertha."

I said, "It'll cost more than seventy-five dollars trying to follow a cold trail."

Bertha Cool shook her head. "That's out. Think up something else."

I picked up my hat, and said, "All right. I will."

My hand was on the doorknob when she called me back. "And get to work on this thing, Donald. Don't mark time while you're trying to think up ideas."

"I am working on it. I've put an ad in the Oakview *Blade* asking for information about Mrs. James Lintig or about her heirs, indicating that someone has died and left her property."

"How much did that ad cost?" Bertha asked.

"Five dollars."

Bertha looked at me over the smoke that spiraled upward from the end of her cigarette. "It's too damn much," she said.

I opened the door, said casually, "It probably is, at that," and closed the door behind me before she could say anything.

I drove the agency car around to the address of Evaline Harris. It was a cheap, three-storied brick apartment house. By the mailboxes was a list of the tenants and call buttons. I found Evaline Harris was in 309, and pressed the button. I had rung the third time when the buzzer announced that the door was being unlatched. I walked in.

There was a lobby stretching across the building and extending back some fifteen feet. It was dark, gloomy, and filled with odors. A door marked *Manager* was on the left. Midway in the corridor a weak electric light glowed over the entrance to an automatic elevator. I rattled up to the third floor and walked back toward 309.

Evaline Harris was standing in the door, peering down the corridor with sleep-swollen eyes. She didn't look either mousy or virginal. She said, "What do you want?" in a voice that was rough as a rasp.

"I'm an adjuster for the railroad company. I want to make an adjustment on that trunk."

"My God," she said. "It's about time. Why pick this hour of the morning? Don't you know a girl who works nights has to sleep sometime?"

"I'm sorry," I said, and waited to be invited in.

She stood in the doorway. Over her shoulder I caught a glimpse of a folding wall-bed let down, the covers rumpled and the pillowcases wrinkled.

She continued to stand in the doorway, doubt, hostility, and avarice all showing in her manner. "All I want is a check," she said.

She was blonde, and I couldn't see any dark line near the roots of her hair. She was wearing wrinkled orange pajamas, a dressing-gown thrown over her shoulders and loosely held in front with her left hand. The back of the hand said she was about twenty-seven. With make-up, her face could have passed for twenty-two. I couldn't get much of an idea of her figure, but she stood with the balanced posture of one who is young and lithe.

She said, "Oh, well! Come on in."

I walked on in. The apartment was smelly with sleep. She jerked the covers back into position, propped herself on the edge of the bed, and said, "The comfortable chair's over there in that corner. Drag it out. I have to move it when I let the bed down. What do you want?"

"I want to get some more particulars on your claim."

"I've given you all the particulars," she said. "I should have asked for two hundred dollars. Then you'd have settled for seventy-five, which is my actual damage. If you're trying to chisel, don't waste your time and mine. And don't ever call me before three in the afternoon."

"I'm sorry," I said.

There was a package of cigarettes and an ashtray on a stand by the head of the bed. She reached out for a cigarette, lit it, and sucked smoke down deep into her lungs. "Go ahead," she said.

I took out one of my own cigarettes and lit up. "I think I can get the claim through the department for you after you've cleared up one or two details."

"That's better," she said. "What are the details? The trunk's down in the basement if you want to see it. One corner's smashed in. Splinters of wood ruined my stockings and one of my dresses."

"Do you," I asked, "have the stockings and the dress?"

She avoided my eyes, and said, "No."

I said, "Our records show that while you were in Oakview, you went under the name of Evaline Dell."

She whipped the cigarette out of her mouth and stared at me with wide-eyed indignation. "Well, of all the snoops! No wonder you're nursing a black eye! What business is it of yours what name I went under? You smashed the trunk, didn't you?"

I said, "In adjustments of this kind, the railroad company has to get a valid release."

"Well, I'll give you one. I'll sign it Evaline Dell if you want. My name's Evaline Dell Harris. I'll sign it Eleanor Roosevelt if that will help."

"You're living here under the name of Harris?"

"Of course I am. Evaline Dell was my maiden name. Harris was my husband's name."

"If you're married, your husband would have to sign with you."

"Bosh! I haven't seen Bill Harris for three years."

"Divorce?" I asked.

She hesitated a moment, then said, "Yes."

"You see," I explained, "if the railroad company made a settlement and got a release, and that release wasn't signed by the person who owned the property, the railroad company would still be liable."

"Are you trying to tell me I don't own my own trunk?"

"Not that," I said. "There's a discrepancy in names. The railroad company insists that discrepancy be explained."

"Well, it's explained now."

I said, "The head of the Claim Department is very particular, Mrs. Harris. He—"

"Miss Harris," she said.

"Very well, Miss Harris. The head of the Claim Department is a stickler for detail. He sent me to find out why you made the trip to Oakview under the name of Evaline Dell instead of under the name of Evaline Harris."

She said sullenly, "Give him my compliments, and tell him to go jump in the lake."

I remembered the expression of avarice in her eyes when she had stood in the doorway. I got to my feet, said, "All right. I'll tell him. I'm sorry I disturbed you. I didn't know you worked nights," and made for the door.

I had my hand on the knob when she said, "Wait a minute. Come back and sit down."

I crossed over to drop ashes off the end of my cigarette into her ashtray and went back to the chair.

"You said you were trying to get the adjustment through for me."

"That's right."

"You're working for the railroad company, ain't you?"

"We'd like to get the adjustment off our books. Of course, if we can't get together, we'll turn it over to our legal department, and let them handle it."

"I don't want a lawsuit."

"Neither do we."

She said, "I went to Oakview on business. It's my business. It's none of yours."

"We're not interested in the business, only in your reason for taking another name."

"It wasn't another name. It's my name."

"I'm afraid I couldn't make that stick."

She said, "All right. I went there to get some information about someone."

"Can you give me the name of the party?"

"No." She hesitated long enough to drop the ashes off her cigarette, and then went on: "A man sent me to Oakview to get some dope about his wife."

"I'd like to check that. Can you give me his name and address?"

"I can, but I won't."

I took out my notebook, and said dubiously, "Well, I *might* put that across for you, but I think the Claim Department's not going to be satisfied. With this confusion about names, they're going to want the whole story."

"Suppose you did put it across? When would I get the check?"

"Almost immediately."

"I need the money," she said.

I kept quiet.

She said, "The information I was after was very confidential."

"Are you," I asked, "a private detective?"

"No."

"What *is* your occupation?"

She said, "I work in a night spot."

"Where?"

"The Blue Cave."

"A singer?" I asked.

"I do a turn."

"Tell me one thing. The husband and wife were not living together?"

"No."

"How long had they been separated?"

"Quite a while."

"Can you give me the name of some witness who knows the facts?"

"What's all this got to do with my trunk?"

"I suppose you completed your business in Oakview, and turned the information over to the husband?"

"Yes."

"Listen, if you want your claim settled fast, give me his name and address, let me call on him, and get his verification. I could include it in my report, and that would satisfy the company."

"Well, I can't do it."

"That, of course, leaves us right where we started."

"Look here," she said. "This was my own trunk, my own wearing apparel. It's my own claim. No one needs to know anything about it. That is, the person who sent me mustn't know anything about it."

"Why?"

"Because it would be taken out of my sal—compensation."

"I see," I said, snapped my notebook shut, put it in my pocket, and closed my fountain pen. "I'll see what I can do," I said dubiously. "I'm afraid the boss will want more information. This is full of holes."

She said, "There's a bottle of Scotch in it for you if you get me a check."

"No, thanks. I couldn't do that."

I got up and ground out my cigarette in her ashtray. She moved her feet over and said, "Sit down here on the bed. You look like a nice boy."

"I am," I said.

She grinned. "What's your name?"

"Lam."

"What's your first name?"

"Donald."

"Okay, Donald. Let's be friends. I don't want to fight with your damn company, but I need the dough. How about putting it across for me?"

"I'll do the best I can."

She said, "That's a dear. How about breakfast? Had anything to eat?"

"Long ago," I said.

"I can fix up a cup of coffee and a little toast if you're hungry."

"No, thanks. I've got a lot of work to do."

"Listen, Donald, try and put it across for me, will you? Who gave you the shiner?"

"A guy socked me."

"Can't you make out a report that'll satisfy that old grouch-face?"

"You mean the claim manager?" I asked.

"Yes."

"Ever met him?" I asked.

"No."

"He's about thirty-five with dark eyes and long, wavy, black hair. Women go nuts over him."

Her eyes showed interest. "I'll doll up and go talk with *him*," she said. "I bet he'd put through a check."

"It might be a good idea," I said, "but don't do it until I've made my report. Perhaps that'll be all you need. If he makes a kick about it. I'll let you know where the beef is and then you can go do your stuff."

"Okay, Donald. Thanks."

We shook hands, and I went out.

There was a grocery store on the corner. I used the telephone to call Bertha Cool's office. Elsie Brand switched the call through to Bertha Cool's private telephone without comment. "Donald talking," I said.

"Where have you been?" Bertha Cool asked.

"Working. I think I've uncovered a lead."

"What is it?"

"This Harris girl is an entertainer in a night spot. Lintig sent her to find out about his wife."

She said, "Donald, what the hell do you mean by having telegrams sent collect?"

"I didn't know there were any."

"Well, there was one, with fifty cents' charges on it."

"Who's it from?"

"How should I know. I sent it back. It wasn't addressed to the agency. It was addressed to you personally. Get it out of your head that I'm Santa Claus."

"What company?" I asked.

"Western Union."

"How long ago?"

"Twenty minutes. It's back at the main office."

I said, "All right," and hung up. I drove down to the main office, and had to wait five minutes while they located the telegram. I paid fifty cents. It was from Oakview and read:

Party you inquired about registered here in hotel under own name. Do I get anything out of it?

Marian

I took an envelope from my pocket, wrote across the face of the telegram: *Bertha: This is it. I'll be at the Palace Hotel in Oakview. Better notify our client.*

I always carried envelopes stamped with special delivery, addressed to the agency, for use in making reports. I put the telegram in one of the envelopes, sealed it, dropped it into a mailbox, and started north, wishing that Bertha Cool would either get a new car or have cases closer to home—and wondering why the devil, with everyone in the country looking for her and after an absence of more than twenty years, Mrs. James C. Lintig should decide to return to Oakview and register at the Palace Hotel under her own name. I wondered if there was any possibility my advertisement in the paper had been responsible. If so, Mrs. Lintig hadn't been so very far from Oakview. Which opened a lot of interesting possibilities.

Chapter Three

I got a few hours sleep in an auto camp, reached Oakview early Tuesday morning, and had breakfast at the hotel dining room. It was a rotten breakfast. I finished the last of my cold coffee and went out to the lobby.

The clerk said, "Why hello, Mr. Lam. Your bag's here at the desk. We didn't know whether you intended to check out. You left suddenly. We were—er—concerned about you."

"You needn't have been. I'll pay my bill now."

He looked at my eye as I handed him some money. "Accident?" he asked.

"No. I was walking through a roundhouse in my sleep. A locomotive hit me."

He said, "Oh," and gave me a receipt and my change.

"Mrs. Lintig up yet?" I asked.

"I don't think so. She hasn't come down yet."

I thanked him and went down the street to the *Blade* office. Marian Dunton came out from behind the partition, and said, "Why, hello—what about it? Good Lord, what happened to your eye?"

I said, "I stubbed my toe. I tried to get you twenty-five bucks. I couldn't make it stick. What's she doing here?"

"Apparently just visiting friends. Remember, I warned you."

"Visiting friends after all this time, and in a hotel?"

"That's right."

"How does she look?"

"I understand she shows her age. Mrs. Purdy, the mother of

one of her old friends, has seen her, and says she looks terrible. Her hair's turned white, and she's put on a lot of weight. Mrs. Purdy says she told her she hasn't had a happy moment since Dr. Lintig ran away."

"It's been twenty-one years," I said.

"Yes, it's a long time—for a person to be unhappy."

I said, "Isn't it—and why did you call my attention to the warning at this particular time?"

"Because," she said, "I don't like being pushed out in the cold."

"Who's pushing you out in the cold?"

"You are."

"I don't get you."

She said, with some feeling, "Don't stall, Donald. Mrs. Lintig is mixed up in something that's important. A lot of people have become interested in her. If you won't take me into your confidence—well, I warned you, that's all."

I said, "How about some information?"

She said, "That depends. Donald, what *did* happen to your eye?"

"I met Charlie," I said.

"Charlie?"

"Yes, you know. Your boyfriend. He resented me taking you out to dinner."

"Oh," she said, lowering her eyes. A smile twitched at the corners of her lips. "Was he jealous?"

"Very."

"Did you hit him first?"

I said, "He struck the first blow."

"Who got in the last blow?" she asked.

"The first was it," I said. "That old proverb to the effect that 'that which is first shall be last' is intended to apply to fist fights."

"I'll have to speak to Charlie," she said. "He didn't hurt his hand, did he?"

"He might have shortened the arm a couple of inches by driving his knuckles back to the wrist bone, but aside from that he's all right. How about my information?"

"What is it you want?"

"The local constabulary," I said. "Do you own a cop about six feet tall, forty years old, around two hundred and twenty, with black hair, gray eyes, a cleft chin, and a mole on his right cheek? He has the disposition of a camel and the execution of a mule. His name wouldn't by any chance be Charlie, would it?"

"We don't own one," she said. "Our cops average about sixty to sixty-five. They're appointed through political pull. They chew tobacco, are suspicious, and their chief duty is to drag in enough fines from out-of-town motorists to offset their salaries. Was it a cop who gave you the black eye, Donald?"

"I wouldn't know. How about killing that ad in your paper?"

"It's too late now. Here's your mail."

She took out a sack of letters tied with a heavy cord.

I said, "Good Lord, I suppose everyone in town wrote me."

"There are only thirty-seven letters here," she said. "That's nothing at all. *Blade* ads get results, you know."

I said, "I need a secretary—someone around twenty-two or twenty-three with brown eyes and brown hair, someone who smiles easily, not just a lip smile, but who throws her whole face into it."

She said, "She'd have to be loyal to her employer, I suppose."

"Oh, yes."

She said, "I don't know anyone who fits the description who would care for the job. However, I'll keep it in mind. How long are you going to be here, Donald?"

"It depends on Charlie," I said. "How about giving me a job for two hours?"

"Doing what?"

"Representing the *Blade*."

She said, "We *could* use a man around twenty-six or twenty-seven, about five feet five, with nice, wavy, dark hair, dark, sensitive eyes—and a black eye. But he'd have to be working for the paper and not for himself."

I said, "You're related to the man who runs the paper, aren't you?"

"Yes. He's my uncle."

"Tell him you've hired a reporter," I said, and started for the door.

"Don't you get us into any libel suits, Donald."

"I won't."

"You're going to see Mrs. Lintig?"

"Yes."

"And you want to approach her as a *Blade* reporter?"

"That's what I have in mind."

She said, "That might make complications, Donald. And I don't think Uncle would like it."

"That's going to be too bad. I'll have to add your uncle as well as Charlie to my list of local enemies."

"Don't you want your mail?" she asked.

"Not now," I said. "I'll see you after a while. The person I asked about couldn't have been a sheriff's deputy, could he?"

"No. They wear big sombreros—and are a pretty decent bunch."

"This man has metropolitan manners," I said, and walked to the door.

She called after me, "If you'll cut me in, I'll work with you."

I said, "I can't cut you in. I told you so. I tried it. It didn't work."

I thought there was a flicker of satisfaction in her eyes, almost a look of relief. "Okay," she said, "you can't say I didn't make the offer." I nodded and let the door click shut.

I went back to the hotel. Mrs. Lintig hadn't been seen in the lobby. The clerk suggested I might phone her.

The house was proud of its telephone system. It had been recently installed to "thoroughly modernize" the house. There was a sign reading *House Telephones* in letters a foot high. Below that sign, on a bench-like desk, was one telephone. I crossed over to it, and the clerk connected me with Mrs. Lintig's room.

Her voice sounded hard and cautious over the line as she said, "Hello."

"Mr. Lam, of the *Blade*. I'd like an interview."

"What about?" she asked.

"How Oakview looks to you after a prolonged absence," I said.

"Nothing about—about my private affairs?"

"Not a word—I'll be right up, if you don't mind." She started to hedge, but I dropped the receiver into place and went on up. She was standing in the door of her room, waiting for me.

She was rather heavy. Her hair was silvered. Her eyes were dark and hard. There hadn't been much sagging to her face, and her eyes glowed with an alert awareness. She gave the impression of having been on her own, where she'd had to look out for herself against all comers.

"You're the man who telephoned me?" she asked.

"Yes."

"What's your name?"

"Lam."

"And you work on one of the newspapers?"

"Yes. There's only one."

"What did you say it was?"

"The *Blade.*"

"Oh, yes. Well, I don't want to be interviewed."

"I think I understand, Mrs. Lintig. Naturally, you resent the idea of having a newspaper pry into your affairs. But you could give us just a few of your impressions on returning to the city—it's been some time since you were here."

"Twenty-one years."

"How does the city look to you now?"

She said, "It looks like the damndest hick burg—to think I spent a part of my life here! If I could only get back the time I wasted here, if I only could—" She paused, peered at me and said, "I suppose that's the wrong thing to say."

"It is."

"I was afraid it was. What should I say?"

"About how the town still retains its distinct individuality. Other cities may have grown faster, but seem to have lost their individuality in the process. Oakview has the distinctive charm which always characterized it."

She peered at me through narrowed eyes.

"I guess you know the answers," she said. "Move over here into the light where I can see you."

I moved over.

She said, "You look young to be a reporter."

"I am."

"I can't see clearly. This hotel wins the prize for being the worst, the poorest excuse for—a bellboy broke my spectacles within fifteen minutes of the time I hit town. He plunked a suitcase right down on top of them, smashed them all to pieces."

I said, "That's too bad. The only pair you had?"

"Yes. I've had to send for more. They should be here today."

"Where," I asked, "are they coming from?"

Her eyes sparkled and glittered at me. "My oculist," she said.

"San Francisco?"

"My oculist," she said firmly, "is sending them by mail."

I said, "So you notice what's happened to the town?"

"Do I!"

"Naturally, it isn't the sort of place you remembered. It must seem a lot smaller."

She said, "It seems—like looking at a city through the wrong end of a telescope. What keeps people here?"

"The climate," I said. "It used to be unhealthy for me, and I moved away for a while. Then I came back and I've never felt better."

She seemed puzzled. "What was the matter with you?"

"Oh, a variety of things."

"You look a little frail, but you seem healthy enough."

"I am. I suppose you're inclined to look at our little city through the eyes of a world traveler. When you left, you were more a part of the surroundings. Now you've become a citizen of the world. Tell me, Mrs. Lintig, how does Oakview compare with London?" She took that right in her stride. "It's smaller," she said, and then, after a moment: "Who told you I'd been in London?"

I gave her my best smile, which seemed wasted on her, probably due to the absence of her glasses. "Your manner," I said. "You have developed a cosmopolitan manner. You don't seem a part of Oakview any longer."

"Good Lord, I should hope not! This place gives me the willies."

I took out a notebook and scribbled a note.

"What's that?" she asked suspiciously.

"Just stating that you said the town was quaint, but had retained its individuality."

She said, "You're tactful, aren't you?"

"A reporter has to be. Have you kept in touch with Dr. Lintig?"

"I wish I had. I understand he's made a lot of money somewhere. After the raw deal he gave me, it wouldn't hurt him any to do something for me now."

"Then you've heard from him?"

"No."

I put sympathy into my voice. "The whole affair must have been a terrific shock to you, Mrs. Lintig."

"I'll say it was. It ruined my entire life. I took it too seriously. I was more attached to him than I realized, and when I discovered his infidelity, I was furious. To think of him keeping that woman right under my nose."

"The records show that he turned over all of his property to you."

"Well, that was just a drop in the bucket. You can't break a woman's heart, ruin her life, and then toss a couple of deeds in her lap, and expect her to go right on as though nothing had happened."

"Yes, I see your point. That case, I understand, has never been dismissed."

"It's dismissed now," she said.

"It is?"

"Yes. What did you think I came to Oakview for?"

"To visit some of your old friends."

"I haven't any friends here. Those I did have have moved away. It seems as though everyone who mattered has moved out of town. What in the world happened to this place?"

"It had some bad luck," I said. "The railroad changed its division point, and quite a few other things happened."

She said, "Humph!"

"I take it then, since you've dismissed the action, you're still married to Dr. Lintig."

"Of course I am."

"And you haven't heard from him during the twenty-one-year period since you left?"

"I—say, I thought you weren't going to talk about this case."

"Not for publication," I said. "I was just trying to get your background."

"Well, you can leave my background out of it."

"The story," I said, "should be treated from a human interest angle—the real evils of divorce and all of that. You and Dr. Lintig were well established here and well thought of. You had a host of friends. Then, out of a clear sky, this thing happened to you. You found yourself faced with the necessity of beginning life all over."

She said, "I'm glad you see it from my viewpoint."

"I'm trying to. I'd like to get a little more of that viewpoint. It would make my story more interesting."

"You're tactful," she said. "I'm not. You know how to write. I don't."

"Have I your permission to use my own judgment then?"

"Yes—no. Wait a minute—I guess not. I don't think you'd better say anything about it. You can say that the action has been dismissed. That's enough. I don't want to have my feelings spread out in print to satisfy the curiosity of a lot of morbid scandal-mongers."

"You didn't do anything. It was Dr. Lintig."

"I guess I was a little fool. If I'd known more about life, I'd have kept my eyes closed to what was going on and continued to live on with him as his wife."

"You mean remained right on here in Oakview?"

She all but shuddered. "Good heavens, no! This town is dead

from its—it's quaint. It's retained its individuality. It's all right for the people who like it."

"Perhaps your travels have brought about a change in you. Perhaps you've changed while Oakview is standing still."

"Perhaps."

"Where are you living now, Mrs. Lintig?"

"Here in the hotel."

"I mean what's your permanent address?"

"Do you want to publish that?"

"Why not?"

She laughed and said, "And I'd have half of the crackpots in town writing to me. No. I'm finished with Oakview, and Oakview can be finished with me. This was a bitter chapter in my life. I want to close it and forget it."

"Then I should think you'd want the divorce to go through so you could have your freedom."

"I don't want my freedom."

"May I ask why?"

"It's none of your business. My God, can't I come to town and handle my own affairs without having the newspapers ask me a lot of personal questions?"

"People are interested in you. A lot of people have been speculating on what happened to you."

"Who?"

"Oh, lots of people."

"Please be more specific."

"Just our general readers," I said.

"I don't believe it. They wouldn't remember a person who had moved away ages ago."

"Have you been discussing the divorce with anyone lately?"

"What if I have?"

"I just wondered."

"You want to know too much, young man," she said. "You promised me that you wouldn't try to pry into my private affairs."

I said, "Just what you'd care to give us, Mrs. Lintig."

"Well, I don't care to give you anything."

"One would think that, in view of the circumstances, a woman as—you'll pardon me, Mrs. Lintig—as attractive as you would have met someone for whom you cared and married again."

"Who said I married again?" she demanded, her eyes hard, black, and glittering.

"It was just speculation."

"Well, the people in Oakview had better mind their own business, and I'll mind mine."

"And, of course, one naturally wonders what happened to Dr. Lintig and to that nurse."

"I don't care a snap of my fingers for what happened to him. I have my own life to live."

"But the effect of dismissing this divorce action is to wipe it off the records. It leaves you legally married to Dr. Lintig. You're now his legal wife—unless there's been a divorce in Reno or—"

"Well, there hasn't."

"You're positive of that."

"I guess I know my own business. I should know what I've done."

"But what has *he* done?"

"It doesn't make any difference what he's done. That divorce action was pending here in Oakview. The Oakview courts had jurisdiction of the entire matter. Until that case was dismissed, he couldn't go anywhere and get a divorce that would be worth the paper it was written on."

"That's what your attorneys have advised you?"

She said, "Mr. Lam, I think we've discussed this matter far

enough. I have nothing to say about my affairs for publication. You wanted to know how Oakview looked to me, and I told you. I haven't had my breakfast yet, and I have a splitting headache because of those broken glasses. That *stupid* bellboy!"

She got up, walked across to the door, and held it open. "You won't publish anything about Dr. Lintig?"

"The dismissal of the divorce action will appear upon the records."

"What if it does?"

"It's news."

"All right, publish it."

"And you're here. That's news."

"All right, publish that."

"And your comments are also news."

"I haven't made any. You did the talking, and I don't care to discuss it. I don't want you to publish a word I've said. Goodbye, Mr. Lam."

I bowed affably. "Thank you very much for the interview, Mrs. Lintig."

She slammed the door behind me as I walked out into the corridor. I went back down to the *Blade* office.

"Do you," I asked of Marian, "keep a rewrite boy?"

"Oh, yes, Mr. Lam," she said, "for the star reporters, we do."

"Where is he?"

"Over in that corner. His name is Mr. Corona, Mr. Smith-Corona."

I said, "Before I go to all that trouble. I've had an interesting interview with Mrs. Lintig. She'll deny it if we publish it, and threatens to sue the paper for libel. Do we publish it or don't we?"

"We don't," she said quickly.

"I could make a swell story out of it, one that would interest your readers."

"Would it get us any new subscribers?" she asked.

"It should."

"And where would they come from?"

"That's taking a low-down, unfair advantage," I said.

She smiled. "Well, we're definitely not progressive, Mr. Lam. My uncle is old-fashioned, and he doesn't like libel suits."

"He told you to go out to dinner with me and get a story," I said. "That shows a nose for news."

She said, "I'm glad you reminded me of my duty. How about that story?"

"No," I said, "if your uncle publishes it, I'll sue him for libel."

"You might at least satisfy my personal curiosity."

"I know you," I said. "As soon as you get the story, you'll quit stringing me along. I prefer to be strung along. Look at the way you showed me how to order dinner."

She said, "My uncle won't let me go out with you unless I get results."

"That," I admitted, "is a thought. I'll try and think up something."

"How did you get along with Evaline Dell's trunk?" she asked abruptly.

I said, "Now wait a minute. One thing at a time. What's this about Evaline Dell's trunk?"

She said, "I have to hand it to you, Donald. You're resourceful. We checked back on Miller Cross and Evaline Dell and found out the names and addresses were fictitious. That's as far as *we* got. Naturally, we checked up on what you'd been doing."

"And found out what?" I asked.

"That you'd been asking questions about the trunk."

"And so?"

"And so we wrote the railroad company. I have a letter here

this morning stating that a claim was made, not by Evaline Dell, but by Evaline D. Harris."

"Did you get her address?"

"Yes. The railroad company gives country newspapers a break now and then."

"Are you going to see her?"

"Are you?"

"That depends."

"What did she say, Donald?"

I shook my head.

She regarded me bitterly for a moment, and said, "You certainly play a funny game, all take and no give."

I said, "I'm sorry, Marian. You wanted to play partners and pool information. I couldn't do it that way. You're working for the newspaper and want a story. I want something else. Publicity wouldn't help my game any."

She drew little aimless diagrams with her pencil on the pad of paper in front of her. After a minute, she said, "Well, we understand each other."

"Your uncle in?" I asked.

"No. He's gone fishing."

"When did he go?"

"Early yesterday morning."

"Then he doesn't know about the big news."

"What?"

"Mrs. Lintig's arrival."

"Oh," she said, "he knew that before he left. He didn't go until after he'd heard about her."

"And he left you on the job to cover the big event and get the paper out?"

She drew more diagrams before she answered. Then she said, "It isn't a big event from a news standpoint, Donald. No one here cares very much about Mrs. Lintig. That's ancient history. The people who knew her moved away. They were the younger set. When business left, they left."

"Just what did happen to this town?" I asked.

She said, "The bottom dropped out. The railroad moved. The Pennant mine struck a water pocket, and the works were flooded. They were never able to pump them out. It's just been a long succession of things like that. After a city starts on the toboggan, people leave."

"Your uncle went through the boom?"

"Oh, yes. He's a native. His feet are anchored in Oakview."

"How about you?"

Her eyes sparkled with the intensity of her hatred. "If I could only find some way to shake the dust of this dead town off my feet," she said, "I'd be on my way so quick it would surprise you." She pointed her finger toward a little closet, and said, "My hat and coat are in there. Show me a way to make a living in the city, and I won't even stop to put on my hat and coat."

"Why don't you come to the city if you feel that way about it, and make some contacts?"

"One of these days I'm going to."

"And what would Charlie say?"

"You leave Charlie out of it," she said.

"I don't suppose your boyfriend would be a big man with a cleft chin and a mole on his cheek, would he?"

She drew diagrams at furious speed. "I don't like to be kidded," she said.

"I'm not kidding. I'm asking."

She dropped the pencil to the counter and looked up at me. "You're playing a game, Donald Lam," she said. "You're not fooling me for a minute. You're smart, and shrewd, and cautious.

There's something big in the wind. If I could find out what it was, I could use it to get out of this town and get established in something in the city. And that's exactly what I'm going to do."

"Under those circumstances," I said, "the only thing I can do is to wish you luck."

"Luck?" she asked.

"Bad luck," I said, and started for the door.

I could feel her standing at the counter, staring at me, wistful and indignant at the same time, but I didn't look back.

I walked over to the hotel. The clerk told me Long Distance was calling. I went to my room, got on the line, and after a ten-minute wait heard Bertha Cool's voice. She was putting on her best wheedling act. "Donald, darling," she said, "you mustn't ever do that again."

"Do what?"

"Walk out on Bertha in a huff."

"I had work to do," I said. "I went out and did it. There'd been too much delay as it was. After this, when a telegram comes in collect, addressed to me, pay for it."

"I will, Donald," she said. "Bertha was in an awful temper. Some little thing had gone wrong and thrown her all out of balance."

"Did you," I asked, "ring me up long distance to tell me about your temper?"

"No, lover. I wanted to tell you that you were right."

"What about?"

"About Dr. Lintig. I've just checked back through the records of the medical board. It took me a little while to get the right line into their office, but I did it."

"What," I asked, "did you find out?"

"In 1919," she said, "Dr. Lintig filed a certificate showing that he had changed his name to Charles Loring Alftmont. So they changed their records accordingly, and he's now practicing at Santa Carlotta—eye, ear, nose, and throat specialist."

I said, "That's fine—only you still haven't told me what you called up about."

Her voice was sugar-coated. "Listen, Donald, Bertha needs you."

"What happened?" I asked.

She said, "In a way, Donald, it's your fault."

"What is?"

"We're fired."

"What do you mean?"

"Mr. Smith sent me a registered letter. He told me that our instructions were to find Mrs. Lintig, not to bother about Dr. Lintig, that he was very much put out at our failure to follow instructions, and that we weren't to proceed any farther with the case."

After a while, when I said nothing, she said, "Hello, Donald. Are you there?"

"Yes," I said. "I'm thinking."

That got action with Bertha. She said, "Well, for God's sake, don't think over the long-distance telephone."

"I'll see you sometime tomorrow," I said, and hung up, while she was still trying to talk.

I sat and thought for the space of a couple of cigarettes, then I picked up the telephone and said, "Connect me with Mrs. Lintig's room, will you please?" The clerk said, "I'm very sorry, Mr. Lam, but she's checked out. She received a telegram and said she had to leave at once."

"Did she leave any forwarding address?"

"No."

"How did she leave, on the train?"

"No. She hired a car—said something about being driven to the nearest place where she could charter a plane."

I said, "Just a minute. I'm coming down. I want to talk with you."

I threw my things into my bag, went down to the lobby, and said, "I have to leave—urgent business. Please make out my bill at once. Now, Mrs. Lintig had some spectacles ordered."

"Yes," the clerk said, "a most unfortunate accident. The hotel agreed to assume responsibility, although I'm not entirely certain we were to blame."

"When those glasses come," I said, "forward them to me at this address."

I scribbled my address on the back of a card. "They may come C.O.D.," I said, "or they may be prepaid. In any event, just forward them to me. If there's a C.O.D., I'll take it up and relieve the hotel of responsibility. I'm related to Mrs. Lintig. She's my aunt—but please don't say anything about it—she's very sensitive, and she used to live here, you know. There was a divorce. I'll pay for the glasses."

"Yes, Mr. Lam. That's very nice of you."

I loaded my bag into the agency car and started out for Santa Carlotta.

Chapter Four

It was exactly nine-five A.M. when I entered the office of Dr. Charles Alftmont. A nurse who radiated hatchet-faced efficiency asked me my name, address, and occupation. I told her I was a traveling man who had developed some eye trouble, and the heavy dark glasses which I was wearing bore out my statement. I gave her a fictitious name and address and told her I wanted to see Dr. Alftmont at once.

She said, "Just a minute," and went through a door into the inner office. A few minutes later, she popped out and said, "This way please. Dr. Alftmont will see you now."

I followed her in through an eye-testing room to where Dr. Alftmont sat behind a desk in a private office that radiated an atmosphere of quiet prosperity.

He looked up. He was Mr. Smith, our client.

Seen without his dark glasses, his eyes matched the rest of his face, a keen, incisive, hard gray. He said, "Good morning. What can I do for you?"

The nurse was hovering around, and I said, in a low voice, "I've been having a lot of eye trouble, doing quite a bit of night driving."

"Where," he asked, "did you get those dark glasses?"

I said, "They're just a cheap pair I picked up in the drugstore. I've been driving all night. The daylight hurts my eyes."

"Worst thing you can do," he said, "driving all night. You're young yet. Some day you'll pay for it. Your eyes weren't intended to stand any such strain. Come into the other room."

I followed him into the other room. The nurse adjusted me in the chair. Dr. Alftmont nodded to her, and she went out.

"Now, just slip off those glasses," the doctor said, "and we'll have a look."

He wheeled a machine with a big lens and a shield in it up in front of my face. He said, "Rest your chin on this strap. Look directly at this point of light. Hold your eyes steady."

He took up a position behind the machine. I slipped off the glasses. He turned various attachments. Lights appeared on each side of the big disc. He spun them slowly, and said, "Now, let's have a look at the other eye," and swiveled the lens over toward my left eye, and went through the process all over again. He made some notes on a pad of paper which he held in his hand and said, "There's considerable irritation apparently, but I see no serious defect in vision. I can't understand why your eyes have been bothering you. Perhaps it's just a momentary muscular fatigue. There's a bruise over the right eye, but the eye itself seems not to have been damaged."

He swung the machine to one side, and said, "Now we'll take a look—" For the first time he got a good look at my face. He stopped in mid-sentence and stared at me with sagging jaw.

I said, "Your wife was in Oakview yesterday, Doctor." He sat looking at me for the space of ten seconds, then he said in that calm, precise voice of his, "Ah, Mr. Lam. I should have seen through your little ruse. Are you at the— Come into my private office."

I got up out of the chair and followed him into his private office. He closed and locked the door. "I should have expected this," he said.

I sat down and waited.

He paced the floor nervously. After a moment, he said, "How much?"

"For what?" I asked.

"You know," he said. "What's your price?"

"You mean for services rendered?"

"Call it anything you want," he said irritably. "Let me know how much it is. I should have known better. I'd heard all private detective agencies resorted to blackmail when the opportunity presented."

"Well, you heard wrong," I said. "We try to give a loyal service to our clients—when our clients will let us."

"Nonsense. I know better. You had no business trying to get in touch with me. I told you specifically that I wanted you to find Mrs. Lintig, to make no effort to locate Dr. Lintig."

"You didn't put it exactly that way, Doctor."

"That was the effect of it. All right, you've found me. Let's quit beating about the bush. How much do you want?"

He crossed over to the other side of the desk and sat down. His eyes bored steadily into mine.

"You should have been frank with us."

"Bosh! I might have known you'd try something like this."

I said, "Now listen to what *I* have to say. You wanted us to find Mrs. Lintig. We found her. We found her very unexpectedly. We wanted to get in touch with you. You wrote in terminating our employment. You have the right to do that if you want to, but there are some things I thought you should know. As a client, you're entitled to a report."

"I fired you," he said with some feeling, "because of your meddling into my affairs."

"You mean tracing you through the state medical bureau?"

"Yes."

I said, "All right, that's done. We've found you. You're here, and I'm here. Now, let's talk turkey."

"That's exactly what I wanted you to do, but understand this, young man, I'm not going to be held up. I—"

"Forget it. Here's the dope. Two other people have been up to Oakview trying to get a line on your wife. One of them was a man named Miller Cross. I can't find out anything about him. The other one, about three weeks ago, was a girl named Evaline Harris, who went under the name of Evaline Dell when she was in Oakview. She's a cabaret entertainer at the Blue Cave in the city. I haven't checked up on the place, but I understand it employs B girls who come out on the stage, show plenty of figure, sing a song or two, just enough to give them an ostensible occupation, and for the rest, make a commission on drinks and pick up what they can on the side.

"I contacted this Evaline Harris. I have her address here in case you're interested. I put it up to her that I was an adjuster from the railroad company. Her trunk was damaged in transit to Oakview. She fell for it. I told her we had to know her business and why she was going under an assumed name. She said she was making an investigation trying to find out about a woman and that she was making that investigation on behalf of the woman's husband. Now then, why didn't you play fair with us?"

There was surprise on his face. "The woman's husband," he repeated.

I nodded.

"Then she's married," he said.

"To you."

"No, no, there must be someone else."

"There wasn't. Mrs. Lintig showed up in Oakview, hired an attorney, and secured a dismissal of the divorce action on the grounds of lack of prosecution. I talked with her—"

"You talked with her?" he interrupted.

I nodded.

"What does she look like?" he asked. "How is she?"

"She shows her age," I said. "I'm assuming she was approximately your age."

"Three years older."

"All right. She looks it, every bit of it She's put on some weight. Her hair is silver-gray. She's a fairly competent-looking customer."

He clamped his lips together. "Where is she now?"

"I don't know. She left Oakview."

His eyes became hard. "Why didn't you follow her?"

I sprang my alibi on him. "Because Bertha Cool had telephoned me and said that we were fired."

"Good heavens, that's the one thing I wanted. I want to know where she is. I want to know about her. I want to know what she's doing, what she's been doing, whether she's married. I want to find out all about her. And you let her slip through your fingers!"

"Because we were fired," I pointed out, patiently. "I thought you acted hastily under the circumstances. I decided to run down to Santa Carlotta and tell you the facts."

He pushed back his chair and paced the office nervously. Abruptly he turned and said, "I simply have to find her."

"Our agency is the best means you have of doing that."

"Yes, yes. I want you to find her. Go ahead and get busy. Don't waste any time. Don't waste a moment."

I said, "All right, Doctor. The next time we get on a hot trail, don't call us off. After all, you have only yourself to thank for this. If you'd trusted us and been frank with us, we could have closed the case within forty-eight hours without any further expense. As it is, we've got to begin all over again."

"Look here," he said. "Can I trust you?"

"I don't know why not."

"You won't try to take advantage of me?"

I shrugged my shoulders and said, "The fact that I'm here, and not asking for a shakedown, is your best evidence of that."

"Yes," he said, "it is. I'm sorry. I apologize, I apologize to you. Explain the circumstances to Mrs. Cool, will you?"

"Yes, and you want us to go right back to work?"

"Right back to work," he said. "Wait a minute. I want the address of that young woman who claimed I'd employed her. It's preposterous. I never heard of such a thing."

I gave him Evaline Harris's address.

"Get started right away," he said.

I said, "All right. Shall we make reports here, Doctor?"

"No, no. Make those reports just as I instructed Mrs. Cool. Make them to Mr. Smith at the address I gave her! Don't under any circumstances let anyone know where I am or who I am. It would be—disastrous."

"I think I understand."

"Get out of town at once. Don't form any acquaintances here. Don't be seen around my office."

I said, "All right. We'll protect you at our end of the line, but be careful with those reports we're sending."

"That's all arranged for," he said.

"And you don't know anything about this Evaline Harris?"

"Good heavens, no!"

"Well," I told him, "it's going to be a job. We're working on a cold trail again."

"I understand. It's my fault, but that's something I've worried about for years, that someone might try to trace me through my professional registration. You were clever—damned clever—too damned clever."

"One other thing," I said. "Who would be interested in giving me a black eye because of the work I'm doing?"

"What do you mean?"

"A man about six feet," I said, "something over two hundred pounds, beefy, but not fat, dark hair, deep-set, gray eyes, a man in the late thirties or early forties, a mole on his cheek, and a fist like a pile driver."

Dr. Alftmont shook his head and said, "I know no one of that description." But he avoided my eyes as he said it.

"He waited for me in my room in the hotel," I said. "He knew all about me. He'd appropriated the agency car, driven it around to the back of the hotel."

"What did he want?"

"He wanted me to leave town."

"What did you do?"

"Made the mistake of trying to yell for the cops."

"What happened?"

"When I regained consciousness, I'd been bundled out of town."

The corners of his lips quivered. His chin moved twice before he said anything. "There m-m-must have been some mistake," he said.

"There was," I said dryly. "I made it."

"You mustn't let anyone know about what you're doing or whom you're working for," he cautioned. "That's imperative."

"Okay," I said. "I just wanted to know."

His eyes were fighting fear as I went out. The office nurse looked at me curiously. My money said ten to one she wasn't Vivian Carter and had never been named as a corespondent in any divorce action.

My breakfast was long overdue. Santa Carlotta was a city on the through coast highway. It catered to the wealthy tourist trade. There were three swank hotels, half a dozen commercial hotels, and flocks of tourist camps. The restaurants were good. I picked one at random.

I saw a placard in the window. Dr. Alftmont's features, looking ten years younger, stared out at the street from that placard. I stood at the window and read the printing on the placard:

ELECT Dr. Charles L. Alftmont for MAYOR.
Clean up Santa Carlotta. Give crooks a one-way ticket.
—Santa Carlotta Municipal Decency League.

I walked in, found a booth, and settled back to the luxury of real orange juice, grapefruit, poached eggs that were fresh and hot on whole-wheat toast that hadn't been made soggy by having lukewarm water poured over it.

Over coffee and a cigarette, the waitress asked me if I wanted to see the papers. I nodded and, after a moment, she came back rather apologetically and said, "I haven't a city newspaper available. They're all in use, but I can give you the local paper, the *Ledger*."

I thanked her and took the paper she handed me.

It was a metropolitan job with wire service, balanced headlines, good make-up, and a fair sprinkling of syndicated features.

I turned to the editorial page and read the editorial, with interest:

The manner in which the Courier *seeks to besmirch the candidacy of Dr. Charles L. Alftmont is probably the best indication available to the unbiased voter of the fear engendered by the candidacy of this upright man.*

It has long been readily apparent to any disinterested observer that the stranglehold which the crooked gamblers and underworld influences have upon Santa Carlotta could not exist without a political background. As yet we are making no direct accusations, but the intelligent voter will do well to watch the tactics used by the opposition. We predict there will be plenty of mud-slinging. There will be many more attempts to besmirch the character of Dr. Alftmont as a candidate. No attempts will be made to meet him on the issues which he has raised. If the city does not need a new police commissioner and a new chief of police, the present administration should be willing to discuss vice conditions fairly and impartially. In place of doing that, our mud-slinging contemporary contents itself with veiled innuendoes. We predict that unless a prompt retraction of last night's editorial is printed, the Courier *will find itself involved in a libel suit. And it may be well for the* Courier *to remember that while political advertising is the sop handed to subservient editors, damages in a libel action are recovered against and payable by the defendant publication.*

The LEDGER *happens to know that the businessmen who are backing the candidacy of Dr. Alftmont and demanding a cleanup are not going to stand an unlimited amount of mud-slinging with no retort save that of turning the other cheek. Last night's slur is a libelous defamation of character.*

It is, of course, an easy expedient to avoid embarrassing questions asked by a candidate, by starting a whispering campaign against that candidate. It does not, however, refute the charges of political corruption which every thinking citizen knows to be well founded. With election less than ten days hence, our adversaries have gone in for mud-slinging.

The waitress brought me a second cup of coffee, and I smoked two thoughtful cigarettes over it. When I paid the check, I asked her, "Where's the city hall?"

"Straight down the street four blocks, and turn to the right a block. You'll see it. It's a new one."

I drove down. It was a new one all right. It looked as though the graft had been figured on a percentage basis, and the boys who were in on it wanted to get plenty—and the principle of the more dollars the greater the graft percentage. It was one of those buildings which had been built for posterity, and the city administration of Santa Carlotta rattled around in it like a Mexican jumping bean in a dishpan.

I found the office marked *Chief of Police* and walked in. A stenographer was clattering away in the reception room. A couple of men were sitting waiting.

I crossed over to the secretary and said, "Who could give me some information about the personnel of the department?"

"What is it you want?"

"I want to make a complaint about an officer," I said. "I didn't take his number, but I can describe him."

She said acidly, "Chief White can't be bothered with complaints of that nature."

"I understand that," I said. "That's why I'm asking his secretary."

She thought that over for a moment and said, "Captain Wilbur is on duty. He can tell you what to do and where to go. His is the next office down the hall."

I thanked her and had started to turn away when my eye caught a framed picture hanging on the wall near the door. It was a long panorama strip, photographs showing the police officers lined up in front of the new city hall. I gave it a passing glance and went out.

Captain Wilbur had the same photograph hanging in his office. I asked an officer who was waiting, "Do you know who took this picture?"

"A photographer here in town, name of Clover," he said.

"Nice work."

"Uh huh."

I went up and scrutinized it, then put my finger on the fifth man from the end. "Well, well," I said. "I see Bill Crane is on the force."

"Huh?"

"Bill Crane. I used to know him in Denver."

He came over and looked. "That's not Bill Crane," he said. "That's John Harbet. He's on Vice."

I said, "Oh. He looks just like a chap I used to know."

When the officer went in to see Captain Wilbur, I drifted out of the door, climbed in the agency car, and drove out of town.

Bertha Cool was just going out for lunch. Her face lit up when she saw me. "Why, *hel*-lo, Donald," she said. "You're just in time to go to lunch with me."

"No, thanks. I had breakfast a couple of hours ago."

"But, lover, this is on the house."

"Sorry. I can't do justice to it."

"Oh, come along anyway. We have to talk, and I want you to try and find Smith. I tried to get in touch with him after I had his letter and found he isn't at the address he gave me. He gets mail there, but that's all, and they don't know anything about him or won't tell me if they do."

"That's nice," I said.

Her eyes grew hard. "Nice, hell!" she said. "That man was on a spot. He was a frightened man if I ever saw one. He was Santa Claus. And now, damn it, he's stuck in the chimney, and our stockings are empty."

I said, "Oh, well, I'll come to lunch if you feel that way about it."

"That's better. We'll go down to the Gilded Swan. We can talk there."

Bertha Cool and I walked out together. I said, "Hi, Elsie," as I held the door open for Bertha Cool. Elsie Brand gave me a nod without looking up. Her fingers never missed the tempo of perfect rhythm on the keyboard.

Over in the Gilded Swan, Bertha Cool wanted to know if I felt like a cocktail. I told her I did, that I was going home and spend the afternoon sleeping anyhow, that I'd driven virtually all night, and that I intended to go around to the Blue Cave in the evening.

She said, "No, you don't, Donald. You stay away from that night spot. You'll spend money there, and Bertha has no money to squander. Unless Smith changes his instructions, we let the matter drop like a hot potato. Not that Bertha is doing so badly at that. She got a retainer in advance, but you hooked me for too damned many expenses, Donald."

I waited until we had a couple of Martinis, then lit a cigarette and said, "Well, it's okay. Smith says for us to go ahead."

Bertha Cool blinked her frosty eyes. "Says which?"

"For us to go ahead."

"Donald, you little bastard, have you found Smith?"

I nodded.

"How did you find him?"

I said, "Smith is Dr. Alftmont, and Dr. Alftmont is Dr. Lintig."

Bertha Cool put down her cocktail glass and said, "Well, can me for a sardine. Now, ain't *that* something?"

I couldn't seem to work up a great deal of enthusiasm over spilling information to Bertha. I'd done too much night driving, and sitting up all night doesn't agree with me. I said, "Dr. Alftmont's running for mayor in Santa Carlotta."

"Politics?" Bertha Cool asked, her eyes turning greedy.

"Politics," I said. "Lots of politics. The man who beat me up and ran me out of Oakview was a man named John Harbet of the Santa Carlotta police force, evidently the head of the vice squad."

Bertha said, "Oh-oh!"

"One of the newspapers has been throwing mud at Dr. Alftmont. The other newspaper intimates that Dr. Alftmont is going to sue for libel. Ordinarily that would be a nice hint, but the way I size it up, the mud-slingers are pretty certain of their ground. They're going to keep on dishing out the dirt and then dare Alftmont to sue them for libel. If he doesn't sue, he's backing down. If he does sue, he has to show damage to his character. When that time comes, what the Santa Carlotta *Courier* will do to his character will be plenty. Alftmont realizes that. He doesn't dare to sue. He wants to find out whether his wife ever remarried or got a divorce."

The expression in Bertha Cool's eyes was like that of a cat wiping canary feathers off its chin. "Pickle me for a peach," she said, half under her breath. "What a perfect setup! Christ, lover, we're going to town!"

"I've already been to town," I said, and settled back against the cushioned bench in the booth, too weary to talk.

"Go on," Bertha said. "Use that brain of yours, Donald. Think things out for Bertha."

I shook my head and said, "I'm tired. I don't want to think, and I don't want to talk."

"Food will make you feel better," Bertha said.

The waiter came, and Bertha ordered a double cream of tomato soup, a kidney potpie, a salad, and coffee with a pitcher of whipping cream on the side, hot rolls and butter, and then said, with a jerk of her head toward me, "Bring him the same. The food'll do him good."

I gathered up enough energy to protest to the waiter. "A pot of black coffee," I said, "and a baked ham sandwich, and that's *all*."

"Oh, no, lover," Bertha said solicitously. "You need some food. You need something to make energy."

I shook my head.

"Something with sugar in it," Bertha said. "Sugar makes for

energy. Some old-fashioned strawberry shortcake, Donald, with lots of whipped cream, some French pastries, some—"

I shook my head again, and Bertha gave up with a sigh. "No wonder you're such a skinny runt," she said, and then to the waiter: "All right. Let him have his own way."

When the waiter had gone, I said to Bertha, "Don't do that again."

"What?"

"Act as though I were a child whom you were taking out to dinner. I know what I want to eat."

"But, Donald, you don't eat enough. There's no meat on your bones."

Arguing with her was going to take energy so I let it go at that, and sat smoking.

Bertha watched me while she was eating. She said solicitously, "You're looking awfully white. You aren't going to come down with typhoid or something are you?"

I didn't say anything. The salty tang of the fried ham made my stomach feel a little better. The black coffee tasted good, but I couldn't manage all of the ham sandwich.

"I know what it is," Bertha said. "You've been eating in those greasy-spoon restaurants up in Oakview. You've knocked your stomach out, lover. Christ, Donald, think of the break it'll be if Dr. Alftmont gets out in front in a political campaign where the citizens can't afford to let him back out, and the other side are gunning for him. We can write our own ticket."

"He's already done that," I said.

"We've got to work fast. It'll mean a lot of night work."

I started to say something, then gave up.

She said, "Don't be like that, Donald dear. Tell me."

I poured out the last of my coffee, finished it, and said, "Get the sketch. Dr. Lintig runs away with his office nurse. She's probably Mrs. Alftmont now, but there wasn't any marriage. It would have been a bigamous ceremony. If they'd tried to solemnize a marriage, that would be a felony. Well, they may have at that. Figure it out for yourself. If Mrs. Lintig is dead or had a divorce, Dr. Alftmont is in the clear. He hasn't committed bigamy, and his office nurse is the legal Mrs. Alftmont. Perhaps there are children.

"But if Mrs. Lintig didn't get a divorce—and she says she didn't—if she's alive and well, all the picture needs is to have her come swooping into Santa Carlotta on the eve of the election. She identifies Dr. Alftmont as Dr. Lintig, the husband from whom she's never been divorced. The woman Santa Carlotta society has recognized as Mrs. Alftmont becomes Vivian Carter, the corespondent. They've been living together openly as man and wife—sweet little mess, isn't it?"

"But," Bertha said, "they have to have Mrs. Lintig in order to pull that."

"Probably," I said, "they already have her. You've got to admit it looks suspiciously like it—her showing up at this time in Oakview, oozing love and affection for her husband, dismissing the divorce action so the records will be cleared."

"Tell me all about that, lover," Bertha Cool commanded.

I shook my head and said, "Not now. I'm too tired. I'm going home and get some sleep."

Bertha Cool reached her jeweled hand across the table to grip my hand with strong fingers. "Donald, dear," she said, "your skin feels cold. You *must* take care of yourself."

"I'm going to," I said. "You pay the check. I'm going to get some sleep."

Bertha's tone was maternal. "You poor little bastard, you're all in. Don't try to drive the car home, Donald. Take a taxi—no, wait a minute. Do you think Alftmont's sending me any more money?"

"He said he would."

Bertha Cool said, "To hell with what they say. It's what they pay that counts. Well, anyway, dearie, take a streetcar. Don't try to drive the agency car."

"It's all right," I said. "I'll need the car tonight. I can drive it."

I walked out and piloted the agency heap out to my rooming house, feeling like the tail end of a misspent life. I climbed into bed, took a big swig of whisky, and after a while drifted off into warm drowsiness.

It seemed that I was just really getting some good sleep when an insistent something kept trying to drag me back to consciousness. I tried to ignore it and couldn't. It seemed to have persisted through an eternity of time in various forms. I dreamed that naked savages were dancing around a fire, beating on war drums. Then there was a respite and I dropped back into oblivion once more, only to have carpenters start putting up a scaffold on which I was to be hung. The carpenters were all women, attired in sunsuits, and they drove the nails to a weird rhythm of *thump thump thump thump—thump thump thump thump—thump thump thump thump.* Then they would chant, "Donald, oh, Donald."

At last my numbed senses came to the surface enough to realize that the noise was a gentle but insistent tapping on my door, and a feminine voice calling, "Donald, oh, Donald."

I made some sleepy, inarticulate sound.

The voice said, "Donald, let me in." The doorknob rattled.

I got out of bed and staggered groggily as I walked over to the closet door for a dressing-gown.

"Donald, let me in. It's Marian."

I heard the words, but they didn't make sense. I walked to the door, turned the key, and opened it.

Marian Dunton came in, her eyes wide with emotion. "Oh, Donald, I was so afraid you weren't here, but the landlady downstairs insisted you were. She said you'd been up all night and were sleeping."

I snapped into wakefulness at the sound of her voice. "Come in, Marian. Sit down. What is it?"

"Something horrible's happened."

I made shift to comb my hair with my fingers. "What is it, Marian?"

She came and stood close to me. "I went to see Evaline Harris."

"Okay," I said. "I gave you that lead. Try and get another one."

"Donald, she's—she's dead! Murdered!"

I sat down on the bed. "Tell me about it."

Marian crossed over to sit beside me. Her words poured out in a low, steady monotone. "Listen, Donald, I've got to get out. The landlady's a suspicious busybody. She said I'd have to leave your door open. You must help me."

I looked at my wristwatch. It was quarter past five. "What's happened?"

"I found where she lived. I kept ringing her bell. Nothing happened."

"She sleeps late," I said. "Works in a night spot."

"I know. Well, after a while, I rang the bell marked *Manager* and asked where I could find Miss Harris."

"Go ahead."

"The manager said she didn't know, that she didn't try to chaperon her tenants, and seemed very crusty.

"I asked if I might run up to her apartment, and she said I could, that it was 309.

"I went up to the third floor in the elevator. As I started

down the hall, a man came out of a room at the far end of the corridor. I don't know—I think it was 309."

"That's probably why she didn't answer the doorbell."

"Donald, listen to me. She was dead."

"How do you know?"

"I went down to 309. The door wasn't locked. It was closed, but not locked. I knocked on it two or three times, and no one answered. I tried the knob, and the door was unlocked. I opened it, and saw—well, a girl was lying on the bed. I thought—well, you know—I said, 'Excuse me,' and went out. I pulled the door shut. I thought I'd better wait for a while, and then come back —you know."

"Go ahead."

"Well, I went back downstairs and out of the building. In about half an hour, I went back and rang the bell again."

"You mean the bell of Evaline Harris's apartment?"

"Yes."

"What happened?"

"Nothing. I rang and rang and didn't get any answer, but I was sure she hadn't gone out because I'd been watching the door of the apartment house.

"While I was standing there ringing the bell, a woman came up the stairs and fitted a latchkey to the door. She smiled at me, and said, 'May I help you?' and I said, 'Yes, thanks,' and walked in right behind her."

"Did she ask you where you were going?"

"No. She was very nice."

"Then what?"

"Then I went up to the third floor again and knocked. Nothing happened. I opened the door and peeked in. She was still lying on the bed in the same position, and—well, something in the way she was lying—I walked in, went over and touched her.

She was dead. There was a cord drawn tightly around her neck. Her face looked awful. It was turned away from the door. Oh, Donald, it's terrible!"

"What did you do?"

"I was in a panic," she said, "because you see I'd gone in once before, a half an hour earlier. The manager knew it. I was afraid that they might think—you know, that I'd done it."

"You little fool," I said. "How long ago was this?"

"Not very long. I'd found out where you lived. I'd telephoned your agency and said I was an old friend, that you'd told me I could locate you there. The girl who answered the telephone told me where I could find you."

"And you came here?"

"Yes, just as fast as I could drive."

I said, "Get in your car. Drive like hell to police headquarters. When you get there, tell them you want to report a dead body. Remember, don't tell them it's a murder, and remember to tell them that you're from Oakview."

"Why the Oakview? I mean why should I tell them about it?"

"Because," I said, "you're going to have to take the part of an unsophisticated country girl."

"But they'll find out that I was up there before—when I asked the manager."

"They'll find that out anyway," I said. "The best way you can stick your neck into a noose is to try to cover up. Don't you understand?"

"Y-Yes," she said dubiously. "Donald, can't you go with me to the police station?"

"Absolutely not. That would be the worst thing that could happen. Forget all about coming here. Forget all about knowing me. Don't mention my name. Don't say anything about the B. L. Cool Bureau of Investigations. Remember now, you'll have to follow those instructions absolutely. Tell your story just as it happened, only tell them that when you found out the woman was dead, you drove *directly* to the police station. Don't let on that you know she was strangled. Say she was dead, that you didn't touch anything. Do you understand?"

"Yes."

"You didn't touch anything, did you?"

"No."

"Who was this man you saw leaving the apartment?"

"I don't know. I can't even be certain he left the apartment. It might have been one of the adjoining apartments, but I *think* it was that one."

"What did he look like?"

"He was rather slender and very straight. He looked dignified."

"How old?"

"Middle-aged. He looked nice."

"How was he dressed?"

"A gray, double-breasted suit."

"How tall?"

"Fairly tall, slender. He was very dignified. He had a gray mustache."

"Would you know him if you saw him again?"

"Yes, of course."

I pushed her toward the door and said, "On your way."

"When will I see you, Donald?"

"As soon as they get done questioning you, give me a ring. Remember not to tell them anything about me or about the agency— Wait a minute. They'll ask you what you wanted to see Evaline Harris about."

"Well, what did I?"

I thought rapidly and said, "You got acquainted with her when she was up in Oakview. She confided in you. She told you she was an entertainer in a night spot here. Remember, you mustn't say a word about Mrs. Lintig. Don't mention anything about the girl making an investigation. Don't let on that you knew she was in Oakview on business. She told you she was up there spending a vacation. You're a country girl, and the more country atmosphere you can pull in, the better it'll be for you. Go in for that rural stuff strong. You wanted to leave Oakview. Everybody does. It's no place for a young woman who has an eye to the future. You wanted to get to the city. You didn't want to work in a night club but you thought Evaline Harris might have some connections and could get you in somewhere. Does your uncle know what you're doing here?"

"No. I'm doing this on my own, Donald. There's a lot of things—a lot of developments that I can tell you about, suspicious circumstances that—"

"Save them," I said. "Seconds are precious. If someone else finds that body before you report it, you're sunk. Remember, you left there and drove to the police station just as fast as you could. You don't know anything about the time. Do you have a wristwatch?"

"Yes, of course."

"Let me see it."

She took it off her wrist. I set the hands back to eleven-fifteen and smacked the watch sharply against the corner of the dresser. It stopped. I said, "Put it back on. Remember, you broke your wristwatch this morning driving down. You dropped it in the restroom of a service station. Think you can put this stuff across, think you understand it?"

"Yes, yes," she said. "I understand it. You're *so* nice! I knew I could depend on you."

"Nix on it," I said. "Get busy. On your way. Don't try to call me here. Call me at the agency. Don't call me while you're under surveillance or from the police station. If it comes to a showdown, you can tell them that you know me and intended to look me up later. You didn't give your name to Elsie Brand, did you?"

"Who's Elsie Brand?"

"The office girl in the agency."

"No, I just told her I was a friend of yours."

I pushed her out into the corridor, patted her shoulder, and said, "Good luck, kid. On your way."

I waited until I heard her go down the stairs and slam the outer door. I was a little afraid the landlady might try to question her.

After the front door slammed, I walked out to the telephone booth in the corridor and called the agency office. Elsie Brand answered.

"Bertha gone home yet?" I asked.

"No, she's just leaving."

"Tell her to wait. Tell her I'm coming up. It's important."

"All right. Did some girl get in touch with you?"

"A girl?"

"Yes. She said she was an old friend of yours. She didn't give her name. She sounded on the up and up, and I told her where you lived."

"All right. Thanks, Elsie. Tell Bertha I'll be right up."

I hung up the telephone, went back to my room, and dressed. I got the motor started on the agency car and fought the afternoon traffic getting up to the office. It was ten minutes to six when I walked in.

Elsie Brand had gone home. Bertha Cool was waiting. She said, "For Christ's sake, Donald, don't sleep all day, and then make me stay in the office all evening. What is it you want?"

"Heard anything from Smith?" I asked.

Her face beamed. "Yes, lover," she said. "He was in. He left me a very substantial deposit."

"How long ago?" I asked.

"Not over half an hour ago. He seemed very, very nice. But he certainly is nervous."

"Exactly what did he want?" I asked.

"He didn't say anything about the political situation," she said, "but I could read between the lines. He said that he wanted us to keep on trying to find Mrs. Lintig, that he was in some other difficulties and was going to need our services, that he wanted to be certain we'd be on the job. You made a fine impression on him, Donald. He said particularly he wanted you to work on his case. He thinks you're very smart."

"How much did he leave?" I asked.

Bertha said cautiously, "It was a nice little sum, Donald."

"How much?"

"What the hell?" she said with sudden belligerency. "I'm running this agency."

"How much?" I asked.

She met my eyes and clamped her chin shut. I said, "Kick through, Bertha. There's more to this than you realize. He wants me to work on his case. You'll be in a fix if you and I part company now."

"We're not going to part company, lover."

"That's what you think."

She thought things over for a while, and then said, "A thousand dollars."

"I thought so. Now, I want you to come with me."

"Where?"

"We're going to call on Evaline Harris," I said.

"Oh, that jane."

"Uh-huh."

"You could do more with her alone, Donald."

"I don't think so. I think this is the time when it needs your fine Italian hand."

"Sometimes my hand gets pretty rough," she said.

"Okay, come on."

She said, "Donald, what's got into you? What's all the rush about? Why are you so nervous?"

"I've been thinking," I said.

"Well," she admitted grudgingly, "that's one thing you *can* do." She got up, crossed over to the closet which held the wash-stand, and started powdering her face and putting on lipstick. I paced the floor impatiently, looking at my watch from time to time. "Did Dr. Alftmont say when he'd arrived in town or when he was going back?" I asked.

"He asked us particularly not to refer to him as Dr. Alftmont, Donald. He said in our office conversation and in memos we must refer to him as Mr. Smith."

"All right. Did he say when he'd come in or when he was going back?"

"No."

"Was he wearing a double-breasted, gray suit?"

"Yes."

"Did he say what he'd come to town for?"

"He said he'd been thinking over your visit this morning and had decided to come down and apologize to me for his letter discharging us and leave some more money."

I said, "All right. All right. Let's go."

'Donald, why *are* you in such a hurry?"

"I think Evaline Harris can tell us something."

"Well, you've had all afternoon. Why get in such a stew now?"

"I was too tired to think clearly. I've just figured the thing out."

"All right, lover. Let's go."

"And I want some more expense money."

"What? Again?"

"Yes."

"My God, Donald, I can't—"

I said, "Listen, this is going to be a big case, one of the biggest you've ever handled. That thousand dollars is just a drop in the bucket."

"Well, I wish I shared your optimism."

"You don't have to, just so I share your take."

"You're working for me, you know, Donald. I'm the agency. You aren't a partner."

"I know," I said.

"You haven't filed a complete expense account on that other yet."

"I will."

She sighed, crossed over to the cash drawer, took out twenty dollars, and handed it to me. I stood with the twenty dollars in my extended hand waiting, and, after a while, she handed me another twenty. I kept waiting, and she sighed, handed me ten more, slammed the drawer shut, and locked it. "You're getting exalted ideas about your value," she said.

I pushed the money down in my pocket, said, "Come on," and tried to rush Bertha down to the agency car.

Trying to hurry Bertha Cool was just that much wasted effort. By the time we got to the agency car, I'd used up enough nervous energy to have gone to Evaline Harris's place and back, and I hadn't made a fraction of a second's difference in Bertha Cool's schedule. She did everything at a certain rate of speed, like a truck that has a governor on the motor.

I slid in behind the wheel, feeling used up. Bertha pulled the body way over on its springs as she hoisted her bulk into the car and settled back against the dilapidated cushions.

I rattled the motor into noise, eased out the clutch, and slid out of the parking lot. Bertha Cool said, "It's still a pretty good car, isn't it, lover?"

I didn't say anything.

It was the slack hour in the business district, and I made time to Evaline Harris's apartment house. A whole flock of machines were parked out in front of the place. The machines had the red spotlights of police cars. I pretended not to notice them. Bertha Cool did. She looked at me a couple of times, but didn't say anything. I led the way to the apartment house and said, "I think it'll be a good plan to ring the manager. In that way we can work a stall and go up to the apartment unannounced."

I rang the manager's bell. Nothing happened. I rang it a couple more times.

A press car came rolling up and double-parked. A photographer with a Speed Graphic and synchronized flashbulb jumped out and ran up the steps. A slender man with the hard-boiled look of a metropolitan reporter came behind him. They tried the door. It was locked. The reporter looked at me and said, "You live here?"

"No."

The photographer said, "Ring the manager, Pete."

They rang the manager's button. When nothing happened, the reporter started pushing buttons at random. After a while they got a customer, and the door buzzed open. They walked on in and Bertha Cool and I tagged along behind them.

"What's the apartment number?" the photographer asked.

The reporter said 309.

I felt Bertha Cool's eyes on me. I nudged her and said in an undertone, "Hear that?"

She said, "Uh-huh."

The four of us got in the elevator. Bertha Cool took up most of the room. The elevator rattled upward.

The third floor was pretty well filled with people. An officer stopped the reporter. The reporter showed him a press card and he and the photographer went on past. The officer pushed his way up to me. "What do you want?" he asked.

I stood staring curiously and said, "Nothing."

"Beat it. Move on. You're blocking traffic."

I said, "I'm looking for the manager. Is she up here?"

"How should I know? I guess so."

"I want to see her about renting an apartment."

"Well, come on back in a couple of hours."

"What's happened here?" I asked.

"Homicide," he said. "Jane in 309. Know her?"

I looked at Bertha blankly. "You don't know anyone here, do you, Bertha?"

She shook her head.

"Okay," the officer said. "Beat it."

"Can't we see the manager?"

"No. I can't hunt her up now. She's probably answering questions. G'wan. Beat it."

We walked back to the elevator. "Well," I said, "someone beat us to it."

Bertha didn't say anything. We rattled back down in the elevator, went out, and got in the agency car.

"Well," I said, "I'll go back to the office and do a little thinking. Do you want me to drop you at your apartment?"

"No, Donald, my dear. I'll go back to the office and help you think."

Chapter Five

We rode back to the office in silence. I put the car in the parking lot and we rode up in the elevator, went into the office, and sat down.

Bertha Cool looked across at me and said, "How did you find out she'd been murdered, lover?"

I said, "What the devil are you talking about?"

Bertha Cool scraped a match on the underside of the desk, lit her cigarette, looked at me, and said, "Nuts."

She smoked for a while in silence, then she said thoughtfully, "Cop cars were scattered all around the joint. You pretended not to see them. You didn't want to ring her apartment. You wanted to ring the manager. You went on up, asked a couple of questions, turned around, and went back down. You knew something had happened. What you wanted to find out was whether the police were there. Going to tell me about it?"

"There's nothing to tell."

Bertha Cool opened a drawer, took out a card, looked at the number on the card, picked up the telephone, and dialed a number. When the party at the other end of the line answered, she said, in that cooing voice of hers, "Mr. Donald Lam has a room at your place I believe, Mrs. Eldridge. This is Mrs. Cool, head of the Cool Detective Agency. Donald works for me, you know. I'm very anxious to find him. Do you know if he's in his room?"

Bertha Cool listened while the receiver made noises, then she said, "I see. About an hour ago, eh? Well, can you tell me if someone called on him shortly before he went out?" Again she listened, and said, "Oh, yes, I see. Can you describe her, please?"

Again Bertha Cool listened, her lids half closed. Beneath them her cold, gray eyes shifted to glance at me then she said, "Thank you very much, Mrs. Eldridge. If he comes in, tell him I was trying to reach him, will you?"

She hung up, pushed the telephone back across the desk, turned to me, and said, "All right, Donald. Who was she?"

"Who?"

"The girl who came to see you?"

"Oh," I said. "That was a girl who went to law school with me. I hadn't seen her for a long time. She heard I was working for you and rang up this afternoon to get the address. Elsie gave it to her."

Bertha Cool smoked for a while, then she dialed another number and when she got an answer said, "Elsie, this is Bertha. Did someone ring up and ask for Donald's address this afternoon?...Who was she? Did she leave her name?...Oh, he did, eh? All right, Elsie. Thanks. That's all."

Bertha hung up the telephone and said, "You told Elsie you hadn't seen this girl."

I said, "All right. Have it that way if you want. I don't believe in letting Elsie Brand in on my love life. This girl was a pal of mine. She ran up and chatted with me for half an hour or so. It was purely social."

"Purely *social*, eh?" Bertha Cool asked.

I didn't say anything.

Bertha Cool smoked some more, and said, "All right, lover. We'll go get some supper. This isn't agency business. It's Dutch treat."

"I'm not hungry," I said.

She smiled. "Oh, well, I'll be generous, Donald. We'll put it on the expense account."

I shook my head. "I don't want anything."

"Well, you can come along and keep me company."

"No, thanks. I want to think."

"Think while you're with me, lover."

"No. I can stay here and figure things out a lot better."

Bertha Cool said, "I see." She pulled the telephone over toward her, dialed a number, and said, "This is B. Cool. Send me up a double clubhouse sandwich and a quart bottle of beer." She hung up the telephone, said, "I'm sorry you're not hungry, Donald. Bertha will sit right here and wait with you."

I didn't say anything.

We sat there in silence, Bertha Cool studying me with half-closed eyes, smoking thoughtfully. After a while there was a knock on the door, and Bertha Cool said, "Open it and let the waiter in."

The waiter from the restaurant downstairs brought in a tray with a double clubhouse sandwich and a quart of beer. Bertha Cool told him to put it on the desk, paid him, gave him a tip, and said, "You can get the dishes in the morning. We're going to be busy tonight."

The waiter thanked her and left. Bertha munched on the sandwich, washed it down with big gulps of beer, and said, "It's a hell of a way to make a dinner, but it will stay my appetite. Too bad you weren't hungry." After she'd finished and had another cigarette, I looked at my watch carelessly and said, "Well, I guess there's no use waiting any longer."

Bertha Cool beamed at me. "I guess you're right. Who was she? Why did she stand you up on the call?"

"A swell jane," I said. "She was going to ring me up for a dinner date. Can't a man step out with a girlfriend without having the whole damned office force trying to chisel in on his love life?"

"Apparently not," Bertha Cool said placidly. "All right, if you want to go, we'll go."

We went down and climbed in the agency car again. I said, "Well, I might as well go to a picture show and kill time that way. Do you want to go?"

"Hell, lover. Bertha's tired. She'll just go to her apartment and get her clothes off and read a book."

I drove her to her apartment. She got out and put a jeweled hand on my left arm. "I'm sorry," she said.

"It's all right," I told her. "The jane didn't call up. I guess she must have called while we were out, and probably some other guy was waiting to begin where I left off."

"Oh, well, Donald, there are lots of women. A young, good-looking boy like you won't have any trouble on that score. Good night."

"Good night," I said.

I turned the agency car and made time back to the office. I looked at my wristwatch. I'd only been gone twenty-five minutes in all. I hoped Marian hadn't called in during that time.

I sprawled out in a chair and was just lighting a cigarette when I heard the sound of a key in the lock of the door. I thought it was the janitor and called out, "We're busy. Let it go until tomorrow, will you, please?"

The latch clicked back and Bertha Cool, calmly placid, came walking into the office. She smiled at me and said, "Thought so," then sailed on through the entrance office to seat herself in the big swivel chair behind her desk. She said, "You and I could get along a hell of a lot better, Donald, if we didn't try to slip things over on each other."

I was just starting to answer that when the telephone on Bertha Cool's desk started to ring. Bertha, with a scooping motion of her thick right arm, pulled the telephone toward her, picked up the receiver, and said, "Hello."

Her eyes were on me, half-closed eyes that glittered like diamonds. Her left arm was out across the desk ready to stiff-arm me back in case I made a lunge for the telephone.

I sat still and smoked.

Bertha Cool said, "Yes, this is Bertha Cool's agency.... No, dear, he isn't here right now, but he told me you were going to telephone and said I'd take the message.... Oh, yes, dearie. Well, he expects to be here in just a few minutes. He said for you to come right up.... Yes, that's right. That's the address. Come right up, dearie. Don't waste any time. Get a taxicab. He wants to see you."

She dropped the receiver back into place and turned to face me. "Now then, Donald," she said, "let this be a lesson to you. The next time you try to cut yourself a piece of cake, cut Bertha in on it, otherwise there's going to be trouble."

"You want in on it, do you?" I asked.

"I'm in," she said.

I said, "You are, for a fact."

She said, "You came to work for me, lover, a little runt that didn't know anything about the detective business. I picked you up when you were down to your last cent. You hadn't eaten for two days when you came to the office. I gave you a job. You're learning the business. You have brains. The trouble is, you don't keep in mind that I'm the boss. You get to thinking you're running the business. It's a case of the tail wagging the dog."

"Anything else?" I asked.

"Isn't that enough?" Bertha asked.

"It's plenty," I said. "Now would you like to know what you've cut yourself in on?"

She smiled and said, "Well, that might help some. No hard feelings, eh, Donald?"

"No hard feelings," I said.

Bertha said, "I stick up for my rights. When I have to fight, I fight to win. I don't hold any grudges. I fight because I want to accomplish something. When I've accomplished it, that's all I ask."

"She's coming up here?" I asked.

"Right away. She said she had to see you right away. It didn't sound like a date to me, lover. It sounded like business."

"It is business."

"All right, Donald. Suppose you tell Bertha what it is. I've declared myself in on the deal, so I'd like to see what cards are in my hand—and what the stakes are. But don't forget that I hold the trumps."

"All right," I said. "You're in on a murder."

"I knew that already."

I said, "The girl you were talking with was Marian Dunton. She was stranded in a hick town up in the foothills. She wanted to get out. She played a hunch that this Lintig case was something bigger than appeared on the surface. She followed my back trail and got a lead by which she figured she could dig up some information."

"You mean with this Evaline girl?"

"Yes."

Bertha said, "Never mind the history. I figured that all out myself. Tell me something I don't know."

I said, "I don't know just what time the post-mortem will show Evaline Harris was murdered, probably about the time Marian Dunton went to her apartment for the first time."

"For the *first* time?" Bertha asked.

"Yes. She opened the door of the apartment and saw Evaline lying on the bed. She thought she was asleep. A man had just left the apartment. Marian thought it wasn't exactly a propitious moment for getting information, so she quietly closed the door and went back to sit in the car where she could watch the door of the apartment house. After half an hour or so, she tried it again. She was bolder that time and more curious. She found Evaline Harris had a cord knotted around her neck and was quite dead. Marian lost her head, could only think of me, and came rushing up to my room to tell me about it. I sent her to the police, told her to say nothing about having been to me, nothing about the agency, nothing about Mrs. Lintig, simply that she was approaching Evaline to see about getting a job in the city, that she thought Evaline was asleep the first time, and had gone out to wait in the car."

"I doubt if she gets away with that," Bertha Cool said.

"I think she will."

"Why?"

"She's from the country. She's a simple, unsophisticated, darn nice girl. It sticks out all over her. She's fresh and unspoiled. She hasn't learned the chiseling tactics of the city. She's just a square-shooting good kid."

Bertha Cool sighed and said, "That's one of your greatest weaknesses as a detective, lover. The women all knock you for a loop. You fall for them head over heels. The fact that you can't get anywhere in a fight is bad enough, but this business of falling for women is twice as bad. You've got to learn to quit it. If you could only do that, your brains would get you places."

"Anything else?" I asked.

Bertha Cool smiled and said, "Now, don't be like that, Donald. This is business, you know."

"All right," I said. "Now *I'll* tell *you* the rest of it. Marian got a pretty good look at the man who was coming out of the apartment. Her description won't mean anything to the police—at least, I hope it won't—but it meant something to me."

"What do you mean?"

"The man who left the apartment," I said, "was Dr. Charles Loring Alftmont, otherwise known as Dr. James O. Lintig. He prefers to have us refer to him as Mr. Smith."

Bertha Cool stared at me. Her lids slowly raised until her eyes were round and startled. She said, so softly that it was almost under her breath, "I'll be stewed for an oyster."

"Now then," I said, "the police don't know anything about the Lintig angle. They don't know anything about the Alftmont angle. There's no particular reason why they should suspect the man whom we will refer to as Smith from now on. But if Marian Dunton should see him or should see his photograph, she'll identify him in a minute."

Bertha Cool gave a low whistle.

"Therefore," I said, "you can play things in either one of two ways. You can turn her loose on her own, in which event the police will sooner or later get a lead to Smith, put him in a line-up, and ask Marian Dunton to identify him, in which event the fat will be in the fire and you won't have any client; or you can keep Marian out of circulation as much as possible, tell Smith what we know, make him give us his side of the story, tell him we're standing between him and a murder rap, get unlimited funds with which to work, and try to clean the thing up."

"Won't that be suppressing evidence, lover?"

"Yes."

"That's serious, you know, for a private detective agency. They'd hook me for my license on that."

"If you hadn't known anything at all about it, they couldn't have held you responsible."

"Well," she said, "I know about it now."

"Yes," I said. "You've cut yourself in on the deal. Marian's on her way up here. It's your play. You know what the cards are now."

Bertha Cool pushed back her chair. "Forgive me, Donald," she said. "I'm going to get the hell out of here."

"No, you aren't," I said. "You answered the phone, and told her to come. I wouldn't have done that. I'd have told her to go to the Union Depot or some place like that, and I'd have met her there. She's probably under surveillance."

Bertha Cool started to drum with her thick, jeweled fingers on the top of the desk. "What a mess," she said.

"You cooked it," I told her.

"I'm sorry, Donald."

"I thought you would be."

"Listen, couldn't you take over and—"

"Nothing doing," I said. "If you hadn't known anything about it, I could have gone ahead and done what I thought was necessary. I could have acted dumb and if anyone had questioned me, they could never have proved anything except that I *was* dumb. Now, it's different. You know. What you know might get found out."

"You could trust me, lover," she said.

"I could, but I don't."

"You don't?"

"No."

Her eyes hardened and I said, "No more than you trusted me a few minutes ago."

There was a timid knock at the outer door. Bertha Cool called, "Come in."

Nothing happened. I got up and crossed through the reception room to open the door. Marian Dunton stood on the threshold.

"Come in, Marian," I said. "I want you to meet the boss. Mrs. Cool, this is Miss Dunton."

Bertha Cool beamed at her. "How are you?" she said. "Donald

has told me the *nicest* things about you. Do come in and sit down."

Marian smiled at her, said, "Thank you very much, Mrs. Cool. I'm very glad to meet you," and then came to stand close by me. She gave my arm a quick, surreptitious squeeze. Her fingers were trembling.

"Sit down, Marian," I said.

She dropped into a chair.

"Want a drink?"

She laughed and said, "I had one."

"When?"

"After they got done with me."

"Was it bad?"

"Not particularly." She glanced significantly at Bertha Cool.

I said, "Mrs. Cool knows it all. Go ahead and tell us."

"Does she know about—about—"

"You mean about your coming to my place?"

"Yes."

"She knows it all. Go ahead, Marian. What happened?"

She said, "I got away with it nicely. I went to the police station and told them I wanted to report a body, and they sent me into the traffic department. Evidently they thought it was an automobile accident. I had to do quite a bit of explaining to two or three different people. They sent a radio car to investigate, and the radio officers called in for Homicide. After that there was a lot of activity, and a nice young district attorney took a statement from me."

"Did you sign it?" I asked.

"No. It was taken down by a stenographer, but they didn't type it out. They didn't ask me to sign it."

I said, "That's a break."

"Why? I couldn't go back on anything I'd said."

"No. But the fact that they didn't tie you up with a signature shows they are taking your story at its face value."

She said, "Mostly they were interested in this man who was leaving the apartment."

"They would be," I said.

"They tried to convince me that I'd really seen him coming out of the door of 309, and that I mustn't say anything to anyone about thinking he might have been coming from another apartment."

"I see."

She went on: "The young deputy district attorney was very nice. He explained that in order to convict a man of murder it was necessary for the evidence to show his guilt beyond all reasonable doubt. Well, you know how it is, Donald. There's a lot of question as to when a doubt is reasonable. Of course, the man *might* have been coming from another apartment, but it didn't look like it, and, the more I think of it, the more I'm certain he came from apartment 309. Now then, if I should just make some slip which would indicate I wasn't dead sure of what I'd seen, a shyster attorney, representing the murderer, would use it to cheat justice. After all, Donald, a citizen has quite a responsibility, and a witness must be willing to take the responsibility of telling things the way he saw them."

I smiled and said, "I see it was a *very* nice deputy district attorney."

"Donald, don't be like that. After all, really those are the facts."

I nodded.

"The police are going to find out all about Evaline Harris. They're going to find out who her men friends were, and after they learn about them, I'll be called on to make some identifications, probably first from photographs."

"They think it was a boyfriend?" I asked with a significant glance at Bertha Cool.

"Yes. They think it was a crime of jealousy. They think that the man who did it had been—well, you know, a lover. You see, the body was lying nude on the bed, and there was no evidence of a struggle. The man must have slipped the cord around her neck and drawn it tight before she knew anything was happening."

"What are you supposed to do?" I asked. "Stick around here or go back to Oakview?"

"I'm supposed to be available," she said. "They investigated me. They telephoned the sheriff at Oakview, and the sheriff is an old friend of mine. He said they could trust me anywhere any time."

"Did they," I asked, "act as though they thought *you* might have been the one who did it?"

"No. Coming to the police station and all that was in my favor, and I acted just the way you told me to—you know, hicky and countrified."

"That's swell," I said. "How about dinner, Marian? Have you eaten?"

"No, and I'm so hungry I could eat a horse."

I grinned at Bertha Cool and said, "Too bad you've eaten, Mrs. Cool. I'll take Marian out to dinner. I'll want some expense money."

Bertha Cool positively beamed. "Yes indeed, Donald," she said. "Go right ahead and take her out. There'll be nothing for you to do this evening."

"I want some expense money."

"Just be sure to be on deck at nine o'clock in the morning, Donald, and if anything turns up tonight, I'll call you."

"That's fine. And the expense money?"

Bertha Cool opened the drawer in the desk. She opened her purse, took out a key to the cash drawer, counted out a hundred dollars in bills, and handed them to me. I kept my hand extended and said. "Keep coming. I'll tell you when to stop."

She started to say something, then handed me another fifty. "That," she said, "is all that's in the drawer. I don't keep any more cash than that in the office." She slammed the lid of the cash box shut, locked it, and closed the drawer.

I said, "Come on, Marian."

Bertha Cool positively beamed at us. "You two go ahead," she said, "and enjoy yourselves. I've had dinner. It's been a hard day, and all I want right now is to get home where I can get into some lounging pajamas and relax. I guess I'm getting old. A hard day uses me up and leaves me limp as a dishrag."

"Nonsense," Marian said. "You're a young woman."

"I have to carry all this fat around with me," Bertha explained.

"It isn't fat. It looks like muscle," Marian insisted. "You're big-boned, big-framed, that's all."

"Thank you, my child."

I took Marian's hand and said, "Let's go, Marian."

Bertha Cool locked the desk, dropped the key in her purse, got to her feet, and said, "Don't bother about taking me home, Donald. I'll go in a cab."

She walked across the office with us with that peculiar, effortless walk of hers which seemed as smooth as the progress of a yacht on a calm sea. Bertha never waddled. She didn't make a hard job of walking. She moved with short steps, never hurrying herself, but keeping up a steady pace regardless of whether it was hot or cold, uphill or down.

When we were in a restaurant, Marian said, "I think she's wonderful, Donald. She seems so competent, so self-reliant."

"She is," I said.

"She looks hard, though."

"You don't know how hard," I said. "And now, let's talk about you."

"What about me?"

"Why did you leave Oakview?"

"To see Evaline Harris, of course."

"Did you tell your uncle that?"

"No. I told him I wanted to take a part of my vacation."

"I thought he'd gone fishing."

"He came back."

"When did he come back?"

She puckered her forehead and said, "Let me see. It was—it was right after you left."

"How long afterward?"

"Just a couple of hours."

"And you started for the city as soon as he got back?"

"Yes."

I said, "All right. Now, where do you fit into the picture?"

"What do you mean?"

"You know what I mean. You said that if I wanted to pool information with you, you'd put in with me, that if I didn't, you were going on your own."

She said, "You know all about that."

"All about what?"

"About how I felt I want to get out of that newspaper. I want to get out of Oakview. I knew that you were a detective—"

"How did you know?"

"I'm not blind," she said. "You had to be a detective. You were working for someone. You were trying to get information, and you weren't simply trying to look up a bad credit or collect a bill—not after twenty-one years."

"All right, go ahead."

"Well, I knew you were a detective, and I knew Mrs. Lintig was mixed up in something big. There's been too much interest in her, and I figured you got that black eye because of trying to find out about her. So I figure if she was that important, it would be a good chance for me, being on the ground, to get in on the ground floor, use my acquaintanceship in Oakview to find out what it was everyone was after, and find out who you were working for, go to your boss with the information, and see if I couldn't get a job."

"What kind of a job?" I asked curiously.

"Being a detective. They have woman detectives, don't they?"

I said, "You were going to ask Bertha Cool to give you a job as a detective?"

"Yes. Of course I didn't know anything about Bertha Cool at the time. I didn't know who your boss was. I thought probably it was one of the big agencies or something like that."

"What do you know about being a detective?"

"I've had to do reporting up there in Oakview, and even if it is a little paper in a one-horse country town, you have to have a nose for news to get by. I'm ambitious and—well, they can't rule you off the track for trying."

I said, "Forget it. Go back to Oakview and marry Charlie. By the way, how is Charlie?"

"All right," she said, avoiding my eyes.

"What did he think of you leaving Oakview and coming to the city to get a job being a detective?"

"He didn't know anything about it."

I kept watching her, and she, feeling my eyes on hers, kept looking at the tablecloth. I said, "I hope you're telling me the truth."

She raised her eyes then in a quick flash, and said, "Oh, but I am." Then she lowered her eyes again.

A waiter took our orders, and brought food. Marian didn't say anything until after she'd finished her soup, then she pushed the plate away, and said, "Donald, do you suppose she'd give me a job?"

"Who?"

"Why, Mrs. Cool, of course."

"She has a secretary," I said.

"I mean as a detective."

"Don't be silly, Marian. You couldn't be a detective."

"Why not?"

"You don't know enough about the world. You have ideals. You—it's silly to even think of it. Bertha Cool takes all sorts of cases, divorce cases particularly."

"I know the facts of life," Marian Dunton said indignantly.

I said, "No, you don't. You just think you do. What's more, you'd feel like a heel. You'd have shadowing jobs. You'd be snooping around, peeking through keyholes, digging down into the muddy dregs of life—things you shouldn't know anything about."

"You talk like a poet, Donald," she said, and tilted her head slightly on one side as she looked at me. "There's something poetic about you, too," she went on. "You have that sensitive mouth, big, dark eyes."

I said, "Oh, nuts."

The waiter brought our salads.

I kept looking at her, and she kept avoiding my eyes. I waited for her to talk, and she didn't feel like talking. After a while she looked up at me and said, "Donald, do you know that man who was coming from Evaline Harris's apartment?"

Her eyes held mine then, steady and searching.

I said, "That's what comes of being coached by the police."

"What do you mean?"

"When you told me about it the first time, you didn't say that he was coming from that apartment. You said he was coming down the corridor."

"Well, he came out of an apartment."

"But you didn't know that it was Evaline Harris's apartment."

"It must have been."

"Do you think so?"

"Yes."

"Do you *know* that it was her apartment?"

"Well—well, not exactly, but it must have been, Donald."

I said, "Tomorrow, after things have quieted down, we'll go up to that apartment house. You come out of the elevator. I'll stand in the doorway of apartment 309 and step out into the corridor just as you leave the elevator. Then we'll try it with the other two doorways."

She squinted her eyes thoughtfully and said, "Yes, it might work. Perhaps Mr. Ellis would like to have me do that for him."

"Who's Ellis?"

"Larchmont Ellis, the deputy district attorney."

"No. He won't want you to do that for him until after he's talked with you a couple of times more. By that time, you'll be positive the man was coming out of 309. Then he'll put on the demonstration to clinch it in your mind."

She said, "He wouldn't do anything like that. He wants to be fair. He's a very nice young man."

I said, "Yeah, I know."

The waiter brought on our meat course, and after he had left, she said, "Donald, I've got to get a room."

"Did the district attorney tell you where you were to stay?"

"No. He said to report at ten o'clock in the morning."

I said, "Look here. I want to keep in touch with you. I don't want to have you hunting me up or running to the agency office, and I don't want to be going to your hotel. Let's go to my rooming house. I'll tell the landlady you're related to me, and ask her to give you a room. I think she has a vacancy. In that way, I can see you once in a while without arousing suspicion."

"Donald, I think that would be swell."

"It's not like a hotel," I said. "It's just a rooming house, and—"

"I know," she said.

I said, "We'll go up right after dinner. I have some work to do, and I'll get you settled first."

"But I thought you didn't have to work. I thought Mrs. Cool said—"

"She doesn't care when I work," I said, "or when I sleep. All she wants is results. If I can get them in twenty-three hours a day, she doesn't object to my doing anything I damn please with the extra hour."

She laughed, then abruptly quit laughing and stared steadily at me. "Donald," she said, "are you working for the man who came out of that apartment?"

I said patiently, "You don't know whether he came out of that apartment or not, Marian."

"Well—look here, Donald. I don't want to do anything that's going to hurt you. Don't you think it would be a swell idea for you to put your cards on the table?"

"No."

"Why not?"

"Then you'd know too much."

"Don't you trust me?"

"It isn't that. You have enough troubles now. If you helped me without knowing you were helping me, no one could make a kick. If you helped me and knew you were helping me and it turned out I was in hot water, then you'd be in right along with me."

She said, "Oh. Then you are working for him."

I said, "Quit talking and eat. I have work to do."

I hurried her through dinner and drove her up to my place. Mrs. Eldridge listened to my explanation that she was my cousin who had come to town rather unexpectedly. I said she might be there for a day or two. I didn't know just how long.

Mrs. Eldridge gave her a front room on my floor. She looked across at me with acid eyes and said, "When you're visiting your *cousin*, leave the door open."

"I will," I said, and took the receipt Mrs. Eldridge handed me.

When she had gone, Marian said, "So we have to leave the door open."

"Uh-huh."

"How much open?"

"Oh, two or three inches. I'm going anyway."

"Donald, I wish you didn't have to go. Can't you stay here for a little while and—and visit."

"No. Charlie might not like it."

She screwed her face up in a little grimace and said, "I wish you'd quit kidding about him."

"But what's his real name?" I asked.

She said, "You've created him. He is entirely your idea. If you don't like Charlie, why don't you think up another name?"

"Charlie suits me all right."

"Then go on calling him Charlie."

I said, "I've got some work to do. I've got to be shoving on."

"Donald, I wish I could get that out of my mind. She had such a beautiful figure, and that cord around her neck—her face was all swollen, and black and—"

"Shut up," I said. "Quit thinking about it. Go to bed and get some sleep. The bathroom is at the end of the corridor."

"When will you be in, Donald?"

"I don't know. Pretty late."

"If I'd sit up, would you look in on me before you went to bed?"

"No."

"Why?"

"I don't want you sitting up, and it may be good and late. Go to bed and get some sleep."

"Will you see me in the morning?"

"I can't promise."

"Why?"

"I don't know what I'll be doing in the morning."

She placed the tips of her fingers on my forearm. "Thanks for the dinner and—and everything, Donald."

I patted her shoulder. "Keep a stiff upper lip. It'll be all right. 'Night."

She came to the door and watched me down the corridor. Mrs. Eldridge was waiting to buttonhole me in the front hallway. "Your cousin looks like a nice girl," she said.

"She is."

"Of course, I like to know something about people who have rooms here, particularly young women."

I said, "My cousin's engaged to a sailor. His boat's due to arrive sometime tomorrow."

Her nose went up in the air an inch or two. "If he calls on her, tell her to keep the door open—or should I tell her?"

"He won't call on her," I said. "His mother lives here. She'll visit him at his mother's. She expected to stay there, only there was some company came in unexpectedly."

Mrs. Eldridge's face thawed into a smile. "Oh," she said, and then after a moment: "Oh."

"Is that all?" I asked.

She said, "Under the circumstances, I won't ask you anything about her. Usually I like to know more details, but under the circumstances it won't be necessary for you to tell me anything at all about her personal affairs."

"I was afraid I'd have to," I said. I went out, climbed into the agency car, and filled it with gas, oil, and water. It was darn near empty on all three.

Chapter Six

I drove down to the Blue Cave. It was a joint. They'd closed up most of the burlesque houses, and those that hadn't been closed had been disinfected so they had virtually no alcoholic content. The Blue Cave was one of the joints which had sprung up in the neighborhood to fill the bill.

The place wasn't particularly wicked as far as anything anyone actually did, but it was plenty wicked so far as intimations of what would be done or could be done or would like to be done were concerned.

I found a table back in a corner and ordered a drink. An entertainer was putting on an expurgated version of a chemically pure strip tease. She had more clothes on when she'd finished than most of the performers had when they started, but it was the manner in which she took them off that appealed to the audience: a surreptitious, be-sure-the-doors-and-windows-are-closed-boys attitude that made the customers feel partners in something very, very naughty. When the applause started getting really loud, she looked questioningly at the manager and put up a hand to the clothes that were left as though asking him if she dared make a clean sweep. He came running forward shaking his head, grabbed her hand, started to jerk her off the stage, then apparently, getting his presence of mind, turned for two or three bows at the audience, and led her toward the dressing room, walking hand in hand.

Shortly after that, the strip-tease dancer was back in circulation, and four noisy men at an adjoining table were very patiently trying to get enough liquor under her belt so that she wouldn't look to the manager for that final signal when the next performance came along.

A woman in the late forties with coal black hair and eyes that were so avaricious I was reminded with each blink of the celluloid tags which shoot up when a sale is rung up in a cash register strolled past my table and said, "Good evening."

"Hello," I said.

"You look lonesome."

"I am."

"On the loose?" she asked.

"Loose as ashes," I said.

She smiled. "I'll see what I can do."

What she could do was indicated by a crook of her finger and a jerk of her head in my direction. In no time at all, a brunette with lots of make-up slid into the chair opposite and said, "Hello. How are you tonight?"

"Fine," I said. "Have a drink?"

She nodded.

The waiter might have been hiding under the table from the promptness with which he answered that nod. "Whisky straight," she said.

"Rye highball," I ordered.

The waiter went away. The girl across the table put her elbows on the tablecloth, interlaced her fingertips under her chin, gave me the benefit of a stare from two very large dark eyes, and said, "My name's Carmen."

"I'm Donald."

"Live here?"

"I'm on the road. I get in once every three or four months."

"Oh."

The waiter brought her whisky glass full of cold tea, gave me a rye highball, and a check for a dollar and twenty-five cents. I nicked Bertha Cool's roll for a dollar and a half, waved him away, and said to Carmen, "Here's happy days."

"Looking at you," she said, and tossed the cold tea down her throat, reached quickly for her glass of water as though the stuff was unusually potent, and then, after a couple of gulps, said, "Gosh, I shouldn't drink. I get funny when I get tight."

"How funny?" I asked.

She giggled and said, "Plenty funny. You haven't been here before, have you?"

"Once," I said. "My last trip into town—and boy, *did* I have a time."

She raised her eyebrows.

"Girl by the name of Evaline," I said. "I guess she isn't here anymore."

She pulled a curtain over her eyes and said, in an expressionless voice, "You knew Evaline?"

"Uh-huh."

She looked me over, then leaned across the table a little closer and said, "Okay, buddy. Forget it."

"Why should I forget it?" I asked.

She nodded vaguely toward the back of the room. "Couple of plainclothes men," she said in an undertone, "making the rounds, asking about the men who knew Evaline."

"Why all the commotion?" I asked.

"Somebody bumped her off this afternoon."

I sat bolt upright in my chair. "This afternoon?"

"Yes. Take it easy, Donald. Don't telegraph the conversation. I'm tipping you off, that's all."

I thought a minute, then surreptitiously slid a five-dollar bill out of my pocket and said, "Thanks, baby. Stick your hand under the tablecloth. I have something I want to say."

I felt her fingers contacting mine, and then the five-dollar bill being gently withdrawn. Carmen's shoulders hunched forward almost even with the table as she slipped the bill down her stocking.

"And my thanks go with it. I have a wife in San Francisco. I couldn't afford to be questioned."

"I figured that," she said. "Evaline was a nice kid. It's a shame. I guess she was two-timing someone who didn't like it."

"How did it happen?"

She said, "Someone got in her apartment, slipped a cord around her neck, pulled it tight."

"That," I said, "is no way to treat a lady."

There was feeling in her voice. "Are you telling me? Christ, when you think of what men are, what they take from a girl, and what they do— Oh, well." She shrugged her shoulders, twisted her red lips into a smile, and said, "This is no way to do. Be happy and keep smiling, or you won't get any customers."

I said, "I guess that's right. You don't get any business being sorry for yourself."

"Not in this racket. You have to put up a smiling front. The boys like girls who are drifting through life without a care in the world. Try and tell them you're in this game trying to support a kid, and she's at home with a bad cough and a fever, and you're worried, and you don't even get a tumble."

"Got a kid?" I asked.

For a moment her eyes moistened, then she blinked back the tears and said, "For Christ's sake, quit it! You'll make my mascara run.... How about another drink? No, wait a minute. Forget it. You slipped me enough so I can afford to give you a break."

"The waiter's looking this way," I said.

"Let him look," she said. "We're entitled to twenty minutes on a drink, more if we want to take it."

"You get a commission?"

"Sure."

"And drink what?" I asked.

Her eyes were defiant. "Whisky," she said, "and don't let anybody kid you on *that* score."

"You do a turn?" I asked.

"Yes. A song, and a few kick steps."

"Who's the woman with the funny eyes?" I asked.

She laughed and said, "That's Dora, the new hostess. I guess Flo was here when you were here before, wasn't she?"

I nodded.

Carmen said, "Dora's a kick, but don't ever kid yourself she isn't on the job. She has eyes in the back of her head. She knows everything that's going on. She's good that way."

"What happened to Flo?" I asked.

"I don't know. She drifted away. I don't know what did happen. Trouble with the boss perhaps. Dora's only been here about a week, but she's taking a hold. Listen, you didn't come here to talk about me and my troubles or about the business. How about a little dance?"

I nodded. The music had swung into a dance. The small strip of floor was crowded with people jostling each other around. Carmen pressed up close against me, opened her eyes wide, slightly raised her head, smirked her lips into a smile, and kept the same expression all the time we were dancing. She danced skillfully, intimately, and with her mind on the child at home who had a cough and a fever. I didn't say anything to change the direction of her thoughts.

After a while the music quit, and we went back to the table. I said to Carmen, "That waiter's looking us over. I have an idea you'd better get commission on another drink."

"Thanks," she said.

I nodded to the waiter, and he came over on the double quick. "Fill them up," I said, and when he had taken the glass, I said to Carmen, "How about Evaline? Did you know her well?"

She shook her head.

"She told me she had some relatives up in the northern part of the state. I can't remember the name of the town."

"No relatives in this state," Carmen said. "She came from the East."

"Ever been married?" I asked.

"I don't think so."

"Was she going steady?"

"Hell, I don't know!" she said, suddenly bringing her eyes to focus on mine. "You talk like a damn dick. How the hell should I know about her? I got troubles of my own."

I said, "You forget that I fell for her pretty hard."

She studied me and said, "You shouldn't have done it. You're too nice a kid to fall for any B girl. Not that we ain't just as good as anybody else, but we have to play our men for what we can get out of them. But hell, you're married and stepping out on your wife, so I guess it's six of one and half a dozen of the other.

"That's a funny thing about people. You've got a home, and you want to step out and sit around where there's music and drinking and entertainment. I have to work in this joint, and I'd give my right arm for a home, a husband, and a lot of housework."

"Why not get the husband?" I asked. "It shouldn't be hard—for you."

She laughed bitterly and said, "Me with a five-year-old daughter. Don't kid yourself, Mister."

"Five years old," I said, putting surprise in my voice.

"You heard me. Cripes, look at Evaline. She was a kid. She had freshness and charm. I can turn on the personality, and put on the warpaint, and— Say, for God's sake, who started this anyway? If you've got the blues, go ahead and get drunk. Start making passes at me and telling stories, but turn off this dark-blue faucet or I'll go nuts."

"Okay, Carmen," I said.

The waiter brought our drinks.

"The plainclothes men talk with you?" I asked.

"Did they!" she said. "They turned me inside out. I couldn't tell them anything. My God, look at us. We play the game on a percentage basis. I'll drift around to a dozen tables in the course of a night. Maybe if I'm lucky, someone will fall for me hard enough to buy me a flock of drinks, and after he gets tight he'll maybe pay for them with a five-dollar bill, tip the waiter, and push the change over to me. That's gravy. Probably he won't.

"There are ten of us girls here, and all of them working the same racket. Evaline was part of that racket. How should I know what men she'd been playing up to? I've got troubles of my own. Wait a minute, I'm going to put through a phone call. You don't care, do you, Donald?"

"Go ahead," I said.

She went over to the phone booth and called. She came back a little later and said, "Well, the kid's resting easier. The cough doesn't seem to be any worse."

"She'll be all right," I said. "Kids run a high temperature over nothing in particular, and snap out of it."

She nodded. "I know, but when it's *your* kid, it's different."

"Any plans for her future, Carmen?"

She laughed bitterly. "I should make plans for *her* future. I can't even figure my own."

I said, "One more question about Evaline. Who was the big beefy guy about six feet tall with the black hair and gray eyes that had such a crush on her? He had a little mole on his cheek.

She told me that if he happened to be in the place when I came back not to make any play for her but to pick one of the other girls and—"

Her eyes stared at me with the fascination of a bird, watching a snake. Slowly she pushed her chair back. Her voice, hardly above a whisper, said, "So you know that, do you? Well, you know just too damn much."

I said, "No. Honest. I—"

"And to think I didn't spot you," she said. "I thought I could tell a flatfoot as far as I could see him."

"Don't get me wrong, Carmen," I said. "I'm not."

She kept studying me as though I'd been a queer-looking fish in an aquarium. After a moment, she said, "By God, I don't believe you are. And if you aren't— Excuse me a minute. I'll be right back."

She got up and went into the women's room. I saw her flash a high-sign to the hostess when she went in. In less than a minute the hostess went into the rest room. After a while the hostess came out and went over to talk with the manager. A few moments later, the manager came strolling casually by.

He paused at my table and looked at the two glasses and at Carmen's empty place. "Being taken care of?" he asked.

"Yes," I said.

He stood there at the table, looking me over. "One of the entertainers?" he asked.

"Yes."

"She run out on you?"

"No. She's putting a little powder on her nose."

"Been gone long?"

"Not very."

He said, "I have to keep an eye on these girls. They— well, you know. I thought you'd been sitting here some little time."

"I have," I said.

"I mean alone."

I didn't say anything.

He said, "You'll understand that I'm trying to look out for your best interests. Let's just take a look and see that your watch and wallet are all right."

"They are," I said.

He stood looking at me with eyes that drooped a little. He was a dark, dapper man with a close-clipped mustache. He wore a double-breasted, gray suit, was a little above average height, and had supple hands with long, thin fingers. He said, "I'd like to have you make sure."

"I am sure."

He hesitated a moment. "I don't seem to place you," he said. "You aren't one of the regular customers."

"I've been here before."

"When?"

"Oh, two or three months ago."

"Have one of the girls at your table?" he asked.

"Yes."

"You don't remember her name, do you?"

I said, "No."

"Carmen was over here, wasn't she—tonight?"

"Yes."

He drew up a chair, sat down, and said, "She's a great girl, Carmen. Winthrop's my name." He shoved his hand across the table at me.

I shook his hand and said, "My name is Donald."

He smiled and said, "I understand. Glad to know you, Donald. My first name is Bartsmouth. My friends call me Bart. How about another drink—this one on the house?"

I said, "That would be swell."

He nodded to a waiter and said, "Fill the gentleman's glass. I'll take straight whisky. Did we treat you all right here before, Donald?"

"Yes."

He said, "I try to run a place which keeps within the law, but the men who come here like action, and I like to see that they get it, as much as I can give them and keep open. You know, I have to depend on customer good will and word-of-mouth advertising."

"That's right."

"How long ago did you say it was?"

"Two or three months."

"I like to have my customers come back—oftener than that."

"I'm out of San Francisco," I said, "a traveling man."

"Oh, I see. What line do you handle?"

"Office safes," I said.

He thought a moment and then smacked his hand on the table. "By George," he said, "that's a coincidence! The safe in my office is an obsolete old bread box, and sometimes our cash receipts run rather high. I've been figuring on getting a new safe. There's nothing I'd like better than to do business with a customer."

"Thanks," I said.

He said, "My business office is on the second floor. There's a flight of stairs back of that door behind the cash register. How about coming up and taking a look at the safe?"

I said, "I wouldn't want to run out on Carmen."

"Oh, I can send word to Carmen."

"No. I would prefer to handle it my way. Suppose I come up in about ten minutes? I think I'm going to get Carmen's telephone number."

"I can give you her telephone number," he said, "and see that she's there when you call."

"Thanks. I'd prefer to handle it my way—the personal touch, you know."

The waiter brought our drinks. I said, "Here's how," and raised my glass. I didn't drink it all, just sipped a bit off the top.

He thought for a minute, then pushed back his chair and gave me his hand again. "All right, I'll be seeing you in about ten minutes. You climb the stairs. It's the first door on the right. Just walk right in."

"Thanks. I will."

His fingers were lean, hard, and strong. His smile was affable. He said, "If you have any trouble with Carmen, let me know."

"Thanks. I don't think I'll have any."

"Neither do I. Okay, Donald, be seeing you later."

He started to walk away, then, after three steps, turned on his heel and came back. He said, "I'll want a pretty elaborate safe, something that's good. I suppose I can get a real good one for around two thousand dollars, can't I?"

"A peach," I said.

"That's fine. You come up and look the place over and appraise my safe. I'll want to turn it in for a trade, you know. But it's an old bread box, and I won't expect too much for it. I'll be reasonable."

"That's fine."

He walked over and said something to the hostess, then walked back of the cash register, pushed open the door, and went upstairs.

I got up and sauntered back toward the kitchen. A waiter said, "The men's room is over there to the left."

I said, "Thanks," and pushed my way out into the kitchen. A Negro cook looked up. I said, "Buddy, the wife just came in the front door. How do I get out?"

"You-all ain't beating a check?" he asked.

"Twenty bucks says I'm not."

"This way," he told me, pocketing the bill.

I followed him past a range out through a narrow, smelly corridor, past the stench of a latrine which said, *Employees Only*, and out into an alley lined with garbage cans. I said to him, "It's going to help a lot if you don't know anything about this afterward."

"Is you," he asked, "tellin' *me*?"

I swung around the alley, back to the street, and walked down to the parking place where I'd left the agency car.

Chapter Seven

It was well after midnight when I pulled into Santa Carlotta. The night had turned cold and I stopped in at an all-night restaurant for a cup of hot chocolate. From a telephone in the restaurant I rang Dr. Alftmont's residence.

The phone rang half a dozen times before a woman's voice, sounding dopey with sleep, said, "Hello."

"Dr. Alftmont's residence?"

"Yes."

"I must speak with Dr. Alftmont at once on a matter of the greatest importance."

"Have you tried his office?"

"His office?" I said in surprise.

"Yes. I think you'll find him there. He was called to his office shortly before midnight and hasn't returned."

"Sorry I disturbed you," I said. "I hardly expected he'd be at his office."

The woman was shaking the sleep out of her voice. She said, "That's quite all right. I understand. Would you care to leave a message in case you miss him at the office?"

"Tell him I'll call him in fifteen minutes if I don't catch him at the office," I said, "and thank you very much."

"It's quite all right," she said again.

I hung up and drove to Dr. Alftmont's office. If I had been a patient the voice of that woman would have made me a lifelong customer.

There were lights on in the building. The elevator was on automatic. I pressed the button and went up to Dr. Alftmont's floor. I couldn't hear any voices as I walked quietly down the corridor, but the oblong of frosted glass in the door of the office was radiating light into the corridor.

I tried the door. It was locked. I knocked a couple of times, and then I heard a door open and close on the inside of the office. I heard steps coming across the floor, then the door opened and Dr. Alftmont stood staring at me. Surprise, consternation, and stark fear took turns registering on his face. The door of the inner office was tightly closed.

I said, "I'm sorry to bother you, Doctor, but a matter of the greatest importance has come up and makes it necessary."

He glanced over his shoulder at the closed door to his private office and seemed puzzled.

I said, "Okay. We can talk right here." I took a step toward him, lowered my voice, and said, "Do you know what happened this afternoon?"

He hesitated a moment, then turned and said, "You may as well come in." He walked to the door of the private office, twisted the knob, and opened it.

I looked into the lighted interior of his testing laboratory. He said, "Go right on through to the private office."

I walked across and opened the door.

Bertha Cool sat over in a big chair near the window. She looked up at me, and her face showed surprise.

I said, "You!"

Dr. Alftmont came in behind me and closed the door.

Bertha said, "Well, well, Donald. You do get around, don't you?"

"How long have you been here?" I asked.

"About an hour," she said.

Dr. Alftmont crossed over to sit behind his desk. "This is terrible," he said, "terrible!"

I kept my eyes on Bertha. "How much did you tell him?" I asked.

"I explained the situation to him."

I said, "All right. Just a minute," and walked around the office, looking in behind the pictures and bookcase, moving the framed pictures out from the wall.

Dr. Alftmont said, "What are you loo—"

I held up a warning finger to my lips, and motioned to the wall.

Bertha Cool got the idea and said, "For God's sake, Donald!"

I didn't say anything until I had completed a search of the office. I said, "I don't see any. Which doesn't mean there isn't any. You have to be careful, particularly of that." I pointed toward the telephone.

Dr. Alftmont started to get up, then sat down again. He seemed completely overwhelmed by the turn of events. I said to Bertha, "Have you concluded your business?"

"Yes," she said, and then added, with a smile, "quite satisfactorily so far as we are concerned, Donald."

"Finished with everything you had to say?"

"Yes," she said.

"All right," I told her. "Let's go."

Dr. Alftmont said, "I'm afraid I don't quite understand."

"I'll be back in about ten minutes, Doctor," I said. "Would you mind waiting?"

"Why—no, I guess not."

I nodded to Bertha. She looked at me rather peculiarly, heaved to her feet, and gave Dr. Alftmont her hand. "Don't worry," she said. "It'll be all right."

"I wish I could share your confidence."

"It's all right. You're in our hands. We'll take care of you."

I said, "Wait fifteen minutes," to Dr. Alftmont and walked

down the corridor with Bertha Cool. Neither of us said anything in the corridor. In the elevator I said, "How did you come up?"

"I hired a car with a driver."

I said, "We'll talk in the agency car. It's downstairs."

We walked out across the strip of dark sidewalk, and Bertha Cool sagged the car over on its noisy springs as she eased herself into the pile of junk. I started the motor, drove down a couple of blocks, and parked in front of an all-night restaurant where we wouldn't attract so much attention. "What did you tell him?" I asked.

"Enough to let him know that we control the situation."

I said, "Where did you leave your car?"

"In the middle of the next block," she said. "The driver's waiting. I told him not to wait in front of the office."

I started the motor on the office heap.

"Didn't you want to talk, Donald?" she asked.

"There's nothing to talk about now," I said. "The beans are spilled."

"What do you mean?"

"I was going to tell him that a witness had seen a man leaving the apartment. I wasn't going to let on that we had any idea of who it could have been. His conscience would have done that."

"If he knows, why shouldn't we let him know that we know?"

"Just a legal difference," I said. "If we were helping him without any idea that he was the one, we'd have been acting as detectives. He naturally wouldn't have climbed out on a limb and told us anything. I suppose now you know it all."

"Yes," she said. "He went down to see her. He wanted to find out who sent her and what she'd discovered and see if he could make a deal with her."

"She was dead when he found her?" I asked.

"That's what he says."

"All right," I said to Bertha, "here's your car. Better drive back. I have a breakfast date at seven-thirty in the morning. I don't think I'll keep it. She's in my rooming house, number thirty-two. Take her to breakfast with you. Stall her along. Get her to give up the room. You'd better get her an apartment somewhere. The D.A. will want to know where she's staying. The way things are now, it had better be away from my joint."

For a moment the self-sufficiency oozed out of Bertha Cool's manner. She said, in something that was almost a panic, "Donald, you'll have to come back with me. You must. I can't control that girl. She's fallen for you. She'll do anything on earth you tell her, and I can't— God, Donald, I didn't know I was laying myself wide open that way."

"You see the point, don't you?"

"I see it now," she said.

"I have work to do here."

"What?"

I shook my head, and said, "There's no use explaining to you. The more you know, the more you talk. The more you talk, the more you put us in a position of being accessories after the fact. I'd have done a damn sight better if I'd held out on you from the start. I tried to, but you insisted on horning in."

She said, "He's wealthy, Donald. I got a check for three thousand dollars."

"I don't care if you got a check for ten thousand," I said. "You're in a jam. If there was a dictograph in that office, you're sunk. Bring your conversation with him up in front of a grand jury, and you can figure how long it'll be before your license gets revoked. After that, you'll be in prison. You won't take me with you—in case that's any consolation to you."

I could see she was frightened. She said, "Donald, come on

back with me. There's nothing you can do here tonight. Leave the agency car. You can drive back with me. It's a warm, comfortable, closed car. You take Marian to breakfast in the morning and get her a nice, quiet apartment somewhere."

I said, "No. Get her both an apartment somewhere and a room in a hotel. She goes to the hotel room once a day to pick up mail and messages. The rest of the time she stays in the apartment."

"Why?" Bertha asked.

I said, "She can't be too accessible. You can figure the play. They have organized vice and organized graft in this city. Alftmont can't be bribed. He's running for mayor. If he's elected, he'll start cleaning up the city. Lots of people don't like that. Some of them are on the police force. They can dig up this scandal and play it either of two ways—to keep him from being elected or make him withdraw from the race, or they can let him be elected and then hold it as a club over his head. They've been working quietly on it for a couple of months. Then he walks right into the middle of a murder. He couldn't afford to notify the police because the newspapers would start asking questions about why he'd gone to the apartment of a night-spot commission girl. He'd figure her trip to Oakview would be dragged out. He knew the local police would try to frame the crime on him, and he had to make a sneak. It just happened he ran into Marian in the hall. That was his hard luck. Our business now is to keep the Homicide Squad from suspecting the case has a tie-in with Santa Carlotta, to keep Marian Dunton from ever seeing Dr. Alftmont."

"That shouldn't be hard," she said.

I laughed. "Remember the man who beat me up and kicked me out of Oakview?" I asked.

"What about him?" she asked.

I said, "His name is John Harbet. He was Evaline Harris's particular boyfriend. He has a tie-in with the man who runs the Blue Cave. He's the head of the Vice Squad in Santa Carlotta. Figure that out."

While she was studying that bit of information, I opened the door of the agency car and said, "Okay, there's your bus. Get started, and don't forget to be on hand to take Marian out for breakfast. And just one other thing. I told that girl to act dumb. She's doing it because she knows it's the thing to do, but don't kid yourself. She's country, but she isn't dumb. And she's a darn nice kid."

Bertha Cool put her left hand on my right arm. "Listen, lover, come back with me. Bertha needs you."

I said, "Any minute now, a cop may come along the street and turn a flashlight on us just to see who we are. Would you like that?"

Bertha Cool said, "Hell, no!"

She scrambled out of the car as though it had been on fire. The driver of her car unwrapped himself from behind the steering wheel and stood holding the door open for her. She gave me one last appealing look, then climbed into the closed car. She sank back against the cushions, and for the moment she didn't look big and hard and competent. She looked like a fat woman in the fifties who was tired out.

I drove around the block, parked the agency car across the street from Dr. Alftmont's office, and went up. He was waiting for me.

I said, "You know too much, and we know too much. Bertha talked too much. I want to talk with you, and I don't want to talk with you here. Let's take a little ride in your car."

Without a word he switched out the lights, locked up his office, and rode down in the elevator with me. His car was parked at the curb in front of the building entrance. "Just where do we go?" he asked in that precise voice of his.

"Some place where we can talk, and where we won't be seen," I said.

He was nervous. "They have a police radio car that investigates parked automobiles."

"Don't park then."

"I can't talk when I'm driving."

"How about your house?" I asked.

He said, "We could talk there."

"Let's go—if it won't inconvenience your wife."

"No, no. It's all right. We can go there." There was relief in his voice.

"Does your wife know anything about the jam you're in?" I asked.

"She knows *all* about it."

I said, "Don't think I'm taking liberties with your personal affairs, but is your wife's first name Vivian?"

He said, "Yes."

No one said anything after that. He drove the car up the main street, turned to the left, climbed a hill, and entered a high-class residential section with modern houses of Spanish-type architecture—white stucco sides and red tile roofs showing to advantage against the dark green of shrubbery—a green which was almost black in the spaces between streetlights.

We turned into the driveway and rolled into the garage of a pretentious stucco structure. Dr. Alftmont switched off the headlights and the ignition, and said, "Well, we're here."

I got out of the car. Dr. Alftmont led the way toward a door which opened on a flight of stairs, then opened another door, and we entered a hallway. The woman's voice I'd heard over the telephone said, "Is that you, Charles?"

"Yes," he said. "I have someone with me."

She said, "A man telephoned and—"

"I know. He's here with me," Dr. Alftmont said. "Won't you come in this way, Mr. Lam?"

He ushered me into a living-room. The furniture was expensive but quiet. The drapes, carpet, and decorations all harmonized in a quiet blend of color.

The woman's voice said, "Charles, let me talk with you a moment, please."

Dr. Alftmont said to me, "Excuse me a moment," and went back down the corridor toward the stairs. I heard low-voiced conversation. It kept up for four or five minutes. Then I heard her asking something of Dr. Alftmont. She kept pleading. He made short answers in a voice which sounded like courteous but firm negatives.

Steps coming down the corridor again; this time there were two people approaching. I got up out of my chair as the woman entered the room. Dr. Alftmont, a step behind her, said, "Dear, may I present Mr. Lam. Mr. Lam, this is *Mrs.* Alftmont."

The accent on the "Mrs." was belligerent.

She had kept her figure remarkably well. She was somewhere in the forties, but she moved with easy grace. The hazel eyes were steady and frank. I bowed and said, "Pleased to meet you, *Mrs.* Alftmont."

She came toward me and gave me her hand. She'd put on a dark blue dress which harmonized with her coloring and set off her figure. Something about my telephone call had made her get up and dress. I'd have gambled she was in bed when I'd called.

She said, "Won't you sit down, Mr. Lam."

I sat down. She and Doc Alftmont took chairs. Alftmont seemed nervous.

Mrs. Alftmont said, "I understand you're a detective, Mr. Lam."

"That's right."

Her voice was well modulated and seemed to come without effort. There was no evidence of strain anywhere about her. Doc Alftmont gave the impression of weighing words with meticulous care lest he betray himself in a moment of inadvertence. She radiated the quiet poise and the calmness of a woman who has never tried to kid herself.

She said to her husband, "Give me a cigarette, Charles," and then to me, "You don't need to mince words, Mr. Lam. I know all about it."

I said, "All right. Let's talk."

Dr. Alftmont handed her a cigarette and held a match. "Want one, Lam?" he asked.

I nodded.

Dr. Alftmont shook out the match, handed me a cigarette, took one himself, and we both lit off the same match. He turned to her and said, "Mrs. Cool was at my office, dear. Mr. Lam didn't come with her. He came—"

"On my own," I interrupted.

Dr. Alftmont nodded.

The woman had kept her eyes on me in steady appraisal. She said, "Go ahead, Mr. Lam."

I said to Doc Alftmont, "I presume Bertha Cool did most of the talking."

He nodded.

I said, "Bertha wanted to convince you you were in a jam, so you'd kick through with some more money. Is that right?"

"Well," he said, after a moment, "it amounted to that."

"All right," I said. "That's *her* end of it. That's taken care of. *My* end is to do the actual work. It's up to me to get you out of this jam. I want you to talk with me."

"What," he asked, "do you want to talk about?"

"I want to know what you're up against, and I want to know what I'm up against."

He glanced at his wife.

She said, "I'm Vivian Carter. We have no children. We're not married legally, although a ceremony was performed in Mexico about ten years ago."

I said to Alftmont, "Tell me about that divorce case."

"What about it?"

"All about it," I said.

He placed the tips of his fingers together and said, "To begin with, my first wife, Mrs. Lintig, was swept into the hectic swirl of social change which came with the war. There was an emotional backwash which resulted in a breakdown of the conventions. There were—" I held up my hand, palm outward, giving him a traffic officer's stop signal, and said to the woman, "Suppose *you* tell me."

She said, easily and naturally, "I was an office nurse for Dr. Lintig. I fell in love with him. He didn't know anything about it. I made up my mind he'd never know. I was perfectly willing to let Amelia—Mrs. Lintig—have the position of wife and the affection of her husband. I asked only crumbs—the chance to be near him, and I kept very much in the background."

Dr. Alftmont nodded vigorously.

"I wanted to serve him, to be where I could help. I was young and foolish. I know the answer to that one now, but I didn't twenty-one years ago. Oakview was in the throes of a boom. New people were coming in. Money was plentiful. There was, as Charles has said, a period of hectic change. Amelia went for it in a big way. She started drinking heavily and became a leader of the younger set. The standards of that social set were different from anything which had ever been known before.

There was drinking, petting, and—and brawling. Charles didn't like it. Amelia did.

"Amelia started to play around. The doctor didn't know that, but he was fed up. He told her he wanted a divorce. She agreed and asked him to get it on grounds of mental cruelty. He filed suit. Amelia didn't play fair. She never did. She waited until I went to San Francisco on some business for the doctor, and then filed a cross-complaint naming me as corespondent, apparently because she thought by beating him to the punch and hitting at me she could get all of the doctor's property, and marry the man with whom she was infatuated at the moment."

"Who was that?" I asked.

Her glance asked permission of Dr. Alftmont.

He nodded. She said, "Steve Dunton, a young chap who was editing the Oakview *Blade*."

I held expression from my face and asked, "Does he run it now?"

"I think so, yes. We've pretty much lost track of Oakview, but I believe he's still there. His niece was working with him on the paper the last I heard."

Dr. Alftmont said, "That was the niece who met me in the corridor of the apartment house, you know."

I dropped ashes from my cigarette into an ashtray, and said, "Go ahead."

"At that time," Mrs. Alftmont said, with just a trace of bitterness in her voice, "there had never been the slightest indiscretion, and Charles had no idea of how I felt toward him. I think Amelia was hardly herself. Her temperament, her irrational mode of living, and the liquor she was drinking made her exceedingly erratic.

"When she filed that cross-complaint, Charles rushed to San Francisco to explain things. I saw right away that he was in an awful spot. Oakview would seethe with gossip. The person who was really the most interested in Mrs. Lintig's divorce was employed on the paper. He was going to see that any circumstances which could be tortured into evidence against Charles were given plenty of publicity. His trip to San Francisco was, of course, the worst move he could have made. At that, we would have returned and fought things out if it hadn't been—" She became silent.

Dr. Alftmont said simply, "I made a discovery. As Amelia had developed those tendencies which were so distasteful to me, I had been gradually falling out of love with her and in love with Vivian. I made the discovery when I met Vivian in San Francisco. After that, I couldn't go back, drag her name through the mud, and—well, we knew we loved each other then. We only wanted to be together. We were young. I wanted to go away and begin all over again. Probably it was foolish of me, although as events have turned out, it was for the best.

"I telephoned Amelia and asked her what she wanted. Her terms were simple. She wanted everything. She'd give me my freedom. I could clear out and begin all over again. I had some travelers' checks, several thousand dollars. She didn't know about those. I'd been afraid of the boom activities of Oakview and had distrusted the bank."

"Then what?" I asked.

He said, "That's virtually all there is to it. I took her at her word. She said she'd go ahead and get the divorce, that I could change my name and start practicing somewhere else, that as soon as the decree was final, I could marry Vivian. I accepted her terms."

"Do you know exactly what happened?" I asked.

"No," he said. "I understand Amelia and Steve Dunton had a falling out. I don't know. She left Oakview and vanished."

"Why didn't you quietly sue for a divorce somewhere else?" I asked.

"She found me," he said. "I received a letter from her stating that she would never let me cast a mantle of respectability over Vivian, that if I ever tried to marry Vivian she would appear and make trouble, that if I ever filed a divorce suit she'd expose the whole thing—by that time, living with Vivian as man and wife, she could have made a perfect case—and a scandal."

"She knew where you were?"

"Yes."

"Why didn't you go ahead anyway?"

"I couldn't," he said. "In the year that we had been living here as husband and wife, I had built up a fairly good practice among the respectable, conservative people. If it had come out that Vivian and I were living together without benefit of clergy, it would have been fatal."

"Then what?" I asked.

"Years passed," he said. "We heard nothing more. I tried to trace her and couldn't. I felt certain that she'd either died or divorced me and remarried. Some ten years ago, Vivian and I quietly slipped across to Mexico and were married. I thought the ceremony would give her a legal standing in the event it should become necessary."

"All right," I said. "Tell me about the political angle."

Dr. Alftmont said, "This city is standing in its own light. Our police force is corrupt. The city administration is honeycombed with graft. We have a wealthy city, good business, and a fine tourist trade. Those tourists are forced to rub elbows with every form of racket. The citizens were tired of it. They wanted a clean-up. I had been instrumental in getting some of the citizens organized. They insisted I should run for mayor. I thought that old scandal was dead and buried, so I agreed to run."

"And then what?"

"Then, out of a clear sky, I received a letter from her, stating that until I made terms with her, I could never be elected, that at the last minute she would, as she expressed it, blow the lid off. She charged that I had cast her into the junk pile and left her a social and financial outcast—although I had done nothing of the sort. I had stripped myself of my property, and—"

"Charles," Mrs. Alftmont interrupted, "that isn't going to help any now. Mr. Lam wants the facts."

"The facts," he said, "were that she wrote this letter."

"What were her terms?" I asked.

"She didn't offer any."

I did some thinking over the last puffs of my cigarette, then ground it out, and asked, "Did she give you any address where you could get in touch with her?"

"No."

"What did she want?"

"First, she wanted me to withdraw from the campaign."

"You didn't do that?"

"No."

"Why?"

"I was in too deep," he said. "Shortly before that letter was received, the opposition newspaper started publishing a series of slurring articles, intimating that my past would stand investigation. My friends demanded that I sue the paper for libel. I was placed in a very embarrassing position."

"Are you," I asked, "absolutely certain that the letter you received was in your wife's handwriting?"

"Yes," he said. "There are, of course, certain changes which are only natural. A person's handwriting has a tendency to change during a period of twenty-odd years, but there can be no question. I have compared the handwriting carefully."

"Where are the letters?" I asked.

"I have them," he said.

"I want them."

He glanced at his wife. She nodded. He got up and said, "It will take a few minutes. If you'll excuse me, please."

I heard his feet slowly climbing the stairs. I turned to Mrs. Alftmont. She was staring steadily at me.

"What can you do?" she asked.

"I don't know," I said. "We'll do all we can."

"That may not be enough."

"It may not," I admitted.

"Would it help," she asked quietly, "if I should step out of the picture—if I should disappear?"

I thought that over for a while, and said, "No. It wouldn't help."

"Stay and take it on the chin?" she asked.

"Yes."

She said, "I don't care a thing in the world so far as I'm concerned, but it makes an enormous difference to Charles."

"I know it does."

"Of course," she said, "if the true facts were known, I think public sentiment—"

"Forget it," I said. "It isn't a question of public sentiment now. It isn't a question of scandal. It isn't a question of extramarital relations. He's facing a murder charge."

"I see," she said, without batting an eyelash.

I said, "I think Evaline Harris was sent to Oakview by a man named John Harbet."

Her eyes were veiled, without expression. "You mean Sergeant Harbet of the Vice Squad?"

"Yes."

"What makes you think so?"

"He was in Oakview. He beat me up and dragged me out of town."

"Why?"

"That," I said, "is the thing I can't figure. When I find out why he did what he did in the way he did, I think I'll have a weapon we can use."

She frowned thoughtfully. "It's very hard on Charles. He's almost frantic. He suppresses himself behind a mask of professional calm. I'm getting afraid of what may happen."

I said, "Don't worry about it. Leave that to me."

Steps on the stairs again, and Dr. Alftmont came into the room with two letters. One of them was dated 1921 and was written on the stationery of the Bickmere Hotel in San Francisco. The other letter had been written two weeks before, and mailed from Los Angeles. Apparently both were in the same handwriting.

I said, "Did you try to reach her at the Bickmere Hotel, Doctor?"

"Yes," he said. "I wrote her a letter. It was returned with a statement that no such party was registered there."

I studied the letter for a while, and then said, "What was her maiden name?"

"Sellar. Amelia Rosa Sellar."

"Did she have any parents living?"

"No, no relatives. An aunt back East had raised her, but the aunt died when she was seventeen. She's been on her own since then."

"I presume you didn't try very hard to locate her when this first letter was written?"

"I didn't employ detectives," he said, "if that's what you mean. I wrote to her at the hotel. When my letter was returned, I took it for granted she'd simply used the hotel stationery as a blind."

"At that time," I said, "she wasn't trying to keep under cover. She had the whip hand and knew it. She wasn't trying to get property then. She was simply trying to keep you from making Vivian Carter Mrs. Alftmont."

"Then why didn't she let me know where I could reach her?" he asked.

I thought that over for a minute and said, "Because she was doing something she didn't want you to know about, something that would have given you the whip hand if you'd found out about it. That's where we'll start our investigation."

I caught a note of quick hope in Mrs. Alftmont's voice. She said, "Charles, I believe he's right."

Alftmont said, "I can believe anything of her. She became selfish, neurotic. Her ego demanded flattery. She was never happy unless some man was paying attention to her. She wanted to be on the go all the time. She was apparently trying to escape any form of routine, any conventional—"

"I know the type," I said. "Never mind putting it in medical terms."

"She is selfish, tricky, deceitful, and unbalanced," he said. "You can expect anything of her. Once she starts, she won't stop anywhere."

I got to my feet and said, "I'm taking these letters. Is there a night train through here for San Francisco?"

"None now," he said.

"How about a bus?" I asked.

"I think there's a bus goes through."

"I've had about all the night driving I want for a while," I said. "I'm taking these letters with me."

"You'll take good care of them?" he asked.

I nodded.

Mrs. Alftmont walked across to give me the pressure of firm, strong fingers on my hand. "You've brought disturbing news," she said, "yet I feel reassured. I want to protect Charles. As far as I'm concerned, I have no regrets. A true, deep love is all the marriage a woman needs. I have always felt married to Charles. If there's to be a scandal, we have each other. As for the murder—you'll have to handle that, Mr. Lam."

"Yes," I said, "I'll have to handle that."

Chapter Eight

It was late Saturday afternoon before I dug up the information I wanted in San Francisco—that the woman I wanted had been a hostess at one of the beach night spots. She'd gone under her maiden name, Amelia Sellar and had lived at the Bickmere Hotel. It was Sunday night when I managed to locate "Let 'Em Ride" Ranigan, who had operated the place and who had acquired his nickname from a tendency to let his bets ride in the crap games.

Ranigan was a genial, age-mellowed soul who had put on a lot of weight, had flowing white hair, and liked nothing better than to smoke a cigar and talk of the "good old days."

Ranigan sat at a corner table over some champagne that would be listed on Bertha Cool's expense account as taxi fare, and became reminiscent.

"You're a young chap," he said. "You wouldn't know about it, but I'm telling you in those days San Francisco was the greatest city in the world. None of the European cities could touch it. Paris couldn't.

"It wasn't because it was wide open. It was because it was tolerant. That's the real spirit of San Francisco. People didn't mind your business because they had business of their own to mind. That was the attitude of the city, the attitude of the people in it. The waterfront was crowded with shipping. There was a big trade with the Orient. No one had time to bother with petty things. It was only the big things that people thought about.

"Nowadays things aren't like that. San Francisco's getting

petty. You hear sirens screaming and police cars tearing through the streets. You tag along to see if it's a riot and find a bunch of cops are picking up a streetwalker for soliciting on the wrong side of the street.

"You go up to one of the big hotels, get in with the hunch that's in the know, and find a poker game in one of the rooms. They aren't playing for gold pieces the way they used to. They're playing for chips, and after you've won all the chips, some piker pays off with an I.O.U.

"You go down to the waterfront, and the old spice, the old tang, the old romance are gone, and—"

I said, "Your glass is empty, Ranigan—here, waiter."

The waiter filled up the glasses. Ranigan tasted it and said, "Nice stuff."

"You used to run the old Mermaid's Roost, didn't you?" I asked.

"I sure did. Those were the days. What'd you say your name was?"

"Lam. Donald Lam."

"Oh, yes. Well, I'll tell you, Lam. If you want to give people the right kind of perspective, give 'em work and give 'em money. Then's when they work hard and play hard. They try to make their money out of business instead of out of chiseling each other. In those days money was flowing in a steady stream. All a man had to do was to get himself a bucket, throw it in the stream, and drag out a bunch of cash. Nowadays there ain't anything like that. Money ain't circulating. You feel there ain't over a thousand dollars in the whole damn city, and everyone is walking around in circles trying to find the fellow that has that thousand. As soon as they find out who it is, they jump on him and take it away from him. Now I remember back in the Mermaid's Roost—"

"You have a real memory," I said. "By the way, someone was telling me about a girl you had working for you who was lucky enough to inherit a million dollars."

He straightened up with surprise. "A million dollars? Working for me?"

"Uh-huh. She was a hostess, there at the Mermaid's Roost. Girl by the name of Sellar."

"Sellar!" he said, squinting his eyebrows together. "Shucks, I had a girl by the name of Sellar who was hostess, but she never fell heir to no million bucks—not that I ever heard tell of. Sellar—Sellar. That's right. That was Amelia's last name. That's who it was. Amelia Sellar."

"She may have got the money after she left you," I said.

"Well, she *might* have," he said.

"Where is she now? Do you know?"

"Nope."

"Any idea where I can find out?"

"No. Those girls drift around and get scattered. I had about the best-looking bunch of legs there was in the city. You take it nowadays, and women don't have pretty legs. They have fashionable legs, but they ain't what you'd call pretty. They ain't the kind of legs a man will spend money over. A woman falls for that slender, streamlined stuff, but it takes real legs to start a man on a spending spree, legs that have curves and class. Now I can remember back in—"

"Don't you keep up with any of your old entertainers?" I asked.

"Shucks, no," he said. "Mostly they were a wild bunch. They came and they went. I saw one of 'em the other day though, girl by the name of Myrtle. She was with me way back in nineteen-twenty. Just a kid she was then, eighteen or nineteen, and believe me, she doesn't look a day older now."

"Where was she?" I asked.

"Taking tickets in a picture show. She certainly is class, Myrtle is. I looked at her a couple of times, and I said, 'Say, your face is familiar. Ain't your mother's name Myrtle?'

"She placed me then and said, 'I'm Myrtle,' and I like to fell over backward. She's married now. Got a kid ten years old, she told me. Of course, they arrange the lights in those little ticket booths so the girls look pretty, but I'm telling you, Mr.—what'd you say your name was?"

"Lam. Donald Lam."

"That's right. Well, I'm telling you, Lam, that girl didn't look a day older than she did when she was working for me, and say, talking about legs—there was the girl that *had* legs. Say, Mister, if I could get a dozen girls like Myrtle and open up a place—but it wouldn't do no good. The coin just ain't in circulation. The business ain't here. It's just like I told you. People are putting in all their time trying to get some of the other fellow's dough away from him. There just ain't any stream of circulating cash where you can throw in a bucket and pull out the dough."

"Where did you say this picture show was?" I asked.

"Oh, it's up on Market Street, four or five doors below the Twin Peaks Hotel."

"What," I asked, "does she look like?"

"Pretty as a picture," he said. "Her hair used to be a lighter shade of red than it is now. She's got it this kind of a dark brown color they're using so much, but she's got that peaches-and-cream complexion, and her eyes are clear blue. God, how that girl could look innocent! And legs! Say, I'm telling you, Mister—what'd you say your name was?"

"Lam. Donald Lam."

"That's right I keep forgetting. It's an odd name, too. Somehow I don't seem to remember names quite as well as I used to.

But shucks, you don't have the personalities to go with them anymore. Why, I can remember back here when San Francisco was just full of men who had personality sticking out all over 'em. Why—"

I looked at my watch. "I've got a train to catch," I said. "It was a real pleasure meeting you. You'll pardon me if I run away—here, waiter. The check please.... Don't let me hurry you, Mr. Ranigan. Just sit and finish that champagne. I'm sorry I have to run, but that's the way it is, you know."

"Sure," he said. "That's the way things are now. If you want to make a dollar, you've got to keep on the run every minute trying to grab it before the other fellow gets it. Things didn't used to be that way. It used to be there was plenty of money for everybody. Nobody begrudged the other fellow what he was making, and when you made anything, you could put it in your pocket. That ain't the way things are now what with government agents coming around and snooping over your books trying to gouge the last penny out of you. Say, we had no sales tax, no income tax, no payroll tax—why, it was a pleasure doing business, and if a government man had ever come in the door and said he wanted to look over our books, he'd have gone out on a stretcher. In those days they used to say, 'What do you think this is? Russia? Get the hell out of here.' And believe me, buddy, the government kept out. Maybe that was why business was so good. Why, I remember one year—"

I shook hands with him and hurried out. I looked back at the door. He was talking to the waiter, telling him over his fourth glass of champagne how good the city used to be.

It was a slack time at the theater. I pushed a twenty-dollar bill through the arch-shaped opening in the glass and placed my lips as close as possible to the round hole.

The girl who sat on the stool by the change machine put

shapely fingers on a series of levers and smiled at me with wide, innocent blue eyes. She looked to be somewhere in the late twenties. "How many please?" she asked. "One?"

I said, "None."

She started to poke the levers and the smile faded from her eyes. "Did you say one?" she asked.

"I said none."

She took her fingers away from the levers, looked at me, and said, "Well?"

"I want to buy twenty dollars' worth of information," I said.

"What about?"

"About the days when you were working in the Mermaid's Roost."

She said, "I never worked there."

I said, "Just a little information between friends."

"You've been talking with Ranigan," she said, "and he's cuckoo. I never worked in his place in my life. He thought I did, and it's part of my duties to kid the customers along."

I gently slid the twenty-dollar bill back and forth. "Couldn't you use twenty bucks?" I asked.

"Of course I could, but—what do you want to know?"

"Nothing that's going to hurt you," I said. "There was a hostess, Amelia Sellar. Do you remember her?"

She reached out with long, tapering fingers, and placed coral-tinted nails on one edge of the twenty-dollar bill. She said, "Yes."

"How well?"

"I knew her quite well."

"Where did she live?"

"At the Bickmere Hotel. She and Flo Mortinson roomed together. Flo was contact girl for a bootlegging ring. She and Amelia were great friends."

"Where's Amelia now?"

"I don't know. I haven't seen her for a long time."

"Did Amelia ever tell you anything about her past?"

She nodded.

"What was it?"

"A small-town background somewhere. She was too fast for the burg. Her husband caught up with her and sued for divorce. She outsmarted him, got all the property, and headed for the bright lights. She had a wad of dough with her. Some man got it."

"Were they married?" I asked.

"I doubt it."

"And you don't know where she is now?"

"No."

"How about Flo Mortinson? Have you heard from her?"

She said, "I saw Flo about three years ago, ran into her on the street—in Los Angeles."

"What was she doing?"

"Hostess in some night spot."

"Did you ask her anything about Amelia?"

"No."

"Know anything else that might help me to locate Amelia Sellar? She's come into a bunch of money—if she can furnish proof that she was never divorced from her first husband."

Her eyes narrowed. "I don't think she ever was divorced," she said. "There was a divorce action filed somewhere, but she walked out on it. Her husband ran away with his mistress. I guess he was entitled to, from what Amelia told me. *She* certainly wasn't overlooking anything. It was a hick town, but it didn't cramp her style—much."

"Did she ever say anything about where her husband was located or what he was doing?"

"No. I don't think she knew. I think her husband went away."

I said, "Okay. Thanks a lot," and released my hold on the twenty-dollar bill.

She said, "Listen. This is under your hat. I've been married twelve years, and my husband thinks I was just out of kindergarten when he married me."

"I know," I said. "It's okay by me."

"Thanks," she said. "Listen, you're a regular guy, and this is just between you and me. If a spotter saw me going south with this twenty, he'd think I was embezzling company funds. Stand up close to the ticket window, will you? Put your arms up on the shelf there."

I did. My shoulders pretty much blocked the window. She raised up her skirts and put the twenty-dollar bill down her stocking. "Thanks," she said.

I said, "I know what Ranigan meant now."

"What?"

"He said if he had Myrtle's legs back, he'd clean up a fortune."

I saw her flush, but she laughed and was pleased. She started to say something, then changed her mind, and, as a customer came up, her face became a smiling mask, with innocent, wide blue eyes, looking up past my shoulder. I stepped away from the window.

From my hotel I called the clerk at the Palace Hotel in Oakview. "How about those glasses that were ordered for Mrs. Lintig?" I said. "What happened to them? You were going to send them to me."

"Gosh, Mr. Lam," he said. "I don't know. They never showed up. I guess she must have picked them up herself."

I said, "Thanks. That's what I wanted to know," and hung up.

In the morning I hired a girl to call up every oculist, every optometrist, and every lens supply house in San Francisco to find out what doctor had sent a pair of lenses to Mrs. J. C. Lintig at the Palace Hotel in Oakview or had a client by the name of Amelia Sellar. I told her to wire me the information at the agency as soon as she had it. I climbed aboard a night bus and caught up on some of my sleep all the way to Santa Carlotta.

I'd left the agency car in an all-night garage that was within two blocks of the bus depot. I walked to the garage and handed my storage ticket to the attendant. He looked it over, then went to the office.

"When did you leave this car?" he asked.

I told him.

"It'll take a minute or two," he said.

I saw him go behind a glass partition and dial a number on the telephone. When he came out, I said, "Listen, buddy, if it's all the same to you, I'm in a hurry."

"Coming right now," he said. He glanced at my ticket and went off on the run. I sat up in front and waited.

A minute or two later he came back and said, "I seem to have some trouble getting your car started. Did you know the battery was run down?"

I said, "No. I didn't know the battery was run down, and if it is, it's because someone here left the ignition switch on."

He said, "Just a moment. We're fully responsible. If there's any trouble like that, we'll give you a rent battery and charge yours up, but you'll have to write out a claim."

I said, "Better give me a new battery because I'm not coming back, and I'm not writing out any claims."

He said, "Just a minute," and ran back toward the rear of the garage. I followed him.

The agency car was back in a corner. The attendant hopped in and started grinding away on the starter.

I said, "Just a minute, buddy. That doesn't sound to me as though the battery was run down. But if you keep on working that starter, it will be."

"The motor doesn't seem to take hold."

I said, "Tell me how much the storage is, and I'll start it. You might try turning on the ignition. That always helps."

He grinned sheepishly, turned on the ignition, and stepped on the starter again. The agency car rattled into life.

I said, "Never mind the stalling. Tell me how much storage I owe, and I'll pay it."

"I'll have to take a look at the books," he said.

"The books be damned," I told him. "Here's two dollars. That'll cover storage. You can fix up the books any way you please. I'm on my way."

He pulled a rag from his pocket and started polishing off the steering wheel. "Your windshield needs a little attention," he said.

I said, "Never mind the windshield. Just get out from behind that wheel and let me get started."

He fumbled around with the choke for a minute, and looked back toward the door. I said, "Do you want this two bucks or not?"

"Of course I want it. Just a minute, and I'll give you a receipt."

"I don't want the receipt. I want the car, and I want to get going."

He got out from behind the steering wheel and stood by the car, looking at the door. I said, "If you'll get away from that car door so I can get in, I'll drive out."

"I'm sorry," he said, but didn't move.

A car, traveling at high speed, skidded into the entrance. I saw a look of relief on the attendant's face. He said, "Okay," and moved to one side.

The car came in the door, ran back the length of the garage, blocking the way out. I saw it was a police car. The door opened and John Harbet got out and came pounding over toward the car in a businesslike way. The attendant said, "I'll get you a receipt," and started to walk away.

Harbet came over to me and said, "So you had to stick your nose into this, eh?"

I said to the attendant, "You stick around. I'm going to want a witness to this."

The attendant said, "I'm sorry. I can't leave the front of the place—the cash register and everything."

He walked away from us and didn't look back. Harbet walked over toward me, and I stepped back into a corner behind the car. "You asked for this," he said.

I slid my right hand toward the left lapel of my coat.

He stopped coming toward me and said, "What are you reaching for?"

"A notebook," I said, "and a fountain pen."

"I told you about your health once," he said. "You didn't listen to me."

"Ever hear about a law covering kidnaping?" I asked. He laughed and said, "Sure, I've heard about it. I've heard about a lot of other laws, too. How would you like to get thrown in the can, wise guy?"

I said, "Throw me in, and I'll bounce right out, and when I do, you know what will happen to you."

He said, "Oh, you think you'll bounce right out, do you?"

"I know it," I said. "Don't think I came into your territory without making plans in advance."

He kept sizing me up and sliding his hand over toward his right hip. He said, "In the first place, I think that's a stolen car. In the second place, a man was killed on the highway a couple of nights ago by a hit-and-run driver. I think this is the car that hit him."

"Try again," I said.

"A man about your build has been annoying women on the streets."

He kept edging closer. Suddenly he jerked out his gun.

I took my hand away from the lapel of my coat. He laughed and said, "I'll just take your rod so you won't get into trouble with it."

He moved up another step and patted the side of my coat, then he laughed and said, "Just running a blazer, eh?"

He spun me around, made certain I had no gun, put his own gun away, and grabbed me by the necktie. "Do you know what we do with wise guys in this city?" he asked.

"Put them on the Vice Squad," I said, "and let them push people around, then something happens, and they get called up in front of the grand jury."

"Don't kid yourself," he said. "I'm not getting called up in front of any grand jury."

He pushed the heel of his right hand against my nose, holding my tie with his left hand. He said, "I have a witness who saw that hit-and-run car making a getaway. The description fits this car. What are you going to do about it?" He was holding his hand up against my face, pushing my neck back.

I said, "Get your hand out of my face." My voice sounded thick and muffled.

He laughed and pushed a little harder.

I swung my right. My arms were a good two inches shorter than his. The swing missed by just that much. He let go of my tie then, and cuffed me with his left. I tried to dodge, and he cuffed me with his right. Then he grabbed me by the coat collar and spun me around.

He said, "Get in that car and drive ahead of me to the police station. Don't try to make any funny moves, or I'll drill you. You're under arrest."

I said, "All right. We'll go to headquarters. Now listen to this. The hotel porter in Oakview saw you carrying me down the corridor. Don't think *I'm* so dumb. Before I left Oakview, I called the Federal Bureau of Investigation. They took fingerprints from the inside of my doorknob and the steering wheel of the car. They don't know yet who those prints belong to. I can tell them."

I saw that I'd jolted him. He stood stock-still. He let go of my collar, and his eyes bored into mine. "You run a damn good bluff," he said. "You made a nice one about having a gun. You're lucky it didn't get you killed."

I said, "That wasn't a bluff. That was a psychological experiment. I thought you were yellow. I wanted to find out. You are."

His face darkened, and he doubled his fist, but thought better of it as I stood my ground. He said, "I'm going to give you one more chance. You're out of your jurisdiction. Keep on your own dunghill and you won't have any trouble. Start messing around in Santa Carlotta and you'll be just a number in a great big house doing a longtime stretch."

I said, "Not by the time I get done telling *my* story, I won't."

He shoved me into the agency car. "Go on, wise guy," he said. "Get started. Right back toward Los Angeles. The next time you come within the city limits, I'll throw the book at you. Savvy?"

"All done?" I asked.

"Yes," he said, and turned around to swagger back to the police car. He backed out, swung the car in a turn in the middle of the block when he hit the street, and drove away.

I blew blood out of my nose onto my handkerchief, drove up even with the office where the attendant was making a great show of being busy. I adjusted my tie and said, "On second thought, I think I'll take that receipt."

He looked nervous. "You won't need a receipt," he said. "It's all right."

"I want one."

He hesitated a moment, then scribbled out a receipt. I looked at it, folded it, put it in my pocket "Thanks," I said. "I just wanted your signature. You may hear from me some day. That's all."

I got back in the car and rattled out of town, taking good care to keep the speedometer needle under fifteen miles an hour until after I'd passed the city limits.

Bertha Cool was in the office when I reached Los Angeles. She said, "Well, for God's sake, where have *you* been?"

"Working."

"Don't ever do that again."

"What?"

"Get away where I can't reach you."

"I was busy. I didn't want to be reached. What's the matter?"

She said, "Hell's breaking loose, and I don't know how to stop it. What's happened to your nose? It's swollen."

I said, "A guy pushed it."

She said, "I've been talking with Marian."

"Well?"

"She's been having daily conferences with the deputy district attorney."

"They haven't said anything about her in the papers yet."

"No, they're not ready for that—but I think they're getting ready for it."

"What's new?"

"They've been talking with her until now she's absolutely convinced that she saw this man coming out of Evaline Harris's apartment."

"Well, he did come out of it, didn't he?" I asked.

"There you go, sticking up for her. You know as well as I do,

Donald, that she didn't see him come out of that apartment. She saw him in the corridor. She doesn't know what apartment he came out of."

"She does now, doesn't she?"

Bertha Cool said, "Yes. She *thinks* she does."

"Is that all?" I asked.

"No. While Marian was talking with the deputy district attorney, a long-distance telephone call came through. It was police headquarters at Santa Carlotta. Evidently they said they thought the case might have a local angle. The D.A. arranged for a conference."

I lit a cigarette and Bertha Cool sat behind the desk looking at me. She said, "You know what that means, Donald. They're getting ready to push our man out in front. Marian will identify him, and then the fat's in the fire. It's too late to do a damn thing. We've got to move fast."

"I've been moving fast," I said.

"What have you learned?"

"Nothing much. Any letters or telegrams for me?"

"Yes. There's a telegram here from someone in San Francisco. It says that no eye doctor or lens supply house in San Francisco had any orders to be sent to Oakview during the period under investigation. I suppose you know what that's all about."

"I do," I said.

"Well, what is it?"

I said, "It's just another figure in the column I'm trying to add up. I haven't the total yet."

"What's it all about?"

"Mrs. Lintig broke her glasses—that is, a bellboy broke them for her. She made a squawk to the hotel. The hotel was going to replace them. She wired for new lenses."

"Well?"

"She left very suddenly before the lenses arrived. I told the clerk to forward the glasses to me as soon as they showed up, that we'd pay the bill."

"Pay the bill!"

"Yes."

"Why did you do that, lover?"

"Because I wanted to see what oculist she patronized. An oculist would have her name and address. Remember, she didn't have the prescription. She simply wired her oculist to send her new glasses."

Bertha Cool stared steadily at me. Her eyes narrowed. She said, "I'm wondering if you're thinking of the same thing I am, Donald."

"What?"

"That perhaps that wire didn't go to San Francisco at all, but went to Dr. Alftmont in Santa Carlotta?"

I said, "I thought of that a long time ago. That's one of the reasons I was so anxious to get the shipment in the original package."

Bertha Cool said admiringly, "You are a brainy little bastard, Donald. You don't overlook many bets. The glasses didn't show up, eh?"

"No."

Bertha Cool said, "That means just one thing, lover. The person to whom she wired for the glasses knew that she wasn't going to be there to receive the shipment, and, therefore, didn't send them."

I said, "Where's Marian?"

"We have her fixed up in a nice little apartment. They've found out quite a bit about the case, and Marian's testimony is most important. She remembers that when she opened the door the morning paper was lying on the floor where it had been pushed through the crack under the door. It was still there when the police arrived. That means the murderer found her in bed."

"What else?" I asked.

"It was a man who killed her. The ashtray by the bed held two cigarette stubs. There was lipstick on only one of them, so the police figure the man sat on the edge of the bed and talked for a while before he killed her. They figure this man had a business matter to discuss. When it didn't go to suit him, he killed her."

"Anything else?" I asked.

"A picture was missing from where it had been stuck in her dresser mirror. The police *think* it may have been a picture of a tall, dark young man with a black mustache. The maid described the photograph as best she could."

"Why was it taken?"

"Probably because the murderer wanted it. I've been trying to put forward the theory, very quietly, of course, that it was a picture of the murderer himself. That would start them looking for a tall, dark young man."

"The D.A. knows where Marian is?"

"Oh, sure. He was keeping her under surveillance. Now he's pretty well satisfied she's on the up and up."

"How often does she go to see him?"

"She's been going once a day."

"I want to talk with her."

"She wants to talk with you. God knows what it is you do to women, Donald, but they fall for you—and you fall for them. You want to be careful with this girl, Donald. She's dynamite."

"What do you mean, she's dynamite?"

"She's all tied up with that deputy district attorney. If he ever turned the heat on her, she'd talk."

"You mean about us?"

"Yes."

"I think she'd be loyal to us."

"Not to *us*, lover, to *you*. And you've got to be careful that young deputy doesn't make her fall for him."

I said, "I want to talk with Marian. Where is she?" Bertha Cool handed me a slip of paper with the address of an apartment house. "Our client is awfully worried, Donald, but he has a lot of confidence in you. I'm glad you had that talk with him."

I said, "So am I. I'm going to see Marian."

"Want me to go with you?"

"That," I said, "is just what I don't want, and you'd better get some new tires for the agency car—or else get a new car for the agency tires—and then throw the tires away."

She said, "I'll do that, Donald, but don't ever go away again where Bertha doesn't know where you are. I've had an awful job trying to hold this thing in line. Our client seems to have more confidence in you than he has in me."

I got up and ground out my cigarette in an ashtray. "While I'm gone, try to find out if a Flo Mortinson was a hostess at the Blue Cave. Locate her, find out about her trunks—if any. Get a room near her."

"All right. Will you give me a ring as soon as you've seen Marian, Donald?"

"It depends. I'm doing everything I can on this case."

"I know, lover, but time's getting short. The thing is going to break any minute now, and when it does, Smith is on the skids for a one-way ride."

"Are you," I asked, "telling me?" and walked out.

Elsie Brand looked up from her typing long enough to ask, "What happened to your nose, Donald?"

"I went to a plastic surgeon," I said, "and he was rough."

Chapter Nine

I went to the apartment house where Marian was staying and scouted around for fifteen minutes before I went in. By that time I was pretty well satisfied the place wasn't being watched.

Marian answered my knock. When she saw who it was, she flung her arms around me and squealed, "Oh, Donald, I'm so *glad* to see you!"

I patted her shoulder, kicked the door shut behind me, and said, "How are things coming?"

"Swell," she said. "Everybody's being wonderful to me. Sometimes I feel like an awful heel not telling them—you know, the—"

I said, "Forget it. You want the murderer to be brought to justice, don't you?"

"Yes."

"Well, if you told them the truth, some smart shyster attorney would tie you up into knots and make a jury think *you* were the one who had committed the murder."

"But they couldn't. I didn't have any motive for murdering her."

"I know," I said. "They might not convict you of murder, but the guilty party would get away. Sit down. I want to talk with you."

"Where have you been?" she asked. "I've missed you so much, and Mrs. Cool has been just frantic. You know, she depends on you a lot. I think she'd be lost without you."

I said, "How about it, Marian? Have they showed you any photographs yet that you can identify?

"No. They've been trying to find out who her friends were. Mr. Ellis, the deputy district attorney, says that he thinks he'll break the case wide open within another twenty-four hours."

"That's nice. Just where was this man when you saw him, Marian? In the hall, coming toward you?"

"No, no, not in the hall. He was just coming out of the apartment. He was pulling the door shut behind him."

"You mean some apartment down at that end of the hall?"

"No, I mean apartment 309, the one where the body was found. There can't be any doubt about it. I've gone over and over the thing in my mind."

"Have you," I asked, "given the district attorney's office a written statement yet?"

"They're preparing one. I'm to sign it late this afternoon."

I said, "Come over here, Marian. I want to talk with you." I patted the arm of my chair, and she came over and sat down. I slipped an arm around her waist and held her hand. "Want to do something for me?" I asked.

She said, "I'd do anything for you."

I said, "This isn't going to be easy."

She said, "If it helps you, it'll be easy."

I said, "You'll have to be darned clever to put this across and make it stick. You'll have to keep your wits about you."

"What is it?"

I said, "When you see the deputy district attorney this afternoon, tell him you've thought of something else."

"What?"

"When you approached the apartment house the first time, before you'd gone in to see the manager and just as you were parking your car, you saw a man come out. He was six feet tall with broad shoulders. He had thick, black eyebrows and gray eyes that were close together. Because his face was so beefy, it made the close-set eyes more noticeable. It's rather a flat face. There was a mole on the right cheek. He had a cleft chin, long arms and big hands, and he was walking very, very rapidly."

"But, Donald, I can't say that now after—"

"Yes, you can," I interrupted. "You've been thinking this thing over. You've been trying to reconstruct it in your mind. You noticed this man at the time because he seemed to be in such a hurry, seemed to be almost running, and it was unusual to see a big man walking so rapidly. Then, of course, the mental shock of finding Evaline Harris chased a lot of things out of your memory. You had to go back and put events together bit by bit so they made a logical sequence."

She said, "Why, that's almost exactly what the deputy district attorney told me I'd have to do."

I said, "Sure it is. They see lots of witnesses who have suffered mental shock, and they understand what has to be done."

She said, "I don't want to do that. It seems unfair. They've been so nice to me in the district attorney's office—I'd have to change the story afterward when I got on the witness stand. You wouldn't want me to commit perjury, would you?"

I said, "Don't you see, Marian? If you tell them this, it will give me more time. They don't want you to sign that written statement until you have everything in it. If you sign it and then something else comes up, a smart criminal lawyer might trap you. He'd ask whether you'd signed a statement and ask you what was in it—demand that it be produced in court. For that reason the district attorney's office doesn't want to break the case until they're sure you've thought of everything."

"Then they'd incorporate this in that statement, and I'd have to sign it?"

"No. You wouldn't have to sign it," I said. "I need the time that can be gained while they're making out a new statement, that's all. If you sign that statement this afternoon, they'll break the case tonight, but if you tell them this, they'll dictate some more stuff to go in the statement and ask you to come back tomorrow to sign it."

She hesitated.

I heaved an audible sigh and said, "Forget it, if it bothers you. I'm in a jam. I thought perhaps you could help me out. I didn't realize how it would seem looking at it from your angle. I'll work out something else."

I got up and started for the door. I'd made two steps when I heard the sound of quick motion behind me, and her arms were around my neck. "No, no, don't go away! Don't be like that! Of *course* I'll do it for you. I told you I would."

I said, "I'm afraid you aren't the type who could make it stick. You would get trapped somewhere."

"Nonsense," she said. "I can do it so naturally and easily that no one will ever suspect. Mr. Ellis likes me. I think he likes me a *lot*."

"Do you like him?" I asked.

"He's nice."

I said, "If you could do it, Marian, it would be a big help to me."

"When do I do it?"

"Right now," I said. "Put on your things, get in a taxi, and go up to the district attorney's office. Tell this deputy you've thought of something else, and tell him about this man. Tell him you thought he might want to put it in the statement."

She said, "I'll go right away. Will you come with me?"

"No. I want to keep out of the picture. Don't say anything about me."

She ran over to the dresser, patted her hair into place, touched up her lips with lipstick, patted a powder puff over her cheeks, and said, "I'll go right now. Will you wait here until I get back?"

"Yes."

"There are some magazines over there and—"

"Never mind the magazines," I said. "I want to sleep."

"All right. Donald, what's happened to your nose? It's bleeding."

I pulled a fresh handkerchief out of my pocket and said, "It got hurt. It's been bleeding every hour or two since."

"It looks all swollen and red—and sore."

"It is swollen and red," I said, "and the reason it looks sore is because it *is* sore."

She laughed and said, "You must be hard to get along with. First it was a black eye, and now it's a swollen nose."

She perched a hat that looked like an inverted flower pot on one side of her head and slipped into a coat.

I said, "How about a taxi? Do you have a phone?"

"Oh, yes, but I can pick one up at the boulevard."

"Better phone," I said. "Then the cab will be here by the time you get downstairs."

She phoned for a taxi, and I pulled up a chair to put my feet on, and slid down into the cushions of the big chair in which I was sitting.

"Now let's get this straight," I said. "Just what are you going to do?"

"Why, tell them exactly what you told me to."

"And you won't break down in the middle of it, and get confused, and then when they start questioning you, tell them that you're doing something someone told you to do, and then start bawling and tell them about me?"

"No, of course not."

"How do you know you won't?"

"Because I can lie when I have to."

"Ever had any experience?" I asked.

"Lots."

"Those were little fibs," I said. "This is going to be different. You'll be lying to a lawyer."

She said, "No. Mr. Ellis will believe me. That's what's going to make it so hard, but he'll have confidence in me. He'll take anything I say as gospel truth. He's awfully nice. I think he likes me, Donald."

I said, "He may be nice, but he's a lawyer. Once you arouse his suspicions, he'll pounce on you like a terrier pouncing on a rat. Now what are you going to tell him?"

"That when I went to the apartment house the first time, I saw this other man coming out, that I hadn't thought it was important before, but now I've been trying to think of everything, and there was something about this man—about the way he acted that aroused my suspicions."

"What did he look like?"

"He was a big man with broad shoulders and thick, bushy, black eyebrows. His eyes were sort of close together, and there was a cleft in his chin. There was a mole on one of his cheeks. I think it was the right."

"What aroused your suspicions?"

"Well, you can't exactly call it that. I noticed him at the time just because I thought there was something unusual about him. Then the shock of finding the body gave me such a mental jolt that it's taken me some time to put things together again. I think this man just slipped my mind."

"You had no idea that a murder had been committed?"

"No, of course not."

"What made you notice him then?"

"Well, it was something about the way he was walking. He

was a big man, and he was walking awfully fast, almost running. And he may have looked back over his shoulder. Anyway, there was something that made me think he was afraid, or something, and he looked at me in the most peculiar way. It gave me the creeps."

"Why didn't you tell me about this before?"

Her eyes, big, wide, and innocent, looked into mine. "Why, I've already told you, Mr. Ellis, because it was such a shock finding the body."

"You might add something," I said, "about the strain of being questioned."

Her eyes smiled at me. "No," she said. "He knows it's not a strain."

"Are you vamping him?"

She considered the coral tips of her fingers. "Well," she said slowly, "he's throwing a mantle of masculine protection about my shoulders, and I'm depending on him. He likes me, and I think he's nice."

I said, "All right. Your cab should be downstairs now. Wake me up as soon as you get back, and, no matter what happens, come straight back here. Make that interview just as short as you can."

"I will," she promised.

I closed my eyes and relaxed. I heard her moving around quietly so as not to disturb me. After a while I heard the door open and close.

I woke up a couple of times just enough to shift my position, and then dozed off again. After a while the chair cramped my limbs, but I was too numbed with sleep to care.

I didn't hear the key click in the door when she came back. The first I knew was when she was on the arm of my chair saying, "You poor darling! I'll bet you're tired out."

I opened my eyes, closed them again to shut out the light, and took my feet down off the chair. I felt her fingertips, soft and cool, on my forehead, caressing back my hair, stroking my eyelids. Gradually I came back to reality. I opened my eyes and said, somewhat thickly, "Did you do it?"

"Yes."

I found her hand and took it in mine. "How about it?" I asked. "Did it go across?"

"What do you mean?"

"Did they believe it?"

"Why, of course they believed it. I told them just what you told me to. You didn't think I could put it across, but I did. I was *very* convincing."

"What happened?" I asked. "Did you get any more on the Santa Carlotta angle?"

"Yes," she said. "Mr. Ellis telephoned Santa Carlotta right away. He said that they'd been waiting to see my written statement. When this new angle turned up, he knew they'd want to be advised."

"You don't know what was said at the Santa Carlotta end of the wire?"

"Apparently nothing," she said. "Mr. Ellis was just reporting. He told me Santa Carlotta thought the case might have a local angle."

"He didn't say what the local angle was, did he?"

"No."

"Do you think he knew?"

"Yes, I think so. It was something he'd evidently discussed with the police there."

I said, "That's fine. Now, what's Mr. Ellis doing to protect you?"

"To protect me?"

"Yes."

"Why, what do you mean?"

"Don't you see?" I said. "Someone murdered Evaline Harris. It was cruel, ruthless, premeditated murder. The police are virtually without clues, except those you've been able to give. When the murderer feels the net tightening about him, the logical thing for him to do is to—" I broke off as I saw the expression on her face. I said, "I was wondering what Mr. Ellis is doing about *that.*"

"Why," she said, with a dismayed look, "I don't think it's even occurred to him."

I looked at my watch, and said, "Well, it's going to occur to him now. I'm going to get in touch with him. You stay right here."

"I could telephone him," she said.

"No," I said. "That's exactly what I don't want you to do. You sit right here and don't say anything. I'm going up to see Mr. Ellis and have a talk with him. I don't care how nice he is, but he has a crust not arranging for your protection—after all the help you've given him, too."

She said, "I just can't believe that I'm in any danger, but I see your point."

I said, "You sit tight. Don't do a thing. Promise me you won't leave this apartment until I get back."

"I promise," she said.

I went over to the mirror, straightened my hair with a pocket comb, picked up my hat, and said, "Remember, don't go out until I get back."

I went down as far as the corner, went into a drugstore, telephoned police headquarters, and asked for Homicide. After a while, a voice said, in a bored monotone, "Yeah, this is Homicide."

I said, in a rapid voice, "This is a tip-off. I'd be in a jam if anyone knew I was giving it. Don't ask my name, and don't try to trace the call."

The voice at the other end of the line said, "Just a minute, I'll get a pencil and paper."

I said, "Nix on that stuff. I told you not to try to trace the call. Get a load of this right now if you want it. If you don't, hang up. When your dicks were making that investigation down at the Blue Cave, they learned everything except about the big beefy guy with the close-set, gray eyes and the mole on his right cheek. Orders have been passed around to lay off of him. No one talked about him. If you want to solve that case, you'd better give the girls at the Blue Cave a *real* shakedown. Ask some specific questions and find out why they were instructed not to say anything about this egg to your investigators."

I slammed up the telephone and walked out. I waited another half hour, hanging around where I could watch the entrance of the apartment house, smoking cigarettes and thinking. It began to get dark and the street lights were turned on.

I went back to Marian Dunton's apartment and knocked excitedly on the door.

She opened it and said, "Gee, I'm glad you're back! I felt— sort of frightened sitting here alone."

"You should," I said. "The D.A.'s office pulled a boner."

"What do you mean?"

"Letting it out about that man whom you described. He's suddenly become the important figure in the case. They've traced him back to the Blue Cave and found that he was friendly with the girl that was killed."

She said, "But I didn't really see him. You made that up."

"Perhaps you did see him," I said, "but just didn't think of it at the time."

"No. I didn't see him. Anyway, I don't remember having seen him."

"Well, he was there all right, and he's the important figure in the case. If you ask me, I don't think that other man you saw had anything to do with it. He didn't look like a murderer, did he?"

"No. He most certainly didn't. I told Mr. Ellis about that. He looked very grave and dignified and respectable, but the more I think of it, the more I think he acted frightened."

"You probably acted frightened yourself," I said. "Suppose someone had seen you coming out of that apartment?"

"I know," she said. "I've thought of that a lot."

"All right," I said. "I've seen Mr. Ellis. I put the cards on the table, I told him exactly who I was and what I was doing and what my interest in the case was, and I told him that I was interested in you. He gave me the job of putting you in a safe place."

"In a safe place?"

"Yes. They don't think this place is safe. Too many people know of it. They don't want to put a guard here because that will attract attention. They'd prefer to have you go some place under another name. I told him I'd take care of it."

"When?" she asked.

"Right away," I said.

"I'll put some things in a bag, and—"

"No, you won't either," I said. "I'll come back and get the things. This case is breaking fast. There isn't a minute to lose."

"But, Donald, surely nothing could happen while you're here, and—"

"Don't ever kid yourself it couldn't," I said. "Every minute you stay here you're in danger. I broke a dozen speed laws getting here. Come on. We can pick up stuff later on." I took her elbow and eased her gently toward the door.

"But, Donald, I don't see why I can't get some things together."

I said, "Please, Marian, have confidence in me. Don't ask questions and don't argue. This means a lot to me."

She said, "All right. Let's go."

We went down the stairs, out the back way through the alley, and around to where I had the agency heap parked. It took me a little while to get it started. I drove directly around to my rooming house.

"You sit here," I said. "Don't get out of the car. I'll be back in a minute."

I ran in and found Mrs. Eldridge.

"We're going to need that room again, Mrs. Eldridge," I said. "My cousin's boyfriend didn't show up. His boat has been delayed. It won't be in for two of three days yet."

"How about the young man's mother?"

"She's been staying there for the last day or two, but some relatives came in, and the beds are all taken."

She said, "All right. She can move back in the same room. How long will you want it?"

"Four or five days."

"Give me three dollars now," she said.

I gave it to her and took a receipt. Then I went out and got Marian. I said, "You're going to stay here again for a while, Marian. I want to be where I can watch you."

"I feel safe here, Donald. It gets pretty lonely being around a big city where you don't know anyone."

"I know," I said.

She said, "I was hoping that when you got back, I'd see more of you. I was lonely—I missed you lots."

I said, "I have a little work to do, then we'll go out and take in a movie, and get some dinner. Are you hungry?"

"Yes."

"Swell," I said. "Give me about an hour, and I'll be back. We'll go out and get something to eat and see a show."

"How about my things?" she asked.

I said, "I'll go up and put your things in a suitcase."

She said, "No, no. Don't do that, Donald. I'll do that later on, but there's some silk pajamas, and a dressing gown, and a toothbrush, and a little overnight case with some creams and lotions in it—don't try to bring anything else, just that. Please, Donald."

I said, "That's swell. Give me your key."

"I want to go with you. I want to pack my things myself."

"It isn't safe, Marian. Can't you understand? I promised Mr. Ellis. He's holding me responsible. If anything happens, it would get me in Dutch with him."

"Well, all right," she said reluctantly.

She gave me the key to her apartment. I said, "In about an hour. So long."

"So long," she said.

I said, "Better check up on the towels, and make sure everything is all right."

She said, "Oh, but it is. I know. I enjoyed being here before. I didn't want to move out, but Mrs. Cool insisted—"

I said, "Okay. Check up on the towels just the same." She went over to the bureau drawer to look for towels, and I slipped her purse under my coat. "Well, I'll be seeing you," I said.

I went back to the agency car, climbed in it, and drove to Marian's apartment. I let myself in, switched on the lights, and went through her purse. There was a compact, lipstick, thirty-seven dollars in currency, some cards printed in the rough-and-ready style of the country newspaper with pale grayish ink in an old English type: *Miss Marian Jean Dunton*. There was a lead pencil, a notebook, a handkerchief, and a key ring with some keys on it that I figured opened doors in Oakview.

I opened the purse and dropped it on the floor. I upset one of the chairs, twisted a rug into a ball, and threw it into a corner. Over near the door, I tapped myself on my sore nose with the side of my hand.

The damn thing wouldn't bleed. It had been bleeding at intervals all afternoon. Now that I wanted it to, I couldn't get it started. Tears smarted my eyes, but my sore nose was as dry as a wildcat oil well.

I screwed up my nerve and tried it again. This time I got results. Blood spilled out, and I walked around the apartment, making certain that a few drops would be where they'd do the most good. Then I had a job stopping it. After a while I got it stopped and started for the door.

The telephone bell shattered the silence.

I walked out and pulled the door shut behind me, leaving the telephone ringing mechanically at regular intervals.

I drove to a drugstore that I knew had a telephone booth. I bought a dozen fresh handkerchiefs, went into the telephone booth, and placed a station-to-station call for the Santa Carlotta police station. When I had them on the line, I said, "Let me talk to Sergeant Harbet, please."

"Who is this talking?"

"Detective Smith, Homicide, Los Angeles," I said.

"Just a minute."

I waited about a minute, and then the operator said, "Sergeant Harbet should be in your office now, Smith. He got a call from the district attorney late this afternoon, and left at once for Los Angeles."

I said, "Thanks. Guess he stopped to get a bite to eat. I want to see him," and hung up.

Things were breaking swell for me.

I called Bertha Cool and said, "Everything's under control. Sit tight. Don't get stampeded, and don't know anything about me."

"Donald, what the hell are you doing now?" she asked.

"Scrambling eggs," I said.

"Well, keep your nose clean. You're clever, but you sure as hell do take chances."

"I'm on my own now," I said. "What you don't know won't hurt you."

She said, "I know so much now I hurt all over."

I hung up, went back to my rooming house, and knocked on Marian's door. She opened it, and I said, "Hi, beautiful. I've just had a break. Bertha's given me a night off. I won't even have to worry about reporting. We can go out and do things.

"I'll have to wait to get your things. I drove to your apartment house, but a couple of men were out front watching the place. I'll have to wait until the coast is clear and try again."

She said, "Donald, I've lost my purse."

I walked in and propped the door open with a chair. "How come?" I asked.

She said, very determinedly, "Someone took it out of this room."

"Nonsense."

"But someone *did*!"

"This is a respectable rooming house. Mrs. Eldridge wouldn't have anyone in here who—"

"I can't help that. I had it when I left the apartment. I'm quite certain that I brought it up here with me."

I pursed my lips into a whistle and said, "That's bad. I bet you left it in the agency car, and I've had the car parked around in a dozen different places on the street. What was in it?"

"Every cent I had in the world."

"How much?"

"All that I had."

I said, "Well, the D.A.'s office told me to take care of your expenses, and I can let you have an advance."

She walked very determinedly over to the chair, jerked it out from under the knob of the door, and slammed the door shut.

I said, "Wait a minute. Your good name will be ruined. Mrs. Eldridge will kick you out for that. She's the kind who puts her offspring out in snowstorms and—"

Marian Dunton came walking over to me. "Now, you look here, Donald Lam," she said. "I'd do almost anything for you. You've been treating me like an unsophisticated little country girl. I suppose I am, but at least I have some human intelligence. You've been nice to me, and I like you, and I have confidence in you, but you can't steal my purse and get away with it."

"Steal your purse!" I said.

"Yes, steal my purse. I know you're a detective. I know you're doing things that you don't want me to know anything about. I know that you've been using me to have the case break the way you want it to break. I figure you're entitled to that much. You gave me the right steer from the start, but you've been lying to me all afternoon, and I don't like it."

I raised my eyebrows, and said, "Lying to you?"

"Yes, lying to me," she said. "I don't think you even went to the district attorney's office. I think you just hung around the apartment house."

"What makes you think that?"

"You told me about how you'd been breaking speed laws," she said, "but your car was stone cold when you tried to start it. You had to use the choke, and nurse it along. I know you never even went near Mr. Ellis. If you want to know how I know, he called me up not more than five minutes before you came back and asked me if I could meet him at his office at ten-thirty tonight. He said some officers from Santa Carlotta were going to be there, and he wanted me to look at a photograph. He didn't say a single thing about you being there or about all that hocus-pocus that you dished out.

"That's okay by me. I have enough confidence in you so that if you don't want to take me into your confidence, I'll play the game the way you want. But when you steal my purse, that's just too much. I had it here in this room when you were here. You walked out, and now it's gone."

I dropped into a chair and began to laugh.

There was indignation in her eyes.

"It's no laughing matter," she said.

I said, "Listen, Marian. I want you to do one more thing for me."

"I've done a lot for you already," she said.

"I know you have. This is going to be hard for you to do, but I want you to do it."

"What?" she asked.

"Believe every word that I've told you."

She said, "You're a city detective and are supposed to know all the answers, but you must think the country is a backwoods. I'd certainly have to be dumb to believe all *you've* told me."

"If you believe it," I said, "and there's any jam, *I'm* the one who's responsible. If you conspire with me, then you've stuck your neck out. Don't you see?"

The indignation faded from her eyes. There was apprehension. "What are you getting into?" she asked.

I met her eyes and said, "I'm darned if I know."

She thought for a while, then said, "Okay. But it makes me look awfully dumb. Under those circumstances, we go to dinner and a movie. What do I do for money?"

I took a wallet from my pocket and handed her some of Bertha Cool's expense money.

"And how about clothes?" she asked.

I said, "You buy a new wardrobe—such as you have to have for the next day or two. And one more thing, Miss Dunton. When I was talking with Mr. Ellis, he said that he thought it would be a bad plan for you to read the newspapers for the next few days."

"Why?" she asked.

"Well, he said that there would be things in it about this case, and that he didn't want you to get a lot of erroneous ideas fixed in your mind from reading the stuff the newspapers would be publishing."

She looked up at me with wide, innocent eyes and said, "Well, I certainly will do exactly as Mr. Ellis suggested. If he doesn't want me to read the papers, then I won't read them."

'That's fine. I know he'll appreciate it."

"Was there anything else Mr. Ellis asked you to tell me?" she asked.

"If there was, I can't think of it now. I—"

I was interrupted by an indignant pounding on the door. I walked over and opened it. Mrs. Eldridge was glaring at me from the threshold. She didn't say a word, but pushed the door open, took a chair, slammed it down so that it held the door open, turned, and pounded down the corridor.

Marian Dunton looked at me and burst out laughing.

Chapter Ten

I dropped in at Bertha Cool's apartment shortly before midnight. She said, "For God's sake, where have *you* been?"

"Out working," I said. "Where's Marian? Do you know?"

"No. I called her four or five times, trying to get in touch with you. I thought you were out with her."

"I went over and saw her," I said.

Bertha Cool stared at me. "Well, can me for a sardine!"

"What's the matter?" I asked.

"That girl did nothing while you were gone but keep Elsie Brand busy answering the telephone. She'd ring up four and five times a day to ask if we'd heard anything from you, when we expected you back, and if we thought you were all right. I'd have bet my diamonds that the first night you were back she'd make you trot her out to dinner and a movie and hold her hand during the performance."

I said hotly, "Marian's a nice girl."

"Sure, she's a nice girl," Bertha Cool said, "but that doesn't keep her from having her head completely turned as far as you're concerned."

"Bunk! She's fascinated by that deputy district attorney."

Bertha Cool snorted and said, "Who was telling you?"

"You were."

"Well, don't fall for that line of hooey. I was just throwing a scare into you. She's stuck on you—nuts over you."

"Well," I asked, "what's new? Have you located Flo Mortinson?"

Bertha Cool nodded. "She's Flo Danzer now," she said. "She

used to be Flo Mortinson. She's staying at the Mapleleaf Hotel, keeps a room there by the month. She hasn't been in that room for about a week, but I'm registered in the hotel and all moved in."

"She have a trunk?" I asked.

"Uh-huh, and I've moved in a trunk big enough to cover hers no matter how big it is. I figured that's what you wanted. Mine's down in the basement. So's hers."

I said, "That's swell. Let's go do a little trunk lifting. What name did you register under?"

"Bertha Cool," she said. "I didn't see any reason for beating around the bush, and someone might know me anyhow."

I said, "We'll have to take a couple of suitcases full of old clothes along with us."

"Why?"

"To act as padding in case your trunk is much too big. We don't want hers rattling around inside of it."

"Why not wait until morning?" Bertha asked. "It's pretty late to pull a stunt like that."

"We can get away with it. Send yourself a telegram before we go over. When the telegram is delivered, it'll give you an excuse to pack your trunk and beat it."

Bertha Cool took a cigarette from the humidor on the table, carefully fitted it into the ivory holder, and said, "I'm not going any further blind, Donald."

"The light," I said, "might hurt your eyes."

"And if Bertha doesn't know where the fire is," she said, "she might get her fingers burned. Bertha wants a showdown, lover."

I said, "Wait until we get that trunk, and then I'll know whether I'm right."

"No. If you're right, it doesn't make any difference. If you're wrong, Bertha wants to know where to find a cyclone cellar. And remember, if you're wrong, Bertha is going to toss you overboard. You're taking the responsibility, and it's your party."

I nodded absently.

"Come on," Bertha said. "Sit down and quit frowning. Give me the lowdown. Otherwise—"

"Otherwise what?" I asked.

Bertha thought for a minute, then grinned and said, "Damned if I know, Donald—unless I pasted you on your sore nose. We're in this together, but Bertha wants to know what she's in and how deep."

I said, "All right. It's just a theory so far."

"Never mind that part of it. I know it's a theory. It has to be, but I want it."

I said, "Here it comes. Mrs. Lintig and her husband split up twenty-one years ago. Mrs. Lintig leaves Oakview. Oakview becomes afflicted with economic atrophy. The town dries up until the money in the bank vaults dies of inaction and loneliness."

"What's all that got to do with it?" Bertha asked.

I said, "Simply this. The Lintigs associated with the younger set. After the town dried up, the younger set moved away looking for more action, more opportunities. The last place on earth where Mrs. Lintig would find any of her own crowd would be in Oakview."

"All right," she said, "I don't follow you all the way, but go ahead."

I said, "For twenty-one years no one in Oakview cares anything about Mrs. Lintig. Then all of a sudden a man shows up and starts asking questions. Two or three weeks later, Evaline Harris shows up and starts collecting photographs. Now, why did she want those photographs? Apparently she snooped out every single photograph in existence that had Mrs. Lintig in it, and bought those photographs."

Bertha Cool's eyes showed interest.

"Then," I said, "she comes back to the city and gets murdered."

"For the photographs?" Bertha asked. "Surely not for those, lover. They aren't *that* important."

I said, "I go to Oakview to look the situation over. Twenty-four hours after I hit town, a cop in Santa Carlotta knows all about it. He shows up, gives me a spanking, takes me out of town, and drops me. Why?"

"So you'd get out of town," Bertha said.

"But why did he want me out of town?"

"So you wouldn't get the information."

I shook my head and said, "No, because he knew Mrs. Lintig was going to come to town, and he didn't want me there while Mrs. Lintig was there."

Bertha Cool puffed thoughtfully on the cigarette for a few seconds, and then said with interest, "Donald, you may have something there."

"I'm pretty certain I have something there," I said. "This big cop is a bully, and he's yellow. If someone had beat him up and kicked him out of town, he'd have been afraid to go back. I've always noticed that people consider the most deadly weapon is one that they fear the most, without regard to what the other man may fear the most. That's psychology and human nature. If a man's afraid of a knife, he figures the other guy is afraid of a knife. If he's afraid of a gun, he thinks a gun is his best bet in a jam."

"Go ahead, lover," Bertha said, her eyes glistening with interest.

"All right. Mrs. Lintig shows up. That was a programed appearance. There was nothing accidental about it. She breaks her glasses or fixes it so the bellboy breaks them for her. She says she's ordered another pair. The other pair never came. Why?"

Bertha said, "I told you about that tonight, lover. It's because the man from whom she had ordered the glasses knew she wasn't going to stay there long enough to receive them."

I said, "No. There's one other explanation."

"What?" she asked.

"That she never ordered them."

Bertha Cool frowned. "But I don't see—"

I said, "She wanted to dismiss that divorce action. She knew her close friends had moved away. But there would be some people left in town who would know her, people she'd be expected to know. They'd be ones who remembered her vaguely, not former intimates, but people who had seen her simply as part of the social background of twenty-one years ago. Twenty-one years is a long time."

Bertha Cool said, "Phooey! There's no sense to it."

"There were no photographs of her available," I went on. "No one could check back on her appearance. What's more, they didn't get a chance. She went to the hotel. From all I can find out, that's about the only place she went. She registered and put in an appearance so the hotel people would know her. She didn't recognize any of her old friends. Why? Because she'd broken her glasses and couldn't see a thing. She put off looking up any of her former friends on that account. She called on a lawyer—a perfectly strange lawyer, by the way—and arranged to have the old divorce case dismissed. She gave me an interview which she hoped would be published in the local press, and she beat it.

"Now get this. This is the significant highlight of the whole business. When Dr. Lintig and his wife had their slip-up, the fly in the ointment was a young chap named Steve Dunton who was running the *Blade*. Steve Dunton was a dashing young gallant, somewhere in the middle thirties. He's in the middle fifties now. He wears a green eyeshade, has put on weight, and chews tobacco.

"Now then, I told Mrs. Lintig that I was a reporter from the

Blade. She didn't even know the paper, and *she never once asked me anything about Steve Dunton*."

"And what was Dunton doing all this time?" Bertha asked.

"He'd quit being a gay blade. He beat it and went fishing. He didn't come back until she'd left."

Bertha Cool said, "Pickle me for a herring, Donald. You *may* be right. If you are, it's blackmail."

"Bigger stakes than that," I said. "Dr. Lintig starts running for office on a reform ticket in a rich little city that's honeycombed with graft. He's too innocent and unsophisticated to know what the opposition would be certain to do—dig back in his past trying to find something sour.

"Naturally, the first thing they looked up was his professional standing. When they started digging into that, they found he'd changed his name from Lintig to Alftmont, so naturally they started looking up Dr. Lintig. They found that Lintig had been registered in Oakview. They went to Oakview and made an investigation. That was when the first man showed up on the job. That was about two months ago, a chap who gave the name of Cross. He was the one who made the original investigation."

Bertha Cool nodded.

"That gave them everything they wanted right there," I went on, "but they couldn't be certain that Mrs. Lintig hadn't died or secured a divorce. They could throw the old scandal in Dr. Alftmont's teeth, but it had all the earmarks of mud-slinging for political purposes. What they wanted to do was to have Mrs. Lintig enter the picture. Then they could play it in either one of two ways. First, they could have her write to the doctor and tell him to withdraw from the campaign. Secondly, they could have her show up and make a statement to the newspapers—not in Santa Carlotta, but in Oakview.

"You can see what would happen then. By showing up in Oakview, it certainly wouldn't look as though it was a case of political mud-slinging. The Oakview papers would publish the statement that she had located Dr. Lintig living under the name of Dr. Alftmont in Santa Carlotta and residing with the corespondent in the divorce action as husband and wife. The Oakview newspaper would telephone Santa Carlotta asking them to verify the tip before they ran it as news. Then Santa Carlotta would let the Oakview paper run it first, and then they'd publish it as an exchange item."

"Then why didn't she tell you that story when you contacted her there in the hotel, Donald?"

"Because she wasn't ready," I said. "She didn't intend to tell the story at that time. That appearance was just for the purpose of laying the foundation. She wanted the people around the hotel to see her and get accustomed to regarding her as Mrs. Lintig."

"Then you think she wasn't Mrs. Lintig?"

I shook my head and said, "The Santa Carlotta police couldn't find her. They found Flo Danzer who used to be Flo Mortinson who roomed with Amelia Sellar in San Francisco. Then they hit a brick wall. Flo knows what it is. They wouldn't have taken the risk of planting another woman as a ringer unless they'd first decided there was no possibility of getting the real Mrs. Lintig."

"But look here, lover," Bertha said, "how did *they* know Steve Dunton would go fishing. He'd have exposed her."

I said, "That's one thing they didn't know. They didn't know it either because Mrs. Lintig never confessed it to Flo, or, what's more likely, because Flo didn't remember such details as names. She knew Mrs. Lintig had been playing around, and that's all."

Bertha Cool smoked for a while in thoughtful silence. "Now

then," I said, "Dr. Alftmont got a letter recently which purported to come from his wife. He says it's her handwriting. I examined that last letter, and it looks like a forgery to me."

Bertha Cool's face lit. "Well, shucks," she said, "there's nothing to it, lover. All we need to do is to prove that Mrs. Lintig is an impostor."

"What good will that do?"

"It'll put Alftmont in the clear, and that's all *we* want."

I said, "It would have a short time ago. It won't now. They're after Alftmont on a murder charge now. Unless we can find some way of beating it, the case is going to break by tomorrow morning at ten o'clock."

Bertha Cool said, "Look, lover. You can do anything with Marian. You can make her look Alftmont square in the face and say that he wasn't the man who came out of that room."

"Wouldn't *that* be nice," I said.

"What do you mean?"

I said, "The other people know all about Alftmont. By this time, they've traced him to Los Angeles. They know damn well he was the man who was in that room. They're just waiting to spring the identification on him. They've told the D.A. here they think the case has a Santa Carlotta angle. He's asked them to lay off until he can get Marian Dunton's mind firmly convinced that the man she saw was coming out of apartment 309 and not out of either of the adjoining apartments. They're ready to shoot now.

"They flash a photograph of Dr. Alftmont on Marian Dunton, and she refuses to identify it. What happens? They give her a regular, old-time third-degree grueling. She can't stand up to that. No girl her age could unless she'd had a lot more experience and a lot more hard knocks than Marian has.

"Marian gets hysterical. She blurts out the whole story or

enough of it so they can fill in all the gaps. They find out that we've been acting as official host and hostess while she's been in the city. They don't bother about asking for an explanation or trying to take your license away. They simply arrest both of us as accessories after the fact, accuse us of trying to bribe and browbeat a prosecution witness, charge us with subornation of perjury, with trying to square a murder rap for Alftmont—and we're all in jail together."

Bertha Cool's eyes showed that she appreciated the logic of my remark, but didn't like the word picture I'd painted. After a minute, she said, "Cripes, lover, let's get out of it. We've done everything we could. We can allege that Mrs. Lintig is an impostor and challenge them to prove it. That will clear our skirts."

I said, "It may clear our skirts, but it won't be getting results for our client."

"I'd rather not get results for our client than spend the next twenty years in the women's penitentiary at Tehachapi."

I said, "What we want to do is to keep out of jail, give our client a break, and let him get elected mayor of Santa Carlotta. What you want is business. With the mayor of Santa Carlotta plugging for you, you've got an asset that's worth a lot of money."

Bertha thought for a minute, and then said, "You went to San Francisco on the bus, didn't you?"

"Yes."

"And left your car in Santa Carlotta?"

"Yes."

"And picked it up late this morning?"

"Yes."

"Then it was someone in Santa Carlotta who pushed your nose back?"

"It was."

"A cop?" she asked.

I nodded.

"The same one who tried to throw a scare into you at Oakview?"

"Yes."

"I don't like it, lover," she said. "A crooked cop can frame you with something you can't get out of."

I grinned and said, "I know it."

"Well, what are you grinning about?"

"I'm grinning," I said, "because that's a game two can play. A clever man can frame a cop so the cop won't have time to frame anyone else. Right now, in case you want to know it, Sergeant John Harbet is a very busy individual, and I wouldn't doubt at all if he was making a lot of explanations."

"Why?" she asked suspiciously. "What's happened?"

"For one thing," I said, "he had been hanging around the Blue Cave with Evaline Harris. When they wanted someone to go up to Oakview and get the lay of the land and pick up all the outstanding pictures of Mrs. Lintig, they sent Evaline. When Evaline got murdered and the police started asking questions about who her boyfriends were, Harbet brought a lot of pull to bear on the management. I don't know how much pull, but it was a hell of a lot, and the word was passed around to the girls not to talk about Harbet. Trying to cover it up that way makes it that much worse when the lid is blown off."

"And is the lid blown off?" she asked.

I nodded.

Bertha Cool looked at me speculatively and said, "Donald, I'd hate to be one to push you in the nose. I have an idea you might find a way to make things awfully uncomfortable for me afterward."

"I would," I promised.

She said, "Come on. Let's go steal a trunk."

"You send yourself a telegram first," I said.

We went around to the Mapleleaf Hotel. The clerk said, "Good evening, Mrs. Cool," and looked at me suspiciously.

Bertha beamed at him and said, "My son—from military academy."

The clerk said, "Oh."

We went up to Bertha Cool's room and sat around for about fifteen minutes, then the telegram which Bertha Cool had sent herself was delivered. We went down to talk with the night clerk. "Very bad news," Bertha Cool said. "I have to take an early morning plane east. I'll have to get my trunk sent up to my room and pack." The clerk said, "The porter isn't on duty now, but I think we can get it up for you."

I said, "I can get it into the elevator if you can find a hand truck."

"There's one down in the basement," he said.

Bertha Cool said, "I'll have to do some packing and unpacking. I'll have to shift baggage around. I want to take just one trunk and one suitcase. Donald, do you suppose you could get that trunk up for me?"

"Sure," I said.

The clerk obligingly gave us a key to the basement. We went down and snooped around. Within two minutes we found a trunk with the initials *F.D.* on it, and a tag: *Property of Florence Danzer, Room 602.*

We opened Bertha Cool's trunk and between us managed to lift Flo's trunk into place. There was quite a bit of room on the sides, and we wadded that with old clothes and newspapers. Then I closed and strapped Bertha's trunk, got it on a hand truck, and got it to the elevator. Thirty minutes later, a taxicab had the trunk strapped onto a trunk rack, and we were headed for the Union Depot. We switched at the Union Depot just so we wouldn't leave a back trail, and went to Bertha's apartment.

The elevator boy dug up a hand truck, and we took the trunk up to Bertha Cool's apartment. I couldn't get the lock picked, but it only took a few minutes to cut off the heads of the rivets which held the trunk lock into position.

We found what we wanted before the trunk was more than half unpacked: a packet of papers and documents tied with a stout cord.

I untied the cord, and Bertha and I went over the papers together.

There was the Lintig marriage license, some letters which Dr. Lintig had written during the courtship while he was still a student in college. There were newspaper clippings, and a photograph of Dr. Lintig and the bride in a wedding dress.

Dr. Lintig had changed somewhat in the twenty-odd years since that photograph had been taken. He was, of course, older, but the change hadn't been as great as might be expected. He'd evidently been an earnest, studious youth who had looked ten years older than his real age.

I studied the face of the woman in the wedding dress. Bertha put my question into words. "Is that," she asked, "the woman you saw at the hotel?"

I said, "No."

"That settles it," Bertha said. "Donald, we've got them licked."

I said, "You keep forgetting the little matter of a murder."

We dug deeper into the pile of documents. I came on some papers written in Spanish. Bertha said, "What are these?"

I said, "Let's see if there isn't a translation appended to them," and turned over the pages. "It looks like a Mexican divorce."

It was.

"Is it any good?" Bertha asked.

"Not much," I said. "For a while some of the states in Mexico established a one-day residential qualification for getting a divorce and provided that the residence could be by proxy. A whole flock of attorneys did a land-office business getting Mexican divorces. The state supreme court punched holes in those divorces whenever the question came up for consideration, but a lot of California marriages had taken place after a Mexican divorce had been granted. Those marriages were so numerous that the authorities simply closed their eyes to their bigamous aspect and let it go at that. The general consensus of opinion is that they constitute a moral whitewash if not a legal justification."

Bertha said, "Now why do you suppose she did that, lover?"

I said, "She wanted to remarry, but she didn't want Dr. Lintig to know of that marriage. She wanted to hold a club over his head. That was why she got the Mexican divorce. That's a bet I've overlooked."

"How did you overlook it?" she asked. "And what was the bet?"

I said, "I'll show you." I went to the telephone, and called Western Union. I dictated a night message to the State Bureau of Vital Statistics at Sacramento, California, asking for information concerning the marriage of Amelia Sellar, and a search of death records for a burial under the married name if any were found.

I hung up the telephone to find Bertha Cool grinning at me. "It looks as though we're getting somewhere, lover," she said.

I said, "You must have a list of operatives who can be called at short notice."

"I do," Bertha said.

"All right. Get a couple of them. Describe John Harbet.

Have them cover police headquarters. I want to know where Harbet goes when he leaves there."

"Won't he go back to Santa Carlotta?" she asked.

"I don't think so," I said. "Not now."

Bertha Cool crossed over to a writing desk and took out a leather-backed notebook. "It may take an hour or so to get them on the job," she said.

"An hour's too long," I told her. "Get people who can go to work immediately. Hire the operatives of another detective agency. Have them on the job within twenty minutes." Bertha Cool started telephoning. I went back to the trunk.

I'd found the rest of it by the time Bertha returned from the telephone, some old stage costumes and some vaudeville publicity photographs of a woman in tights with autographs written on them, *Lovingly, Flo.*

I studied the pictures. "Add twenty years and forty pounds," I said, "and that's the woman I saw in Oakview, the one who was registered as Mrs. James C. Lintig."

Bertha Cool didn't say anything. She walked over to the kitchenette and brought out a bottle of brandy.

I looked at the date on the seal of the bottle. It said 1875.

Chapter Eleven

Bertha Cool had just finished pouring her third brandy at the end of an hour, when the telephone rang.

She looked at her wristwatch, and said, "That's prompt action. One of the operatives reporting on Harbet."

She picked up the receiver and said, in that crisp, official voice of hers, "Yes, this is Bertha Cool talking. Go ahead."

I couldn't hear what was coming over the wire, but I could see the expression on Bertha Cool's face. I saw the lips tighten, the eyelids lower. She said, "I don't do any driving myself. That can be verified."

There was another long period of silence while Bertha Cool sat listening at the telephone. Light scintillated from the diamonds on the hand that held the receiver. She avoided looking at me. After a while she said, "Now listen, I'll have to check up on my records to find which operative was driving the car at the time you mention and where the car was in operation. Personally, I think there's some mistake but.…No, I'm *not* going to the office now. I'm in bed. It wouldn't do me any good if I went there. I couldn't find the records. My secretary has charge of those.…No, I'm not going to have her disturbed at this hour, and that's final. It isn't *that* important. Nine times out of ten, witnesses who take license numbers are mistaken.…Yes, by ten o'clock in the morning.…All right, nine-thirty then. That's absolutely the earliest.…I have several operatives. I have two or three out on a case now.…No, I can't tell you their names or the nature of the case. That's confidential. I'll look up my car records in the morning and advise you. I won't do anything until then."

She hung up the telephone. Her eyes swung around to rivet on me. They seemed as glittering as her diamonds. "Donald, they're turning on the heat."

"What?" I asked.

"Santa Carlotta has telephoned the police here asking for cooperation. They've found a witness to a hit-and-run case. The witness has given the license number of the automobile. It's the agency car. They looked it up on the registrations."

I said, "I didn't think he'd go that far."

She said, "You're in a spot, lover. They'll railroad you sure as hell. Bertha will stick by you and give you what assistance she can, but the case will be tried in Santa Carlotta. It's a felony. They'll pack the jury."

"When," I asked, "did it happen?"

"Day before yesterday."

"The agency car was stored in a garage," I said. "I have a signed receipt for the storage."

"The police came. They looked it up. The garage attendant says you came and took the car out after it had been in less than twelve hours, that you were gone with it for about two hours, and then brought it back, that you seemed excited. He doesn't know you by name, but he's given a description."

I said, "The damn crook threatened to do that, but I didn't think he would."

"Well," she said, "he has. He—"

The telephone rang again. Bertha Cool hesitated, then said, "What the hell, lover? I've got to answer it."

She picked up the receiver, and said, "Hello," cautiously. This time she didn't give her name.

Her attitude relaxed somewhat as she listened. She picked up a pencil and made notes on a pad of paper. Then she said, "Just a minute. Hold the line," and cupped her hand over the mouthpiece.

She said, "Harbet left headquarters. The operative tailed him to an apartment hotel on Normandie. The name of the apartment hotel is the Key West. Harbet went in. It's a swanky place with a night clerk on duty who announces callers. Harbet gave the name of Frank Barr. He told the clerk to ring apartment forty-three A. Forty-three A is occupied by an Amelia Lintig who registered as from Oakview, California. What do we do next?"

I said, "Keep him on the line. Let me think. It's either a preliminary conference or else it's an official visit. They're getting ready to turn on the heat all along the line. Election is day after tomorrow. Tell your operative to stay on the job until we get there."

Bertha Cool said, into the receiver, "Stay on the job until we get there.... Just a moment."

She looked up at me and said, "Suppose Harbet comes out before we get there?"

"Let him go," I said.

Bertha Cool said into the receiver, "Let him go," and hung up.

I picked up my hat. Bertha Cool struggled into her coat, put on a hat, and then looked at the two glasses of cognac on the table. She picked up one of the glasses, and motioned me toward another.

I said, "It's a crime to drink that stuff fast."

Bertha said, "Well, it would be a greater crime to let it go to waste."

We exchanged glances over the glasses, and drank the smooth, clear, amber liquid.

On the way down, in the elevator, Bertha Cool said, "Every step we take gets us in that much deeper, Donald. We've got our necks stuck out pretty damn far."

"It's too late now to pull them back in," I said.

She said, "You're a brainy little squirt, all right, but the trouble with you is you don't know when to stop."

I didn't argue it. We got a taxi and drove over to where the agency car was parked. We went out to the Normandie address in the agency car. Bertha spotted the operative. He said, "The man I was tailing went out. I followed your instructions and let him go."

I said, "All right. Stay on the job. If a woman about fifty-five with gray hair, black eyes, and weighing about a hundred and sixty pounds comes out, tail her. Station your partner in the alley. If he sees any woman who answers that description leave the house, have him tail her."

"Check," he said.

His partner said, "I haven't a car."

"Take the agency car," I said. "Park where you can watch the alley. She may come out that way."

I said to Bertha, "Come on. We'll go in and phone for a taxicab."

Bertha looked at me for a moment, then heaved her bulk out of the agency car. I took her arm, and we walked across the street toward the apartment house.

I said, "You go in alone. Turn your grande dame manner on the clerk. Find out when the telephone operators come on duty at the switchboard, and get their names and addresses."

"He'll get suspicious," she said.

"Not if you play it right. You're trying to check up on your nephew. He has a crush on a girl who works on the switchboard at the Key West Apartments. You want to check up on her. If she's a good egg, you'll give him your blessing and not change your will. If she's a fortune-hunter, you'll get rough. Flash your diamonds in the clerk's eyes. Be sure you get all the girls' home addresses."

"What's the idea?" she asked.

I said, "It's something I have to think over."

Bertha Cool's big diaphragm rippled as she heaved a sigh which seemed to come from her boot tops. "God, Donald," she said, "before you started working for me, I used to get a decent night's sleep once in a while. Now I couldn't sleep even if I had the bed and the chance."

I said, "Your only chance of getting out of this mess is to do what I tell you."

"That's what's got me into it so far."

I said, "Suit yourself," and turned my back.

She stood there on the sidewalk, her eyes sparkling with anger. Then she turned without a word and sailed majestically into the lobby of the apartment house. I casually walked past the door and looked in after she'd been gone a minute or two. She was standing at the counter, her hands playing with a fountain pen, her diamonds sending out splashes of light. Bertha had an air of haughty condescension which seemed to be getting across. I hoped she'd remember not to pull any profanity.

After a while, a taxi drove up. Bertha stayed on inside, talking with the clerk. The cab driver went in. A few minutes later, Bertha Cool came out through the glass-paneled door to the sidewalk, walking in that smooth-flowing manner which was so characteristic of her.

The cab driver on one side and I on the other helped her get in the cab.

"Where to, ma'am?" the driver asked.

"Straight down the street," I said. "Drive slow."

I got in the cab. The driver pulled down the flag and started.

"Get them?" I asked.

"Yes, it's easy."

"Tell me about the day operator."

"Her name's Frieda Tarbing. She lives at 119 Cromwell Drive. She comes to work at seven o'clock in the morning and stays on until three in the afternoon. She's a good scout with sex appeal. The afternoon operator's a pill, but highly efficient. Frieda Tarbing isn't quite as skillful, but she's easy on the eyes. The clerk is quite sure that she's the one who is in love with my nephew, says the afternoon operator isn't in love with anyone."

"That," I said, "makes it easier."

I slid back the window in the partition and said to the cab driver, "119 Cromwell Drive."

Bertha Cool settled back against the cushions and said, "I hope to God you know what you're doing, lover."

I said, "That makes two of us."

She half turned her head, swung her eyes all the way around to look at me under half-closed lids. "You get me in any more jams, lover, and I'll wring your damn neck."

I didn't say anything.

The cab made time through the deserted streets. The place we wanted was an apartment house with an individual bell signal on the front panel. I found the Tarbing name and held my finger against the button.

While I was ringing the bell, I said to Bertha Cool, "It's up to you to get us in. Tell her you have to see her, that there's money in it for her. She won't let a man in at this hour of—" A speaking-tube next to Bertha's ear shrilled into a whistle, and then a voice, which didn't sound too annoyed, said, "What do you want?"

Bertha Cool said, "This is Mrs. Cool. I have to see you about a business matter—a chance for you to pick up some money. It'll only take just a minute. I can run up and explain the situation to you and be out, all inside of five minutes."

"What sort of a business proposition?"

"I can't explain it to you here. It's very personal, but there's a chance for you to pick up a nice little piece of change."

The voice through the speaking-tube said, "All right. I'll bite. Come on up."

The electric door-catch release buzzed into action. I pushed open the door, and held it for Bertha Cool.

Coming in from the fresh air of the night, the apartment-house corridor was thick with smell. We found an elevator, rattled up to the fourth floor, and walked back to Frieda Tarbing's apartment. There was light showing over the transom, but the door was closed and locked.

Bertha Cool tapped on the panels.

"Who is it?" a voice asked.

"Mrs. Cool."

The voice on the other side of the door said, "I'll have a look at you first."

The bolt turned, a chain rattled, and the door swung back about three inches, leaving a crack just big enough for a pair of dark, sparkling eyes to take in Bertha Cool's big frame. Bertha moved her hand so that the diamonds glittered, and Frieda Tarbing rattled the chain loose, and said, "Come on in—good heavens, I didn't know there was a man with you! Why didn't you say so?"

Bertha Cool sailed on into the room and said, "Oh, that's just Donald. Don't mind him."

Frieda Tarbing went back to the bed, kicked off her slippers, pulled the covers up, and said, "Find a couple of chairs that haven't clothes on them. Perhaps you'd better close the windows."

Her hair was too dark to be brown. It wasn't exactly black. Her eyes were alert, curious, and bubbling with life. She'd wakened from a sound sleep looking as fresh as though she'd just come back from a morning walk. It was a face that could get by anywhere. She said, "All right. What is it?"

I said, "My aunt has just rented an apartment at the Key West Apartments."

"What's your aunt's name?"

"Mrs. Amelia Lintig."

"Where do I come in?"

I said, "My aunt is a widow. She has a lot of money and very little sense. A man who intends to grab off all her cash is making a play for her. I want to put a stop to it."

The eyes looked me over without any particular enthusiasm. She said, "I see. You're a relative. You hope that some day auntie will kick off and leave you the dough. In the meantime, she wants to play around and use it up. You don't like that. Is that right?"

"That," I said, "is not right. I don't ever want a dime of her money. I just want her to be sure what she's getting into. If she wants to marry this fellow on her own, that's all right by me. But apparently he's blackmailing her. He has something on her. I don't know what it is. Probably it's something serious. I think he's convinced her that she could be called as a witness against him or he could be called as a witness against her on some kind of a criminal action, but I wouldn't be knowing about it."

"What do you want me to do?"

"Listen in on her telephone tomorrow morning."

"Nothing doing."

I said, "You listen in on the switchboard when she talks with this chap. If they're billing and cooing, that's quite all right by me. I step out of the picture. But if he's holding something over her head or talking about a crime, I want to know about it. There's one hundred bucks in it for you."

"That," she admitted, "is different. How do I know there's a hundred bucks in it for me?"

"Because," I said, "you get the hundred bucks right now. It's easier for us to take a chance on you than for you to take a chance on us."

She said, "It would cost me my job if anyone knew about it."

"No one," I said, "will ever know about it."

"What do you want me to do?"

"Just notify me when she calls this man. If it's a mushy conversation, I step out of the picture. If it's blackmail, I want to put the cards on the table with her and say, 'Look here, Aunt Amelia, you give me the lowdown on this before you do anything rash.' "

Frieda Tarbing laughed, extended her hand, and said, "Gimme."

I said to Bertha Cool, "Give her a hundred."

Bertha, looking as though she had a mouthful of vinegar, opened her handbag, counted out a hundred dollars, and handed the bills over to Frieda Tarbing.

"When you see me," I said, "don't let on that you know me."

She said, "Say, listen, if you think *I'm* that dumb, maybe I'd better coach *you* a bit. This is absolutely between us. I need the hundred bucks, but I need my job, too. Don't make any dumb plays. The day clerk has been making passes at me, didn't get to first base, and is just looking for a chance to trip me up on something."

I said, "It'll be okay. I'm going in to see Aunt Amelia early in the morning. When I go out, I'll slip you a note with a number on it. When you get the dope, call me at that number. If the conversation sounds like a mushy, romantic one, you simply say, 'You've lost that bet.' If it sounds as though there's a crime mixed up in it, say, 'You've won your bet.' "

"Okay," she said. "Open that window as you go out, and switch out the light. I'm going to get another forty winks before the alarm goes off. Bye-bye."

She rolled up the bills, shoved them in the pillowcase, and straightened out on the bed.

I opened the window, then the door. Bertha Cool switched off the lights. We went out into the corridor, and Bertha Cool said, "Think of having a disposition like that at this hour in the morning. Donald, if you want to take the advice of one who has seen something of the world, go marry that girl before someone else beats you to it."

I said, "I've heard of goofier ideas, at that."

"What do we do now?" Bertha asked.

I said, "We go back to the taxi. I go out to the Key West Apartments and keep the operatives on the job to make certain nothing slips. You go back to your apartment and grab a little sleep. I don't dare to show up around the office because they'll nab me on that hit-and-run charge. You stay away from that office appointment with the cops. Show up at the Key West about nine or nine-thirty, and we'll go in and have a talk with Aunt Amelia."

"What are we going to talk about?" Bertha asked.

I said, "I think I know the words, but I don't know the music—yet. I'll have to think it over. Keeping a watch on that apartment house will give me a chance to think."

We climbed in the taxi, and I told the driver to take me to the Key West, and then take Bertha to her apartment.

As we were rolling along, Bertha said, "Do you think she's going to skip out tonight, Donald?"

"No. Not one chance in a hundred, but we can't afford to gamble on one chance in a thousand."

Bertha Cool said, "Are *you* telling *me*," and settled back against the seat cushions.

The cab driver deposited me at the Key West Apartments. I said goodbye to Bertha Cool and walked over to sit with the operative who was watching the front of the apartment house.

He was a man about fifty-five with twinkling blue eyes, a face like a cherub, and a detailed knowledge of underworld graft and corruption that made the ordinary racket sound like a Sunday school picnic. He'd worked with the government for fifteen years, and I listened to him talk until daylight showed in the east. The palm trees in front of the Key West Apartments began to take color, and a mockingbird started pouring its song into the dawn.

I'd heard all I wanted of prostitutes, dope fiends, pimps, and gamblers. I said, "If your insides are as cold as mine, you'll want some hot coffee."

I could almost see him start to drool at the mention of the coffee.

I said, "You'll find an all-night restaurant down the street three blocks, to the left two blocks. It's a little joint, but you can get good coffee there. I'll sit here and watch. Don't be in a hurry. This is a slack time. If she'd been skipping, she'd have made a break earlier."

"That's damn white of you," he said.

"Don't mention it."

He climbed out of the car and stamped his feet to get circulation in them. I settled back on the cushions and quit thinking about the case, about murders, criminals, politics, and frame-ups. I watched the east get brassy, saw the sun come up and send its first rays, turning the white stucco of the apartment house into a golden glow.

After a while the mockingbirds quit singing. I saw people beginning to move around in the apartment house, windows being closed, curtains being pulled.

The operative came back and said, "After I got there, I figured I might as well have breakfast, so you wouldn't have to relieve me. I hope I wasn't too long. It took a hell of a while to get what I wanted."

I said, "It's okay. Get in, sit down, and keep quiet for half an hour. I've got some thinking to do."

We sat side by side in the car while the morning began to hum with activity.

Shortly after seven o'clock I walked around to the alley and relieved the other operative while he got breakfast. When he came back, I took time out to walk down to a service station, go in the washroom, and freshen up a bit. I walked around to the restaurant and had some ham, eggs, and coffee. Then I went back to the Key West and waited for Bertha.

Chapter Twelve

Bertha showed up in a taxi about nine-thirty. I thought she looked plenty worried. She came over and told the operative, "There'll be a relief for you in half an hour. Give me a ring shortly before five and I'll let you know whether you work tonight."

He said, "Thanks."

Bertha said, "You can go wash your hands while we're in there. She won't leave while we're there."

The operative said, "Thanks," and added with a grin, "My hands are clean. Lam held the fort for a while early this morning."

Bertha looked me over and said, "Donald, you look like hell."

I didn't bother to say anything.

Bertha said, "Drive around to the alley and tell the operative who's watching the back that I'll have a relief for him. Tell him to call up shortly before five. You can leave the agency car out in front."

She looked at me. "Okay, lover?" she asked.

"Okay," I said. "What's new?"

We started across the street toward the entrance of the apartment house. She avoided my eyes. "Come on," I said. "Let's have it. What's new?"

"A telegram from the Bureau of Vital Statistics."

"Saying what?"

"Amelia Sellar married John Wilmen in February of 1922. She was never divorced. There's no record of the death of either Amelia or John Wilmen. Where does that leave us, Donald?"

"Right in front of the Key West Apartments," I said, "with a tough job on our hands."

"What are we going to say to her?"

"It'll depend on how she reacts. You let me take the lead. Then you follow my play. I've been doing a lot of thinking. Today is probably the time they intend to spring their trap. There's just time enough before election to let the news get exaggerated by word-of-mouth gossip. There isn't time for any refutation."

"Had breakfast?" Bertha asked.

"Yes."

The day clerk at the desk smiled at us. I nodded and walked past him to the switchboard. Frieda Tarbing looked up with a perfectly blank face.

"Will you ring Mrs. Lintig," I said, "and tell her that her dutiful nephew is in the lobby. Please ring very quietly because if she's asleep I don't want to disturb her."

I saw a quick flicker of comprehension on Frieda Tarbing's face. "Ring quietly?" she asked.

"Very quietly," I said.

"I get you," she said.

The clerk gave us the once-over then turned away. Frieda Tarbing went through motions at the switchboard and said, out of the corner of her mouth, "Do you really want me to ring?"

"No," I said.

She raised her voice, and said, "Mrs. Lintig says for you to go right up. It's forty-three A on the fourth floor."

I thanked her, and Bertha Cool and I walked into the elevator. An elevator boy shot us up to the fourth floor. The Key West was an apartment that had just a touch of swank. The service was quietly efficient.

We walked down to 43A, and I knocked on the door.

Almost immediately we heard motion on the other side of the door, and I said to Bertha Cool, "Today's the day all right. She's up and ready. Probably she's due to drive up to Santa Carlotta and be there by afternoon. They'll let the story break this evening."

The door opened then. The woman I'd seen in Oakview stood on the threshold. She stared at me frowning, then suddenly recognition dawned on her face. I noticed that she wasn't wearing spectacles.

"Good morning, Mrs. Lintig," I exclaimed cordially. "You'll remember me. I'm from the *Blade* in Oakview. A friend of yours, Sergeant Harbet, told me he thought you'd have a story ready for me."

She frowned and said, "I didn't know he wanted it published in Oakview. I didn't— Do you know Sergeant Harbet?"

"Sure," I said. "We're old buddies."

She said dubiously, "Well, come in."

I said, "This is Bertha Cool, Mrs. Lintig."

Bertha Cool flashed her diamonds, and Mrs. Lintig smiled all over her face. "So pleased to meet you, Mrs. Cool. Won't you come in?"

We went in. I closed the door and noticed there was a spring lock that clicked into position. I said, "I don't know the details. I understand the Santa Carlotta paper is to publish it the same time we do."

"And who was it sent you?" she asked.

"Why, John," I said. "John Harbet. He said you knew all about it."

"Oh, yes," she said. "You'll excuse me if I'm a little cautious. Here's the story. I think you know the first part of it, how my husband ran away and left me absolutely destitute."

"Didn't you get some property?" I asked.

She snapped her fingers and said, "A mere sop! I didn't get enough money out of it to keep me for two years. It's been twenty-one years since he ran away with that hussy. I've been searching for him, trying to find him. The other day I located him, and where do you think he was?"

"Santa Carlotta?" I asked.

She said, "Is that a good guess or did John tell you?"

"It's more than a good guess," I said.

"Well, he's in Santa Carlotta, all right, under the name of Dr. Charles Loring Alftmont. He's living shamelessly and openly with that Carter girl, and they have the crust to pose in the community as man and wife, but the most startling thing of all is he's running for mayor. Can you imagine that?"

I gave a low whistle.

She said, "Now, I don't want to be vindictive, but I certainly am not going to have this creature dropping a mantle of respectability over her scarlet shoulders, and then adding insult to injury by becoming the Mrs. Mayor of Santa Carlotta. I think my husband will withdraw from the campaign on the eve of election. If he does, you understand the story isn't to be published."

I said, "I understand. John told me all about that. I promised to hold it until I got a release."

She said, "Of course, you can play up the local angle."

I said, "That's fine. That'll make a nice story. Now, about this Evaline Harris who came up to Oakview, and was subsequently murdered. I understand she was doing some work for you, trying to find out about your husband."

The woman's face became a cold mask of suspicion. "John didn't tell you that," she said.

"Why, yes," I said. "That is, not in so many words, but he dropped some remarks which led me to believe that was the case."

She said, "What did you say your name was? I've forgotten."

"Lam," I said. "Donald Lam."

She said, with growing suspicion in her eyes, "John never mentioned to me that he had a friend on the newspaper in Oakview."

I laughed and said, "He didn't know where I was until just the other day. I've known John for years."

She reached a decision and said, "Well, John certainly didn't tell you anything about that Harris girl because he didn't know anything to tell. I never saw her in my life."

"You're certain of that?" I asked.

"Yes, yes," she said. "Why not?"

I said, "That's funny. Because she worked as an entertainer at the Blue Cave, and you were employed there as hostess."

She caught her breath.

I said, "I'm trying to get this straight for our paper. I don't want to make any mistake and publish something that doesn't click."

Her eyes narrowed. She said, "You're lying to me. You don't know John Harbet."

I laughed easily and said, "Any time you think I don't! John and I are just like that." I held up two fingers.

In a low, hoarse voice she said, "You get out of here! Both of you!"

I drew up a chair and sat down, nodded to Bertha Cool, and said, "Have a chair."

The woman said, "I said for you to get out of here."

I said, "Sit down and keep your shirt on. We're going to ask you some questions."

"Who are you?" she asked.

I said, "We're detectives."

She sat down as though the strength had oozed out of her knees. She looked at me with a face that was filled with despair.

I said, "It's been rather a long, tedious trail, Flo, but we've unraveled most of it. You roomed with Amelia up in San Francisco. You found out all about her life history, and after she married Wilmen, you got possession of her papers, probably out of a trunk she'd left with you, or you may have stolen them. Anyway, you got them."

"That's a lie," she said.

I said, "Recently, the political ring that was controlling Santa Carlotta wanted to find Mrs. Lintig. There was money in it. You were approached. You couldn't find Amelia Lintig; perhaps because she's dead, perhaps because she's moved out of the state. But you convinced them you could do a good job of impersonation. You knew all about her background.

"You had certain things on which you wanted to check. You were pretty close to Evaline Harris who was working in the night spot where you were hostess. You arranged to send her up to Oakview and have her make the investigations. Particularly you wanted her to pick up all of the photographs of Amelia Lintig that could be found."

"You're absolutely crazy," she said.

I said, "Now we go on from there. Evaline Harris came back with the photographs all right, but she also had an overpowering curiosity. She was a chiseler, and she was greedy. Her trunk had been smashed in shipment. She knew you'd never consent to having her make a claim for damages because you didn't want anyone to trace her, but, without consulting you, she went ahead and made the claim. You found out she'd been traced. That caused a lot of trouble.

"John Harbet was giving you instructions. You were going to him for advice. He knew all about Evaline Harris. When he first started looking for Amelia, the trail led to you. While he was giving you the once-over, he hung around the Blue Cave.

He was friendly with Evaline. He worked with her, coaching her and giving her instructions on what she was to do in Oakview."

She said, in a dull, mechanical voice, "That's a lie."

"No, it isn't a lie. It's the truth. It can be proved. Now then, when Evaline Harris left that back trail by putting in a claim with the railroad company for her damaged trunk, Harbet blew up. That was when Evaline Harris tried to cut herself in on the deal. She wanted some coin to keep from talking—and that's why she was found strangled in bed. Now then, Flo Danzer, it's your move."

She came toward me. "God damn you, get out of here, or I'll claw your eyes out. I'll scratch your face. I'll—"

Bertha Cool's big arm swung around like a pile driver. She caught a fistful of Flo's hair, jerked her head back, and said, "Shut up, or I'll knock your teeth down your throat. Sit down in that chair and stay there. That's better."

Bertha Cool relaxed her hold on the woman's hair.

For a moment they glowered at each other, Bertha Cool towering over the woman in the chair. Then Bertha said, "I can be just as tough as you are. You've had a background which gives you a strong stomach, but you haven't seen anything yet. I'm *really* hard."

Flo Danzer said, "It's a damn lie, but it makes a good story. I suppose it's a shakedown. What do you want?"

Bertha Cool said, "Don't go near Santa Carlotta. Don't have anything—"

"Wait a minute," I interrupted. "That Santa Carlotta business is out anyhow. We'd show her up for an impostor within five minutes after she made the claim. What we want right now is to clean up this murder."

"What do you want out of me?" she asked.

"I want the facts on the Harris murder," I said. "I want everything you know."

She started to laugh then, and I could see hard defiance in her eyes. "Well, go jump in the lake," she said. "You've run a damn good bluff, and it's got you nowhere. You win on one thing. I'm not going to stick my neck out in Santa Carlotta. John Harbet will just have to get along without me. As far as the rest of it is concerned, you're barking up the wrong tree, and if you don't think I know what I'm doing, just stick around and I'll call the cops."

"A fat chance of *you* calling the cops," I said.

She said, "That shows all you know about it. If you'd waited until this afternoon when I'd driven to Santa Carlotta and given my statement to the *Courier*, told them I had come for a settlement with Dr. Alftmont, and *then* disappeared, you'd have had something you could pin on me, and—"

"You were going to disappear?" I asked.

Her laugh was a sneer. She said, "Of course I was. For a smart dick, you're awfully dumb about some things. I couldn't let Alftmont lamp me. He'd know I wasn't Amelia as soon as he saw me. I was going to tell my story to a newspaper reporter. I was going to say that I had an appointment with Dr. Alftmont. Then I was going to disappear. It was going to look as though I'd been bumped off, and the evidence was going to point to Alftmont. About the time he was denying that, we were going to connect him up with Evaline Harris, and the police down here were going to accuse him of the Harris murder. The witness would identify him, and that would have been all there was to it. Public opinion would have been divided over whether he'd killed me or not, but when they added the Harris business on top of it, he wouldn't have stood a chance.

"Now then, that's all there is to it. Alftmont murdered Evaline. I hope they hang a first degree on him for that. He tried to get some information out of her, and she wouldn't kick through. The party got rough. Don't kid yourself about Dr. Charles Loring Alftmont. He's a killer. I'm no tin angel myself, but I can't stomach murder. If you'd waited until this afternoon, you could have pinched *me* for something. As it is, I'm in the clear. You can't do a damn thing. If you don't get out of here, I'll call the cops."

I said, "When did you last see Evaline Harris alive?"

She said, "About twenty-four hours before she was murdered. I told her to watch out for Alftmont."

"Why?"

"Because I knew he was dangerous."

"Then you knew that Alftmont could find her?"

She squinted her eyes. "I knew some detectives were working on the case. I found out that Evaline had been a greedy little bitch, and couldn't resist the temptation of trying to pick up a piece of change from the railroad company. That was the worst of Evaline. You could never trust her. Lots of the girls in her racket pick up steady boyfriends who make regular donations—not Evaline. She was too greedy, and she couldn't resist blackmail. As soon as she'd get her hooks into some nice young chap, she'd find out all about him, and then start blackmailing. You couldn't control her for a minute. She couldn't control herself. It was like dope. She wanted to chisel."

I said, "When the police found her body in the apartment, they found she'd been on an all-night party and was sleeping late. The newspaper was under the door. That means she hadn't got up. There were cigarette stubs and an ashtray by the bed. One of them had lipstick on it. One of them didn't.

"Evaline slept with a package of cigarette and matches by the bed. She always had a cigarette first thing after she woke up. I know that.

"Now then, I figure someone went to see Evaline. It was

someone she knew. She sat down on the bed, and they talked. The talk didn't go to suit this man, and he slipped a loop over her neck—and I think you know who that man was."

"Sure, I do," she said. "It was Dr. Alftmont. He'd traced her—probably through that claim she'd made to the railroad company. He went down to see her. He was willing to be reasonable with her, but he found out she was just a tool, that there was a bigger game afoot. He couldn't buy her off, so he croaked her. Now then, you can either get the hell out of here, or I'll call the cops, and I mean it."

I said to Bertha, with a surreptitious wink, "Well, the police are working on that package of cigarettes and on the cigarette stubs, using that new iodine process for developing fingerprints. Don't kid yourself. They're going to get the prints of the man who called on Evaline. Won't it be too bad if those are the prints of Sergeant Harbet of the Santa Carlotta police force, and won't it be funny if Harbet drags Flo Danzer into the picture."

"Don't be silly," Flo Danzer said. "How's he going to drag me into the picture? I'll stand up on my two feet and admit everything I did—I went to Oakview and said I was Mrs. Lintig—so what? Maybe I *intended* to work some blackmail on Dr. Lintig. Maybe I didn't. I haven't asked anyone for five cents in cash. And don't kid yourself John Harbet is ever going to get dragged into this thing. Dr. Alftmont is the one who's holding the bag on this rap. He lost his head and killed Evaline."

I nodded to Bertha, got up, and started over toward the door.

"Come on, Bertha," I said.

She hesitated.

"Come on. We're going down to the district attorney's office and put the cards on the table. We're going to get a warrant for

Flo Danzer and John Harbet on criminal conspiracy. We can prove the conspiracy, and her going to Oakview and registering as Mrs. Lintig was an overt act. She isn't in the clear. She only *thinks* she's in the clear."

Bertha said, "Now listen. I—"

I raised my voice. "Come on," I said. "Do as I say."

I flung the corridor door open.

Getting Bertha Cool out of that room was like pulling a bristling dog away from another dog who's trying to pick a fight. Bertha Cool finally came out into the corridor, but she didn't want to come. She was mad clean through. She didn't like the way I was playing the game, and she wanted to stay and have it out with Flo Danzer.

Flo Danzer didn't say anything. She'd got control of her face now, and it was set in an expression of tight-lipped hostility.

Out in the hallway, Bertha said, "My God, Donald, what's the matter with you? You've called the turn on her, and she's just about ready to cave."

I said, "No, she isn't. You two women will start fighting. We haven't enough cards to call for a showdown."

"Why haven't we?"

"Because we can't *prove* anything. All we can do is bluff. Remember, the object of this visit was to make her call Harbet. She'll call him now. What she'll say over the telephone will make that switchboard operator's hair stand right up on end. She'll be listening in on that conversation. By the time we know what's said over the telephone, we'll be ready to call for a showdown. Then we'll have some proof. Now, we're just running a bluff."

We went down in the elevator. I paused at the switchboard to say, "Thank you very much," and added in a lower voice, "I'll ring you in fifteen minutes."

Bertha Cool paused at the clerk's desk to flash her diamonds. "You have very lovely apartments," she said, with that gracious smile of hers, and the clerk came out from behind the shell of icy reserve to smile all over his face. "In case you're interested," he said, "we have one or two choice vacancies."

"Perhaps a little later," Bertha Cool said, nodding with just the right amount of condescension, and sailing majestically out of the door, which I deferentially held open. She looked for all the world like Mrs. Million-bucks taking her pet diamonds out for an airing.

I indicated the agency car. Bertha Cool said, "To hell with that bunch of junk. He may be looking out of the door. We'll get a taxi."

"We won't find one cruising along here," I said.

"We'll stop at a drugstore and telephone."

I said, "Let's go up and see Marian," and then watched Bertha Cool's face out of the corner of my eye.

She said, "No, lover, we can't go see Marian."

"Why not?"

"I'll explain to you later. You haven't seen the morning papers."

I said, "No. I've been on the job all night."

"I know, Donald. Now listen, we can't go to the office. We can't go to your place. We can't go to Marian's place. I'll telephone for a taxi. You go back and tell the relief operatives to telephone reports in to me at the Westmount Hotel. We'll go there."

I said, "What's in the morning papers? I'd better buy one."

"Not now, lover," she said. "Just keep your mind on this."

I said, "All right. You get the cab and pick me up."

I walked back to the operatives on duty and told them to report to Bertha at the Westmount Hotel, and, in case there was no answer there, to ring the agency and report to Miss Brand.

I was halfway back to the drugstore when Bertha showed up with a taxi. I climbed in, and we drove to the Westmount Hotel in silence. Bertha had a morning paper clamped under her arm, but she wouldn't let me see it.

Chapter Thirteen

We registered as Mrs. Cool and Donald Cool. Bertha said, "My nephew and I would like two rooms with a connecting bath. I'm expecting some telephone calls. Please be certain they're handled without delay. Our baggage will come later."

She flashed her diamonds again, and the gang in the hotel fell all over itself giving us service.

In the rooms, I waited until the bellboy had left and then put through a call for the Key West Apartments. When I heard Frieda Tarbing's voice on the line, I said, "Call Bertha Cool at the Westmount Hotel for any tip-off. We're in six-twenty-one. Better make a note of the number."

"Very well," she said. "There's nothing at present. I'll call you back."

I said, "Are you always as good-natured when you're pulled out of a deep sleep?"

"Was I good-natured?" she asked.

"Yes. Mrs. Cool said you were one woman in a million, that I'd better lay siege to your heart and marry you before some other guy grabbed you off."

Her laugh was melodious. "There's merit to the idea," she said.

"I thought so," I told her.

Suddenly her voice changed to that of impersonal efficiency. "I have the message. I'll see that it's delivered," she said. "Thank you."

I hung up, and Bertha Cool, sprawled out in the overstuffed chair with her shoes kicked off and her stockinged feet elevated to another chair, looked at me and shook her head. "It's a gift," she said.

"What is?"

"Making women fall for you."

"They don't fall for me," I said. "I was just kidding her along. I don't even know whether she liked it."

"Nuts," Bertha said, and fitted a cigarette into her cigarette holder.

I walked over to the bed where she'd placed the morning paper and opened it. The news was on the front page. A key witness whom the district attorney's office had been keeping under cover in the Evaline Harris murder case had disappeared. Circumstances made the police believe she'd been the victim of foul play. Police were "combing the city." There was the usual amount of newspaper hooey: The police were following a definite lead and expected to have important disclosures to make before midnight. The witness, it seemed, had disappeared just as the police were ready to "break" the case. The police had hinted that developments of a most startling nature were to be anticipated.

I put on an act for Bertha. "My God," I said, "if anything's happened to her! Do you suppose the police were so damn dumb they didn't anticipate something like this? Good God, here they were dealing with a murderer, and this girl was the key witness, and they left her entirely unguarded. Of all the damn fool plays I've ever heard or seen, that takes the cake!"

Bertha said, "Keep your shirt on, lover. She's all right."

"What makes you think so?"

"The only person she could have identified was our client. You know that he wouldn't do anything like that."

I read through the article and said, "There was blood in the apartment!"

Bertha Cool said, "Don't worry, Donald. She's all right. If they'd wanted to kill her, they'd have simply killed her there in the apartment, and the police would have found her body. The fact that she isn't there means that she's alive. The police will find her. They're pretty thorough, you know, when they get on the job."

I started pacing the floor and said, "I'd like to think you're right."

"Don't get all stewed up," she said. "There's nothing you can do to help. We've got this other thing to handle. You've got to keep your mind clear."

I paced the floor for a while, smoked a couple of cigarettes, and went back to read the paper again, and then went and stood looking out of the window.

Bertha Cool smoked in comfortable silence. After a while she called the office and talked with Elsie Brand. She hung up and said, "The cops are looking for you at the office, lover. I guess those boys in Santa Carlotta mean business."

I let on that the information didn't even interest me. After a while she said, almost musingly as though thinking out loud, "For a little runt, you draw a hell of a lot of water."

"What do you mean?"

She said, "I was running a detective agency. It was a run-of-the-mill agency. Most of the better-class outfits won't handle political stuff, and won't handle divorce stuff. I'd handle anything. My business wasn't always the most savory, but it was a nice, routine business. I made some money out of it, not a hell of a lot, but enough to get by. You enter the picture. I hire you to work for me, and the first thing I know, you're dragging me so deep into murder cases that I'm in right up to my neck. I've ceased to be a detective and become an accomplice. The tail's not only wagging the dog, but it's shaking hell out of him."

I said, "Forget it. You're making money, aren't you!"

Bertha Cool looked down at her big, firm breasts, at her big thighs, and said, "I hope I don't lose weight worrying. I was so comfortable the way I was—just like a foot in an old shoe, and now look at me. Lover, do you know that if we don't pull this case out of the fire, we're going to be in jail?"

I said, "There's lots of ways of getting out of jail."

Bertha said, "Put that in writing and send it to the guys up in San Quentin. They might be interested."

I didn't say anything, and we sat for a while in silence. First Bertha'd look at her wristwatch, then I'd look at mine. Then I'd look out of the window, and Bertha would light another cigarette.

The street in front of the hotel furnished the only variation. A bakery wagon made some deliveries. An occasional housewife would sally forth to do some shopping. A couple of elderly people who looked like tourists spending a few months in Southern California strolled out of the hotel, got in a car with a New York license plate, and drove leisurely away. The sky was blue and cloudless. The sun beat down, throwing intense, black shadows which gradually shortened.

I went back to the bed, propped myself up with pillows, and read the rest of the news in the paper. Bertha Cool sat in the chair, to all outward appearances calmly serene.

When I threw the paper down and went to stand at the window again, she said, "For God's sake, quit fidgeting. It doesn't get you anywhere. You're too nervous, too intense. Sit down and relax. Rest while you can. You've been working on this case day and night. You're nervous. There's no percentage in getting nervous."

I went back to the bed, punched the pillows into shape, stretched myself out, and said, "I'm going to try and get forty winks. I don't think I can, but there's a lot of work ahead of us. Lord knows when I'll have a chance to sleep again."

Bertha Cool said, "It's a good idea. Hand me the financial section, lover—not that it means a damn thing. Those financial writers diagnose history with a condescending attitude that makes you think they knew what was going to happen all along, but try and pin them down to anything definite in their predictions. Listen to this. 'In the event the European situation remains static, it is the consensus of opinion that the market has a healthy tone and securities are due for a steady, persistent advance. The domestic political situation, while still far from reassuring, shows evidences of a trend toward the better, at least the swing of the pendulum to the left has been checked. However, it is to be remembered that business generally is far from optimistic, and the attempts of various parties to gain political power or perpetuate the powers already enjoyed will doubtless exert a retarding influence upon any recovery which might be expected.'"

She said, "Bah," and dashed the paper to the floor.

I made myself as comfortable as I could on the bed, but knew I couldn't sleep. My brain was racing as though I'd had an overdose of coffee. My mind picked up a dozen different possibilities of the situation, carried them through to disastrous conclusions, and then dropped them to pick up some other possible development. I tried lying on my left side for a while, then rolled over to my right side. Bertha Cool said, "For Christ's sake, stay in one position. You can't sleep rolling around that way."

I tried staying in one position. I looked at my watch. It was almost eleven.

Bertha Cool said, "Perhaps we'd better ring the Key West again."

I said, "I don't think so. We don't want to make the clerk suspicious. Remember, he's in love with Frieda Tarbing, and inclined to be jealous. Probably they don't allow her to make personal calls while she's on duty."

Bertha said, "For God's sake, shut up and go to sleep."

I lay there thinking. I'd turned the heat on Harbet, and Harbet had turned the heat on me. Taken by and large, there was a lot of fire, and someone was due to get his fingers burned. I thought of Dr. Alftmont sitting up in Santa Carlotta on the eve of election with a sword hanging over his head. I thought of the woman who was posing as Mrs. Alftmont, the wife of an eye, ear, nose, and throat specialist who had built up a good practice, who had achieved some social recognition in the inner circle of a snobbish city, wondered what she was thinking as she waited—waiting without knowing what was going on.

It occurred to me that those people could rest more easily because they had confidence in me. Even Bertha Cool was able to shift part of her responsibilities to my shoulders. I had no one to whom I could pass even a part of the load.

I thought of Marian Dunton and wondered if she was getting along all right. I didn't dare to call her—not with Bertha Cool in the room, and I knew Bertha Cool well enough to know I couldn't make a sneak and put in a surreptitious telephone call. I thought of what a loyal friend Marian was, of how she'd realized I was playing a game and using her as a pawn, but, like the good scout she was, she'd drifted along—laughing brown eyes—the shape of her lips—the smile that seemed to come so easily—her white teeth—

The ringing of the telephone brought me up out of a sound sleep. I rolled off the bed and staggered as I tried to stand up. My eyes, drugged with slumber, refused to focus. A telephone was ringing—that telephone bell was the most important thing in my life—Why?—Who was calling?—Where was the telephone?—What time was it?—Where was I?—

I heard Bertha Cool's calmly competent voice saying, "Yes. This is Mrs. Cool," and then, after a moment, "All bets are off? We'll be right over."

She hung up the telephone and stood looking at me with her forehead puckered into a frown. "Frieda Tarbing," she said. "She goes off duty in an hour. She wanted to remind me. She said that it looked as though all bets were off."

Having something definite to work on steadied me. I went over to the washstand and splashed cold water on my face and into my eyes. I said, "Ring Elsie Brand at the office and see if one of those operatives has made a report. There must have been a slip-up some place. She's gone out."

Bertha rang the agency office, said, "Hello, Elsie. Spill me the dope," listened for a while, and then said, "You didn't hear from those operatives?....All right. Thanks. I'll call you back after a while."

She hung up and said, "More cops looking for you, lover. Some looking for me. Nothing from the operatives."

I smoothed my hair back with my pocket comb, looked at my soiled and wilted shirt collar, and said, "My God, Bertha, I *can't* be wrong! We exploded that bombshell under her. She must have communicated with Harbet. She had to—"

"She didn't," Bertha said.

I said, "Well, there's only one thing to do. Go over and make another crack at it. We're in so deep now we've got to start moving. We can't do anything else. Here, I'm going to put through a telephone call."

I grabbed up the telephone and called the number of my rooming house. A maid answered the phone and I said, "Let me speak to Mrs. Eldridge, please."

After a while I heard Mrs. Eldridge's voice, that peculiar, cynical voice which I'd know anywhere. I said, "This is Donald. I wonder if you'd mind asking my cousin to come to the telephone. I wouldn't bother you, only it's important."

Mrs. Eldridge said acidly, "Your cousin, Donald, turned out to be Marian Dunton, a witness who was wanted by the police in connection with a murder case. They took her away three hours ago. I think they're looking for *you* now. If you're going to use my rooming house as—"

I slammed the receiver back into its cradle.

Bertha Cool looked at me and said, sweetly—too damn sweetly—"Your cousin, Donny boy?"

I said, "Just a friend. I passed her off as my cousin."

"That number you called was the number of your rooming house."

"I know," I said.

Bertha Cool stood staring at me. Her eyes narrowed until they were mere glittering slits. "Humph," she said at length, and then, after a moment, added, "*I'll* say they fall for you. Come on, lover. We're going places. It may not be the wisest thing to do, but at least it's *something* to do. We may be here all day without getting a call. There's one thing you didn't figure."

"What?" I asked.

She said, "I've been thinking it out while I was sitting here. Suppose Harbet has a date to call at the Key West Apartments, this afternoon, pick up Flo Danzer, and take her up to Santa Carlotta?"

"Then the operatives would have reported that she'd gone out. I figured that possibility."

"Yes," Bertha said, "but if she knew Harbet was coming, she'd wait for him instead of telephoning."

I said, "Well, come on, let's go. We can't get in any deeper than we are now."

Bertha Cool said, "God, how I wish you were right," and unlocked the door.

We went out into the corridor. Bertha calmly and methodically locked the door. "How about a taxicab?" I asked.

"There's a taxi stand in front of the hotel," she said.

We went down through the lobby. The clerk said, "Your baggage hasn't shown up yet, Mrs. Cool. Do you want me to do anything about it? I can arrange with a transfer company—"

"Nothing, thank you," Bertha said and swept on past him.

There was a taxi at the stand in front of the hotel. Bertha heaved herself into the seat. I said to the cab driver, "Key West Apartments and make it snappy."

We rode along for a block or two in silence. Then Bertha Cool said, "Why in hell you didn't fix it up so the police wouldn't think she'd been kidnaped is more than I know. If she wanted to come down where she could live with you, why the hell didn't you have her think up a good stall which would fool cops. The way it is now, you're headed for the big house, and it doesn't make a damn what happens to this murder case. You—"

"Shut up," I said. "I'm thinking."

She said, "Well, I'm paying you wages. Think about the case we're working on. Think about your own troubles in your time off."

I turned on her. "You give me a pain. I *am* thinking about business problems, and *you* try to get me started on my personal problems. Shut up."

"What are you thinking about?"

"Shut up."

When we were within a few blocks of the Key West Apartments, I said, "We're all nuts."

"What is it now, Donald?" Bertha Cool asked.

"Those cigarette stubs in Evaline Harris's apartment. One of them had lipstick on. One of them didn't. Police jumped at the conclusion that that meant a man had been in the room. It doesn't mean any such thing."

"Why not?"

I said, "She'd been out late the night before. She was sleeping late. She was still asleep when someone gave her door a buzz."

"What makes you think so?"

"The paper under the door."

"I see. Go ahead."

I said, "You don't keep lipstick on when you go to bed, do you?"

"No."

"Neither did Evaline Harris. She removed her make-up and got into bed. Her visitor came before she had a chance to put any make-up on. They sat on the bed and talked. Her visitor was a woman. It was the caller's cigarette stub that had the lipstick on it."

The cab driver pulled into the curb in front of the Key West Apartments. "Want me to wait?" he asked.

I said, "No," and handed him a dollar.

Bertha Cool was staring at me with steady, wide-eyed intentness.

I said, "You know what that means."

Bertha Cool nodded.

"All right. Let's go."

She pulled herself out of the cab. Out of the corner of my eye I saw one of the detectives parked just behind the agency car keeping the place under surveillance. Bertha saw him too, but didn't even bother to signal him.

As I held the door open for Bertha Cool, I said, "Keep the clerk busy for a minute."

Bertha nodded and moved over to the desk. The clerk came

forward to greet her. I walked past him to say in a low voice to Frieda Tarbing, "Didn't she call?"

"Not a peep. Shall I go through the motions of ringing?"

I saw the clerk cock an ear in our direction, and I said in a loud voice, "Oh, don't bother to ring. Aunt Amelia is expecting me. We'll go right on up."

She raised her voice. "According to the rules," she said, "I have to ring."

The clerk said, "That's all right, Miss Tarbing. They can go right up," and he smiled at Bertha.

Bertha gave him one of her most gracious smiles, and I stood to one side while she eased her avoirdupois into the elevator. I followed her. The elevator door clanged shut and we shot upward.

We left the elevator and walked down the corridor. Bertha Cool said to me, "Any ideas?" and I said, "We've got to really get rough with her this time."

Bertha said, "All right then, lover. You keep out of it. When it comes to getting rough with a woman, I know some fine points that would never occur to a mere man. If it's getting rough you want, just stand to one side and watch Bertha do her stuff."

We knocked on the door and waited. There was no sound from the inside. The transom was tightly closed.

I knocked again. Bertha said, "This is a swank place. There's probably a button here somewhere—here it is."

She pressed her finger against the button. Still nothing happened. Bertha and I exchanged glances. Then we listened at the door for any sound of motion. We pounded again, and nothing happened.

Bertha said, "That damned operative went to sleep on the job and she sneaked out on us."

I tried to keep my face from showing what I was feeling.

We pounded on the door again and Bertha Cool rang the buzzer some more. Then she said grimly, "Come on down with me, lover. I want you to hear what I have to say to that snake's-belly sitting in that car."

I tagged along behind. There was nothing else to do. We'd taken half a dozen steps when suddenly Bertha Cool stopped and sniffed. She turned and looked at me.

"What is it?" I asked, and then I caught it, just a faint whiff of gas.

I ran back to the apartment door and dropped to my hands and knees, put my cheek against the carpet, and tried to look under the door. I couldn't see a thing, just a black strip beneath the jamb of the door. I took a long-bladed knife from my pocket, opened the blade, and inserted it in the crack. It struck some obstacle.

I jumped up, dusted off the knees of my trousers with the palms of my hands, and said, "Come on, Bertha. Let's go."

We went to the elevator and down to the lobby. I walked up to the clerk and said, "I'm afraid something's wrong with my Aunt Amelia. She told me to come back at this time, that she'd be here waiting. I went up and pounded on the door and couldn't get any answer."

The clerk was very affable. "She's probably gone out," he said. "She'll be back in a little while. Would you like to wait in the lobby?"

I said, "She was expecting me. She said she'd be there."

Frieda Tarbing said, "I'm quite sure she hasn't gone out."

"Give her a ring," the clerk said.

Frieda Tarbing flashed me a quick glance, then plugged in a line, and worked a key back and forth. After a few minutes, she said, "She doesn't answer."

The clerk said, "Well, there's nothing I can do—"

"I thought," I said, "that there was a faint odor of gas in the corridor."

The affable smile dissolved from the clerk's face. I saw his eyes get big and his face change color. Without a word, he reached under the counter and took out a passkey. "Come on," he said.

We went up. The clerk tried fitting the passkey to the door. It didn't work. He said, "The door's bolted from the inside."

Bertha Cool said, "Donald, you're thin. You could smash out the glass in that transom, and drop through, and open the door."

I said to the clerk, "Give me a leg up."

He said, "I'm not certain we should resort to extreme measures—"

Bertha Cool said, "Here, lover. I'll give you a boost." She picked me up as though I weighed no more than a pillow. I pulled a handkerchief from my pocket, wadded it around my hand, and smashed in the glass of the transom. A blast of gas came out to strike me in the face.

I said to Bertha, "Slip off your shoe, and give it to me. I can hang on up here."

I clung to the transom ledge with one toe resting on the doorknob. Bertha Cool slipped off a shoe and pushed it into my hand. I beat out the glass with the heel, then dropped the shoe and slid through the transom.

The gas was terrible. It stung my eyes and made me gag. The room was darkened with the shades all drawn and the drapes pulled into place. I had a glimpse of a bed, and the inert figure of a woman sprawled over a writing-desk, her head on her left hand, her right hand stretched out across the desk.

I held my breath, ran across to the nearest window, jerked

the shades to one side, opened the window, stuck my head out, and got a breath of air. I ran across to the other window, opened it, and did the same thing. Then I ran out into the kitchen. The gas stove was going full blast. I could hear the hissing sound of escaping gas. I shut off all the valves and opened the kitchen window.

From the door I could hear the clerk calling, "Open up," and Bertha Cool's voice came drifting through the broken transom, "He's probably overcome by gas. You'd better run down and call the police."

There were steps running down the corridor, and then Bertha Cool's voice, sounding as calm as though she'd been giving me orders over the telephone, saying, "Take your time, lover. Make a good job of it."

I went over to the desk. Flo Danzer had been writing. There was one letter addressed to Bertha Cool. It was in an envelope. I ran over to the window, took out the letter, and glanced through it. It was a long, rambling account of how she had tried to pose as Amelia Lintig. I saw the name John Harbet, saw the name of Evaline Harris, and then to my dismay saw the name of Dr. Alftmont, of Santa Carlotta.

I slipped the letter back into the envelope, hesitated a moment, then sealed the envelope. I whipped out of my pocket one of the stamped, addressed envelopes with a special delivery stamp in the upper right-hand corner which I used for making out agency reports. I pushed the whole business into this envelope, sealed it, and said to Bertha, "Over the transom."

I sailed it up. I heard Bertha say, "What do I do with it, lover?" and I said, "Take it over to the mail chute, drop it, and forget it."

I heard Bertha Cool's step in the corridor. I was feeling giddy and nauseated. I ran to the window and took a deep breath. Then I went back and looked under Flo Danzer's head. There was a piece of paper underneath it. She'd been writing, evidently when the gas overcame her. There was a pen in her hand.

I wanted to ease that letter out and see what it contained. I could get the words: *To whom it may concern:* The writing seemed to be badly scrawled.

Wind was taking out some of the gas smell, but it was still awfully thick. My eyes were smarting and I felt strangely light-headed. I heard a man's voice in the corridor saying, "There's a terrible odor of gas," then a woman's voice, and then I heard the sound of steps running down the corridor, and the clerk's voice saying, "The police will be here, also an ambulance. Here, break that door down. The man inside has been overcome."

I figured that was the best I could do now. I heard the sounds of bodies slamming against the door. I ran toward the window and dropped down to the floor. I closed my eyes and, as though in a daze, heard the door crash inward and people were running toward me. Someone picked up my shoulders. Someone else picked up my feet. I was carried out to the corridor. People were running around, and a woman was screaming.

I felt fresh air on my face, and Bertha Cool saying, "Here, put him out on that window ledge. Hang onto his feet. He may drop."

I inhaled great lungfuls of fresh air and opened my eyes. People were milling around. I heard the clerk say, "Poor chap. It was his aunt—" There followed a confused interval of blurred half-consciousness, and then I heard the sound of a siren. A few minutes later, officers from a radio car were in charge. After a while an ambulance came. People went into the room and came out.

I looked up into Bertha Cool's face and said, "Remember to give them her name. She's Amelia Lintig of Oakview."

"It's on the register, lover," Bertha said.

"Be sure to see they get it right," I said.

After a while I tried my legs. They were a little wobbly. A man in a white coat said, "How are you feeling, buddy? Think you can get down to the ambulance under your own power?"

"I want to stay here with my aunt," I said.

Bertha Cool said, "It's only partially the gas. He's been under a terrific strain worrying about his aunt. He knew she was despondent."

The white-coated man stuck a stethoscope on my chest, said, "Here, we've got to get him out to the air."

I pushed him away and said, "I want to know what's happened."

"You can't go in there," the ambulance man said.

"I've got to."

Bertha Cool said cooingly, "Poor boy. It was his *favorite* aunt."

I went into the room. Radio officers were in charge. One of them said, "It's too late to do anything here. The body isn't to be touched until the coroner comes. Who shut off the gas?"

"I did," I said.

The clerk said, "They broke in the transom at my orders. I knew it was the only thing to do."

Bertha Cool glanced at me meaningly. "You'd better go in the ambulance, lover," she said.

I looked at Bertha, and said, "I can't. There's an important letter—"

"I know, lover," she said. "Leave it to Bertha. She'll take care of it."

The ambulance man put an arm around my shoulders. "Come on, buddy. Your heart is taking an awful beating. You got quite a dose of gas. If you could only smell your own breath, you'd realize it. You smell like a gas house."

I went down to the ambulance. Strained, white faces in the lobby eyed me as though I'd been some alien creature. I stretched out on the cot in the ambulance. I felt a needle prick my arm, and heard the scream of the siren.

After a while I began to feel better and realized that the ambulance was the safest place for me—that and the receiving hospital. The police were looking for me in too many different places on too many different charges.

Chapter Fourteen

Bertha Cool called on me in the receiving hospital. "I have a cab waiting, lover, any time you feel like trying to leave. How are you?"

The nurse looked at my chart and said, "He's suffering from a general run-down condition as well as the shock and the gas."

Bertha said, "It's no wonder. Poor boy. He's been working twenty-four hours a day, and he isn't built for it."

The nurse said to me, "You must take things easier."

I said, "I'm better now. I think I can leave."

The nurse said, "Just a minute. I'll get the doctor's permission."

She walked down the corridor. I heard the whir of a telephone dial, and then she started talking, saying something in a low voice which I couldn't understand.

I said to Bertha, "Wise me up."

Bertha, with an eye on the corridor, said, "You doped it out right. She committed the murder."

"How about the confession?" I asked. "Did it mention Alftmont?"

Bertha said, "No. The confession was unfinished and unsigned, but it was in her handwriting. It was one of those 'to whom it may concern' things. It started right out by saying that she was the one who had murdered Evaline Harris."

"Did it mention Harbet's name?"

"No. That was in the letter she wrote and addressed to me."

"Are we going to have to use that letter?"

"I don't think so."

"If we do," I said, "remember that we had left her a stamped, addressed envelope, and told her to drop us a line about some other matter. She mailed the letter herself and—"

Bertha Cool said, "For God's sake, Donald, don't think everybody is dumb. I got the play as soon as you threw it over the transom. We aren't going to have to use it. It's nice, but it's dynamite."

"She says something about Harbet in there," I said.

"Spilled the whole beans. All about how Harbet wanted to bring pressure to bear on Dr. Alftmont."

I said, "I want to put in a telephone call for Harbet. I'll tell him confidentially that we have—"

Bertha said, "You'll have a hell of a time reaching him. Harbet has taken a powder. The D.A. here telephoned Santa Carlotta about the suicide. Harbet got up from his desk, walked out, and hasn't returned. He won't return."

I thought that over. "I wanted to be the one to tell him," I said.

"You're a vindictive little cuss, Donald."

"What did she say happened to the real Mrs. Lintig?"

"She didn't know. Amelia married Wilmen, and went down into Central America somewhere. They never showed up again. Amelia left her trunk with Flo. Flo kept it in her place for a while, then put it in storage, and finally went through it and took out what she wanted. She figured Amelia was dead."

"But she can't prove it."

"No."

I said, "That's what I was afraid of. Insist that this woman is Amelia Lintig. Perhaps we can get by with it and get a certificate of death."

Bertha said, "There you go again, Donald, thinking you have to point out every play for me. For Christ's sake, don't you give me credit for—"

The nurse came back down the corridor. A doctor was with her. The doctor said gravely, "I'm sorry, Mr. Lam, but orders are that as soon as you're able to leave here, you're to go to the district attorney's office."

"You mean that I'm under arrest?"

"It amounts to that."

"For what?" I asked.

"I don't know," he said. "Those are orders. I think that you've been under a great strain lately. You are wiry and strong. Organically you're as sound as a nut, but your nerves can't stand the terrific whipping you've been giving them lately. I dislike to have you subjected to any undue strain, but those are orders. A detective is on the way to pick you up."

I said, "Can Mrs. Cool go along? I'd like to have her corroborate parts of my story."

"I don't think so," the doctor said. "You'll have to ask the detective about that."

He went away. The nurse kept sticking around. After a while a detective came in and said, "Come on, Lam. We're going to run over to the district attorney's office."

"Who wants me over there?"

"Mr. Ellis."

I said, "What's the charge?"

"I don't know that there is any."

Bertha Cool said, "He's intensely nervous. He's in no condition to be questioned or bullied."

The detective shrugged his shoulders.

Bertha Cool took my arm and said, "I'll come right along, Donald."

The detective said, "You can go as far as the D.A.'s office. After that, it's up to Mr. Ellis."

We went to the district attorney's office. A secretary said Mr. Ellis wanted to see me, and Bertha Cool tagged right along.

The secretary said, "Only Mr. Lam," but Bertha couldn't hear her. Her attitude was filled with the maternal concern of a setting hen. She held open the door of the office marked *Mr. Ellis* and said, "Go right on in, Donald," as though she'd been talking to a five-year-old child.

I walked in. Mr. Ellis was one of these good-looking, God's-gift-to-women guys. I looked at him and could tell his story with that one glance—a nice college boy, an athlete by the looks of his shoulders and the bronze of his complexion, a football player for dear old Southern California, a model student with a high scholastic record, friends everywhere, and a habit of ingratiating himself with his professors. They'd manipulated him into the district attorney's office as a deputy, and he was filled to the collar button with the abstract legal lore of a law school.

He said, "Mr. Lam, your activities in this case have been rather remarkable."

I said, "Haven't they?"

He flushed.

I said, "It's an awful shock to learn that my own aunt is guilty of a murder."

"And, by a remarkable coincidence," he said, "in a case which you were investigating."

I raised my eyebrows and said, "A case *I* was investigating?" and looked blankly at Bertha Cool.

Bertha Cool said, "There's some mistake. Donald is working for me. We weren't investigating any murder."

"Why did he go to Oakview?" Ellis asked.

Bertha said, "I don't know. That was private business. He asked for time off. It had something to do with finding his aunt. They'd been estranged for a while, and he wanted to look her up. He found her in Oakview, you know."

Ellis frowned and said, "Yes. I know." And then, after a moment: "Perhaps, Mr. Lam, if you had no interest in the Evaline Harris murder, you'll be kind enough to tell me why you took it on yourself to run Miss Dunton into your rooming house as your cousin, and—"

"Because I thought she was in danger," I interrupted. "I formed a friendship with Miss Dunton while I was in Oakview."

"So it would seem," he said.

I said, "I got worried about her. She told me that she could identify a man she had seen leaving that apartment. Of course, at the time I thought that he was the murderer—sort of took it for granted, you know."

"That's a nice story," he said, "but I happen to know that you were trying to keep her out of circulation. You were hiding her so we couldn't find her."

"So *you* couldn't find her!" I exclaimed. "Good heavens! I don't know— Oh, yes, I told her that I was going to notify you of her new address. That's right. I forgot to do that. This business with my aunt came up and—"

"What business with your aunt?" he interrupted.

I said, "She was going to marry a man who was only interested in her money. I wanted to investigate him. I spoke to Mrs. Cool about it, and she said that she'd use the agency and see what could be done."

Ellis picked up a telephone and said, "Send Miss Dunton in."

A few moments later there were quick steps in the hall and Marian Dunton opened the door. I think she expected to find us there. She smiled and there was concern on her face. "Donald, how are you?" she asked, and came over to give me her hand. "I heard you were at the receiving hospital. You're white as a sheet."

I took her hand, and her left eye, the one that was farthest from Ellis, closed in a slow, solemn wink.

She said, "You're trying to do altogether too much and you're worrying too much, Donald. When you got worried about me, you should have communicated with the authorities instead of taking it on yourself to—"

"That'll do. Miss Dunton," Ellis said sternly. "I'll ask the questions. I'd prefer that the information came from Mr. Lam."

I said, "What information do you want, Mr. Ellis?"

"How did that apartment get all mussed up?"

"What apartment?"

"The one where Miss Dunton had been staying."

I said, "I wouldn't know."

'You wouldn't know anything about the blood either?"

"Oh, yes," I said. "I know all about that. You see, I'd been having terrific nosebleeds at intervals during the day. I went up to pack some things for Miss Dunton and my nose started to bleed. I had a lot of trouble with it, trying to stop it. I was afraid I was going to have to go to a doctor. I couldn't take her things. I was holding my nose. I left the apartment, headed for a doctor's office, but my nose stopped bleeding before I found one."

"And you never did get back to pick up Miss Dunton's things?"

"To tell you the truth, I didn't. I started back, and came to the conclusion someone was watching the apartment. I was afraid he would shadow me and find out where Miss Dunton was staying."

"And you didn't push the furniture around?"

"Why, no," I said. "I don't know what you're talking about. I do remember I fell over a chair. I was holding a handkerchief to my face, you know."

Ellis said, "It looked as though there'd been a struggle in that apartment. Miss Dunton's purse was lying open, and—"

"He told me he'd dropped my purse when he had the nosebleed," Marian said.

Ellis frowned, but his eyes, meeting Marian's, couldn't hold a stern expression. He said, "Let me do it, please, Miss Dunton."

"Oh, very well," she said in a hurt voice.

Ellis couldn't get up any steam after that. He was licked. Five minutes later, he said, "Very well. The circumstances are exceedingly strange. After this, Mr. Lam, if you want to protect any witness who is in communication with our office, simply advise the office and don't take the responsibility on your own shoulders."

I said, "I'm sorry, but I did what seemed best at the time."

I glanced at Bertha Cool, and then decided I might as well get the whole thing straightened out while I was about it. I said to Bertha, "What was this about some charge on a hit-and-run case being made against me?"

She said, "Some officers were trying to pick you up at the agency office."

Ellis said hastily, "That's quite all right. That matter has been taken care of. You can simply ignore that. An officer at Santa Carlotta telephoned in a short time ago. The witness who saw the car made a mistake on the license number."

I said to Bertha, "Well, I guess we can go."

Marian said, "I'm coming along, Donald, if you don't mind."

Ellis said, "Just a minute, Miss Dunton. I'd like to ask you a few more questions, if you please—after the others leave."

Bertha Cool said, "It's all right, Marian. We'll be waiting for you in a taxi down at the main entrance."

Walking down the corridor, I said to Bertha Cool, "Do you have that letter Flo wrote with you?"

Bertha said, "Do I look that simple, lover? That letter's in a safe place. How about notifying our client?"

"Too dangerous," I said. "A lot of heat has been turned on. Our lines may be tapped. Let him read it in the papers: '*Amelia Lintig of Oakview Confesses to Murder of Night-Club Entertainer and Commits Suicide.*' "

Bertha Cool said, "You're never going to get away with this aunt business, lover. They'll nail you on that."

I said, "They're going to have a sweet time doing it. She really *was* my aunt."

Bertha Cool looked at me in surprise.

"You don't know anything about my family or antecedents," I said.

"And what's more, I don't want to," Bertha hastily told me. "This time you're on your own."

"That's swell. Just remember that."

We waited in the cab for about ten minutes, then Marian came down looking rather flushed and elated. She flung her arms around me, and said, "Donald, it's so *good* to see you. Gosh, I was afraid you were going to make the wrong play with Mr. Ellis. I'd already squared things for you. I told him we'd formed a very close friendship, and that you were really concerned about me."

"How did they locate you?" I asked.

"I think it's that landlady of yours," she said. "She read the morning papers with a description of the missing witness. I don't think she trusts you entirely, Donald."

Bertha Cool said, "I think it'll be a good idea for you to get another rooming house, lover."

"Mrs. Eldridge will have already arranged that," I said. And then to Marian: "Did you have any trouble with Mr. Ellis?"

"Trouble?" Marian laughed. "Good heavens, no! Do you know what he wanted to ask me when he requested me to remain behind?"

Bertha Cool said, "It's an even money bet he asked you to marry him."

Marian laughed and said, "No, not that—not yet. He's a very conservative young man, but he did ask me to go to dinner and a show tonight."

There was silence for a while. Marian kept looking at me as though waiting for a question.

Bertha Cool asked it. "What did you tell him?" she asked.

Marian said, "That I had a date with Donald."

Bertha Cool sighed, and then, after a moment, said, in an undertone, "Can me for a sardine."

Chapter Fifteen

It was all more or less routine to the coroner. He had some witnesses who identified the body as that of Flo Danzer, the night-club hostess, but I explained to him that that was a name taken by Aunt Amelia after she'd left John Wilmen. I put the whole history together for him. She'd left Oakview as Mrs. Lintig, had taken her maiden name of Amelia Sellar, had secured a Mexican divorce, had married John Wilmen, had left John Wilmen, taken the name of Flo Danzer, and more recently had gone back to using the name Amelia Lintig. I told him about her trip to Oakview, and the clerk and the porter at the hotel, whose expenses to the city had been donated by the agency, identified the body absolutely.

After the autopsy, they turned the body over to me. I went with it to Oakview for interment. Quite a few people turned out for the funeral. That wasn't so good. I explained that I thought the mourners were sincere, but there were a lot of curiosity-seekers and morbid persons who had attended the funeral, so I was going to keep the coffin lid closed. I thought Aunt Amelia would want it that way.

It was a nice funeral. The preacher said what things he could, and stressed the fact that at the last Amelia had repented of the crime and had made the supreme atonement, that justice was divine, and that who was there among us to condemn.

Bertha Cool sent a nice floral wreath, and there was a huge pillow of flowers marked: *From an old friend.*

I didn't try to trace the pillow. If I had, I felt quite certain that Marian's Uncle Stephen would have been found at the paying end of the bill, but Uncle Steve wasn't at the funeral.

Afterward, when I dropped in at the office to say goodbye to Marian. I could hear the typewriter laboriously clacking away behind the partition. I wondered who it was.

"A new reporter?" I asked.

She said, "That's Uncle Steve. He wanted to write the obituary himself. It seems that he used to know her."

I raised my eyebrows.

Marian looked at me steadily. "Donald," she said, "was she *really* your aunt?"

"My favorite aunt," I said.

She came closer to the counter, so that her uncle couldn't hear me, and pushed her hands out across the partition. Her eyes were wistful. "When," she asked, "am I *ever* going to get to see you?"

"Almost any time," I said. "Bertha's landed a job in the city for you."

"Donald!"

"It's a fact," I said.

She came around the counter.

From the back room came the labored *clack-clack-clack* of the typewriter as Stephen Dunton wrote out the obituary of the woman with whom gossip had connected his name twenty-one years ago.

In an envelope in my inside coat pocket was a certified copy of the death certificate. The envelope was addressed to Charles Loring Alftmont, Mayor of Santa Carlotta, and, right at present, that envelope was being badly wrinkled by the pressure of Marian Dunton's body as she hugged me to her, but I thought it would be a touching gesture to hold up mailing the envelope until I could include a clipping from the Oakview *Blade*.

"Oh, Donald, you darling!"

"Bertha did it," I said. "The newspaper picture helped—the one with the legs. What'll Charlie say?"

"Charlie?"

"Charlie, the boyfriend."

"Oh." She looked up at me and laughed. "I tied a can to him. He was too much of a stick. He liked it here."

"When did all this happen?" I asked.

Her face was tilted up to mine. "The day after you took me to dinner in the hotel. He was there in the dining room, seated right behind you—I thought perhaps he'd given you the black eye."

"That was Sergeant Harbet. Say, did your Uncle Steve deliberately run away from my aunt?"

"Yes. He's sensitive about his weight, his baldness, and his rural background. He figured she'd been living in cities, was sophisticated and smart, that she'd look on him as a country boy—"

She broke off abruptly as the typewriter behind the partition quit clacking.

Steve Dunton had finished writing the obituary.